Praise for *The Prince and*

"This is a story of forgiveness, grace, and redemption, ... tells it in a creative and believable way, which is a hallmark of her writing. The details she adds generate deep emotion and lead to a satisfying ending."

Booklist

Praise for *Miriam's Song*

"An inspiring and uplifting read about hope, faith, and perseverance. . . . To be captivated by such a compelling story, so much so I did not want to put it down, attests to the writer's storytelling ability."

Interviews & Reviews

"I really loved the story and the writing style of Jill Eileen Smith. She is a master storyteller of Bible stories and really keeps the reader captivated."

Life Is Story

"*Miriam's Song* by Jill Eileen Smith is a beautifully written biblical story. . . . I was hooked. Jill Eileen Smith's writing is superb."

Urban Lit Magazine

"A novel based on detailed and meticulous research combined with a keen eye for historical detail."

Midwest Book Reviews

Praise for *Star of Persia*

"Real people with real flaws and palpable emotions play at your heartstrings in this unforgettable telling of the Bible's greatest Jewish heroine. Jill Eileen Smith's conversational style makes Esther's story relatable, its complex history understandable, and its details fascinating. A must-read for every biblical fiction fan."

Mesu Andrews, Christy Award–winning author
of *Isaiah's Daughter*

"In *Star of Persia*, Jill Eileen Smith breathes new life into the tale of Queen Esther, and those whose lives entwined with hers, by weaving together richly crafted descriptions, well-researched historical detail, and her usual flair for retelling biblical stories with a fresh perspective."

Connilyn Cossette, ECPA bestselling author of the
Out from Egypt and Cities of Refuge series

"This beautifully written novel creates a deep context for the biblical story of the Jewish orphan Hadassah. . . . Smith's latest will be of great interest to fans of historical fiction, especially those interested in biblical times, as well as readers who enjoy new perspectives on women figures from the past."

Booklist

DAUGHTER
OF
EDEN

Books by Jill Eileen Smith

THE WIVES OF KING DAVID

Michal
Abigail
Bathsheba

WIVES OF THE PATRIARCHS

Sarai
Rebekah
Rachel

DAUGHTERS OF THE PROMISED LAND

The Crimson Cord
The Prophetess
Redeeming Grace
A Passionate Hope

The Heart of a King
Star of Persia
Miriam's Song
The Prince and the Prodigal
Daughter of Eden

When Life Doesn't Match Your Dreams
She Walked Before Us

DAUGHTER
OF
EDEN

EVE'S STORY

JILL EILEEN SMITH

Revell
a division of Baker Publishing Group
Grand Rapids, Michigan

Published by Revell
a division of Baker Publishing Group
Grand Rapids, Michigan
RevellBooks.com

Printed in the United States of America

Library of Congress Cataloging-in-Publication Data
Names: Smith, Jill Eileen, 1958– author.
Title: Daughter of Eden : Eve's story / Jill Eileen Smith.
Description: Grand Rapids, MI : Revell, a division of Baker Publishing Group, [2023]
Identifiers: LCCN 2022020825 | ISBN 9780800737641 (paperback) | ISBN 9780800742614 (casebound) | ISBN 9781493439669 (ebook)
Subjects: LCSH: Eve (Biblical figure)—Fiction. | Adam (Biblical figure)—Fiction. | LCGFT: Bible fiction | Novels.
Classification: LCC PS3619.M58838 D38 2023 | DDC 813/.6—dc23/eng/20220428
LC record available at https://lccn.loc.gov/2022020825

Most Scripture used in this book, whether quoted or paraphrased by the characters, is from The Holy Bible, English Standard Version® (ESV®), copyright © 2001 by Crossway, a publishing ministry of Good News Publishers. Used by permission. All rights reserved. ESV Text Edition: 2016

Some Scripture used in this book, whether quoted or paraphrased by the characters, is from THE HOLY BIBLE, NEW INTERNATIONAL VERSION®, NIV® Copyright © 1973, 1978, 1984, 2011 by Biblica, Inc.® Used by permission. All rights reserved worldwide.

This is a work of historical reconstruction; the appearances of certain historical figures are therefore inevitable. All other characters, however, are products of the author's imagination, and any resemblance to actual persons, living or dead, is coincidental.

Published in association with Books & Such Literary Management, www.booksand such.com.

Baker Publishing Group publications use paper produced from sustainable forestry practices and postconsumer waste whenever possible.

23 24 25 26 27 28 29   7 6 5 4 3 2 1

In loving memory of my mom, Shirley R. Smith,
who left this earth two days before I completed the final draft
of this book. My mom gave me a love for books and was my
greatest cheerleader. She read every book until this one, which
her earthly eyes will never see. But just knowing she is with
Jesus is all that matters to me. She loved her family well.
June 27, 1923–March 7, 2022

Also in loving memory of my brother, Dennis,
who read all of my books and who, like Eve, left this
earth realizing afresh how much God loved him.
November 8, 1943–July 10, 2021

And to those who wonder what God's creation of the
world might have looked like . . . to those who wish
they could say to Eve, "Don't eat the fruit!"
This book is for you.

The heavens praise your wonders, LORD,
    your faithfulness too, in the assembly of the holy ones.
For who in the skies above can compare with the LORD?
    Who is like the LORD among the heavenly beings?
In the council of the holy ones God is greatly feared;
    he is more awesome than all who surround him.

Psalm 89:5–7 NIV

The Unseen Realm

The first time he opened his eyes, light, brilliant and pure, moved in colored ribbons about him. Sounds like thunder and whispers joined in melodic tones. Scents came from the surrounding colorful foliage, and he could taste the breeze swirling in the air. He blinked and stood, taking in the garden, the mountains, the city shining like a jewel in its midst.

"You are Michael," a voice like a song said behind him.

He turned, facing the sound, and there before him stood a being majestic and beautiful, His eyes like glowing flames.

Instinctively, Michael bowed low, aware that there were others like him all bowing before this being. *Who are You?*

Your Maker and Creator, came the response deep within him.

"Rise," the Creator said, and a host of beings rose with Michael. He looked about and then observed his own form, noting slight differences between himself and others among the throng.

"You are My messengers, angels of every rank, each with specific duties to serve My Father." The Creator pointed to a place lifted high in the distance, where a clear liquid substance flowed from a fiery, living throne. "The Ancient of Days," the Creator said. "Some of you will serve Him directly and sit on His council."

Michael briefly met the Creator's gaze, enveloped by euphoric feelings. *You are worthy and mighty and holy*, he said without speaking aloud.

"I am Adonai Elohim, the Son of the Father, who is the Ancient of Days. I am the Alpha and Omega, the Beginning and the End. You are the heavenly host, His servants." The Creator looked at each one, nodding and speaking the names of some. "Gabriel, Michael, come."

Michael stepped closer, and another bearing his same qualities drew alongside him. They bowed low again.

"You are My archangels," the Creator said. "You have access to My Father and will stand in His presence. You are two among many princes and will have duties and power above the others." He stretched His arm toward the path leading up to the throne of God and beckoned them to go.

Michael walked beside Gabriel along a floating path above a crystal sea as the Creator spoke to others behind them.

"Lucifer," Adonai Elohim called, and Michael turned to glimpse a dazzling angel stepping close and bowing low. "You are a guardian cherub of Eden on the holy mount of God."

Michael looked at Gabriel. "What is Eden?"

Gabriel shrugged. "I am newly created as you are. I have no idea. Perhaps the Ancient of Days will tell us."

They continued to float above the crystal sea until at last they came to stand in the presence of God. The throne's fire came from spinning wheels at its sides, and the Ancient of Days sat upon it, magnificent. Cherubim sang His praise, saying, "Holy, holy, holy is the Lord God Almighty, who was and is and is to come."

The sea beneath them illumined a great chasm of darkness in the space far below. The Spirit of God hovered over the face of the deep, and the Creator, Son of the Almighty, joined them, surrounded by millions of angels in God's throne room. Thunder erupted when the Ancient One spoke to the hovering Spirit and the Son in a language the created ones could not understand.

Suddenly the Spirit's hovering ceased, and He moved in ethereal beauty about the throne room, speaking to the Ancient of Days and Adonai Elohim in tones and utterances, like groans too deep for words.

Until . . .

"Let there be light," God commanded, all speaking in one voice. The ribbons of light swirled, and the crystal sea beneath them showed the deep no longer dark. Light, not nearly as bright as the heavenly colors but brilliant enough to displace the darkness, exposed the swirling chaos so all could see. The mass of waters was visible now, yet still it remained black as night.

Then God separated the light from the darkness and called one day and one night. There was no form or foundation to the light or darkness, just separation to show those watching what God was doing.

Suddenly an explosion of commands came from the center throne. An expanse separated waters from waters, and a lower heaven emerged beneath the throne room's glassy floor.

A measuring line stretched across the deep, and in the course of time, God set the cornerstone and built the foundation for what He would soon call "earth."

The morning stars sang as they watched the changes God made of the chaos, and Michael joined the angels as they shouted for joy when the boundaries were set for the beauty they knew was coming. How could anything the Almighty made be anything but glorious? Everything Michael could see, including the body that belonged to him, was beautiful and pure, and he marveled as he watched. What was God creating here?

In sudden yet seemingly slow progression, dry land appeared, and the waters were placed behind invisible doors, unable to reach beyond their boundaries to touch the ground. Vegetation bearing seeds to procreate and trees of every imaginable design sprouted from the new ground, bearing fruit of every glimmering color.

Sun and moon and stars, lesser lights than the light of heaven, appeared in the expanse to mark days and nights and seasons.

Time began when God marked the first day, evening and morning, and Michael pondered what time meant.

He held his breath as living beings appeared in the sea and on the land. He laughed outright and joy filled the heavens at some of their strange images. How different the earth was from the heavens.

Silence followed the creation of the last of the creatures for a heavy moment, until at last God spoke again in a loud whisper. "Let us make *adam* in our image, after our likeness. And let them have dominion over the fish of the sea and over the birds of the heavens and over the livestock and over all the earth and over every creeping thing that creeps on the earth."

Humankind? What would these image-bearers look like? Would they shine like the jewels and brilliance of the heavenly hosts? Michael leaned forward to watch as Adonai Elohim slipped through heaven's barrier and knelt in earth's dust.

What was He doing?

His shining appearance blocked their view until He knelt further and breathed into the air. No, not the air, for a moment later, Adonai Elohim took a hand and pulled a being to its feet.

The human didn't look like God in any way. *How is this Your image-bearer?* Michael wondered. But the Creator did not respond to his question.

He yearned to understand as Adonai Elohim walked the *adam* throughout the earth and showed him all that God had made. By the time the new sun had moved toward the edge of the sky, Adonai Elohim had put the *adam* to sleep and lifted a hand to another *adam*, one like the first and yet not the same.

A million of the heavenly hosts now crowded along the edges of the crystal floor, the sea of God's throne room, watching, listening in silence and awe as the voices sounded again, quieter this time.

"Be fruitful and multiply and fill the earth and subdue it," God said to the new *adams*, "and have dominion over the fish of the sea and over the birds of the heavens and over every living thing that moves on the earth. Behold, I have given you every plant yielding seed that is on the face of all the earth, and every tree with seed in its fruit. You shall have them for food. And to every beast of the earth and to every bird of the heavens and to everything that creeps on the earth, everything that has the breath of life, I have given every green plant for food."

Then Adonai Elohim guided the *adams* and placed them in a garden, which had missed Michael's notice until this moment. A garden flourishing and glorious, matching the beauty of heaven. Was this Eden?

A collective sigh came from the heavenly hosts, mirroring his own feelings. And then as suddenly as He had left heaven, Adonai Elohim returned to His throne beside the Ancient of Days, and the Spirit hovered in the air between them.

"It is very good," God said.

"Glory, glory, glory to the Lord God Almighty, who was and is and is to come," the cherubim sang, and the angels danced.

Sometime later, as Michael stood in God's presence, he approached the Creator and bowed low. "Is this garden where You have placed the *adams* the Eden You spoke of?"

"Yes," He said. "It is the garden of God."

1

The woman laughed at the spray of water tingling her skin as the man, Adam, ducked under a waterfall and pulled her in with him. The cascade of sparkling liquid fell from the land high above them and flowed in rushing rivers going off in four directions.

"Swim with me," he said, kissing her hand. Before she could respond, he released his grip and used his tawny, muscled arms and sturdy legs to propel himself ahead of her through the waters of the Pishon.

"You think you can outpace me, do you?" She dove beneath the clear surface and swam as the frogs did. She was soon at his shoulder. He turned to her, his smile wide, and at the way he looked at her she nearly lost her ability to think.

He took advantage of her brief distraction and pushed ahead, until they both fell silent as they raced the length of Havilah, which circled Eden. At last, barely winded, Adam climbed onto the shore and offered her his hand. She took it and found herself enveloped in his wet arms, his dark shoulder-length hair dripping onto her bare skin.

His kiss filled her with intense joy, and in a moment she pulled him to the lush grasses beneath them as they came together once again as man and wife. It was what the Creator had told them to do, to be fruitful and multiply and fill the earth, though there had yet to be any fruit of their lovemaking.

Perhaps this time.

She rested in the crook of Adam's arm sometime later, gazing at the waters that hung in white cumulus clouds above them. The waters below misted the ground, keeping it lush and green, making caring for the garden rewarding work. They had spent the morning tending the trees and pruning vines. The seed-bearing plants and trees would reproduce themselves, but the animals always needed tending.

The woman looked at her husband and brushed a tendril of wet hair from his eyes. "This is a good place Adonai Elohim has given to us."

He leaned up on one elbow, bent over her, and kissed her nose. "We have not even begun to discover all that is hidden here. Didn't He tell us there are gold and precious stones in Havilah like the jewels that adorn the heavenly messengers? Tomorrow, after we care for the animals, let us return and search for them." His eyes gleamed like the dark of polished onyx, a stone they had recently found on one of their walks.

"Tomorrow might be too soon," she said, cupping his chiseled cheek. "One of the ewes is due to give birth, and didn't the Creator say the council would meet in the evening, after our walk in the cool of the day?"

Adam looked into her eyes, his gaze drawing her closer, if that were possible. "What would I do without you to remind me? I had forgotten about the ewe."

"But you recalled the meeting?"

He nodded. He had known the Creator before she had, and the Creator had told him things, explained the earth and Eden to him even before she drew her first breath. Was it not in the naming of the beasts of the field and every living thing that they found no one to complete Adam?

"You have named the animals. Why have you not named me?"

she asked. While his name was connected to the earth and she to him, she often found "woman" somewhat wanting.

He kissed her, pulling her out of her musings. For a moment she wondered if he would embrace her again, but he stood instead and pulled her to her feet.

"I did name you," he said, intertwining their fingers. "You are woman because you were taken out of man."

"But you are Adam. Even the Creator says so." She didn't mean to pout, but suddenly she wanted something more, something unique to describe her.

"Let me think on it." He sifted her hair between his fingers and gazed on her with such love that suddenly "woman" did seem enough. What else could he call her anyway? He was an *adam* as she was, yet she was very different.

"Shall we walk back to the place where Adonai Elohim meets us, or do you want another chance to show me you can swim faster?" He chuckled at the look she gave him, then placed his arm about her. "My woman, taken out of man. You are everything I could have imagined and so much more."

She leaned against him, content. She had no need to compete with him except for the sheer joy of using her strength and feeling the freedom of her limbs. To race him allowed her to laugh at his playful ways. The cheetahs did not laugh like Adam did, nor the ostrich, though they could outrun her.

"Let's walk along the river on the way back," she said, smiling up at him. "Perhaps we will see some of the gold of Havilah along the way."

He led her to the bank of the rushing waters, both searching the grasses and the dirt beneath. But they reached the center of Eden too soon, having spotted nothing.

Then the woman heard the sound of the Creator walking nearby. She turned to Adam and took his hands. "He's here!" Delight filled her, for she dearly loved these moments, far more than finding gold in the rivers or in the land.

"Yes!" Adam said.

They hurried to meet Him, hand in hand. This was her favorite time of day.

Adonai Elohim appeared in the center of the garden not far from the Tree of Life. They hurried closer, and she fell at His feet and kissed them. Gratitude to Him for creating her always overwhelmed her when she saw the beauty of His face. His body, which He assumed in order to walk among them, was like theirs, only His torso was like topaz, His face like lightning, His eyes like flaming torches, His arms and legs like the gleam of burnished bronze, and His voice like the sound of a multitude. And yet they did not fear His brilliant presence. When He spoke to them alone, sometimes He spoke in whispers.

"Where have you been today?" He asked as He always did when they met. Today His voice sounded like Adam's in tone and strength.

"We swam the length of the Pishon throughout the land of Havilah," Adam answered as he draped one arm over her shoulder.

"It is beautiful there, though we did not see the gold or onyx or bdellium near the river. But I can swim as fast as Adam. Next time I will win." She glanced at Adam, then turned to hold Adonai Elohim's fiery gaze.

Adonai laughed, and they joined Him.

"My wife loves to compete with me, and I love to catch her." Adam gave her an affectionate look. "We had hoped to return tomorrow to search out the jewels and gold You have placed there, but my wife has reminded me that one of the ewes is about to give birth, so we will remain near until her time."

They continued to walk throughout the vast garden, passing near a forest of trees where small animals approached the Almighty, all eager for His attention. He knelt to touch each one. As the woman watched, her heart ached with love for Him and the way He cared for even the smallest of His creatures.

The sun in the expanse above them grew lower in the west, and the air cooled their glowing skin. Adonai Elohim led them back toward Eden's center, then up a nearby rise in the land, when all at once an opening in the trees illumined the path with unearthly light. He motioned them to follow Him, and as had happened several times before, they found themselves on the mountain of God and entered a place not of the earth and yet still part of the earth. As if God's heavenly dwelling place had come to tabernacle with them on this vast and marvelous planet.

Angels of varying ranks came and knelt before Adonai Elohim, each one larger and stronger than they, each one colorful and shining like translucent jewels. The woman watched in awe as each angel spoke to Adonai Elohim in a language she did not understand. His nod or smile caused each one to bask in His approval.

The angels moved and took seats in a circle fanning away from the Creator while Adam stood near the throne, as Adonai had indicated. She clasped Adam's hand as she always did in these meetings, standing open and unashamed before the angelic group. Adam had spoken once or twice at these gatherings, but she had been too caught up in the awe of looking from one angelic being to another to open her mouth. The archangel Michael held the highest rank, but Lucifer seemed to shine brighter, like a star of the dawn. Gabriel, a third powerful angel, stood near Adonai Elohim's throne.

The council of God was present, and her heart grew light with joy. If she could have flown like the Spirit of God who moved in the midst of them, she would have done so for the unsurpassable thrill of being in God's heavenly presence. How privileged they were to be here.

The discussion carried on around her about things she could not comprehend. The heavens they spoke of were apparently above the clouds in the earthly expanse, far, far above them. The council of God normally met there, Adam had told her, except for these rare occasions when God wanted to bring heaven to earth.

Adam glanced at her, his heart in his gaze. Such love moved and breathed in this place. Such acceptance and beauty. How could they possibly take it all in?

"I never want to leave," she whispered in his ear.

"I can take Adam and his wife to the jewels of Havilah, my King," one of the lesser angels offered, drawing her back to their discussion.

"Or perhaps I could show them," Lucifer interjected, "since I am a guardian of the garden of God."

She looked at the angels and wondered why any of these beings would want to show her and Adam the things of earth when they preferred to discover the glories of its depths on their own. She heard Adonai Elohim speak, more in her heart than in His usual audible voice, assuring her that she could explore the space He had created for them, to the farthest reaches of the land in Eden and the surrounding rivers.

He then declined the angels' offer, affirming that she had not imagined His voice in her heart.

Love for the Creator rose anew within her. How blessed she was to glimpse what His highest heavens must be like—where many millions of angels and other hosts resided. Was Eden as beautiful? Would God ever show them heaven as well as earth?

But no. God had created earth for the *adams*, humankind, to fill and subdue it and tend to the growing and living things. This was their domain under His authority, the place where He would reside with them.

God with us, she thought. What more could she ever want?

2

Dawn broke over the eastern ridge of the bluest sky the woman had ever seen, giving her and Adam the light they needed as the ewe bore down to deliver a slimy, wet lamb into the grasses beneath her. The ewe quickly turned to lick the birthing fluid from the newborn lamb's wool.

"How wonderful and perfect she is," the woman exclaimed, clapping her hands and throwing herself into Adam's arms. "I want one!"

"You want a lamb?" Adam laughed at her attempt to pout.

"A baby, silly man! Birthing can't be so hard. The ewe showed little effort, and look, the lamb is already standing."

The lamb found her mother's teats and began to drink the milk she would need to sustain her life. The woman looked at her own breasts, then compared them to Adam's. She would definitely be the one to nurse a child and find her body filled with milk as easily as the ewe had. Obviously this was the Creator's design.

Adam cupped her face in his hands and kissed her, caressing her softly. "I would give you a child, my love. But I suspect Adonai Elohim is the one who will give us that life. One day He will quicken your womb." He took her hand, and together they walked among the small flock of sheep that had already produced six ewes and two rams.

"Why does He wait, I wonder?" she asked. "Chipmunks and bears and even Behemoth have mated and borne offspring." She loved to watch the long-necked gentle giants that rested in the shade of the Gihon, where the trees hung low and plants were plentiful.

"He does not tell us everything." Adam nibbled her ear, and she squirmed away from him, laughing.

"Perhaps He is waiting for something." She could not imagine what, but she rarely questioned the Creator. When she did, it was only to understand the things in the garden or to ask Him to tell them again how He had made each thing. If He wanted more *adams*, would He not simply speak them into existence or form them with His hands, as He had them?

Then again, she did not think so. Any new creatures would not spring from the earth but be born as the lamb had been.

She took Adam's hand and intertwined their fingers. "Our God is very creative." She smiled and coaxed him along the path toward the Gihon. "Let us go and see the other animals." Joy bubbled in her at the delight in his eyes. "I want to see Behemoth's new young."

She released his hand and took off running before he could say another word. He chased her through the soft grasses. They stopped short as the slow waters of the Gihon met their ears.

"I'm faster on land," she said, doing a little dance.

"And I'm faster in the water." He reached for her and lifted her up, twirling her around.

A high-pitched sound met their ears, causing Adam to set her down. He glanced toward the tall rushes. "Her offspring is talking to her." He crept near the river's edge, and she followed close behind him.

They bent low in the shade of a nearby lotus and watched as the young, long-necked lizard took a bite of the plant, just as its mother had done a moment before. "They are so big and powerful," the woman whispered. "Her tail is as strong as a cedar. Her thighs are so thick. Who could stand against her? And yet, she is so gentle and graceful." The beasts wouldn't hurt them, but she wasn't sure the mother would want to play as she had before, having a young one so new.

"They are among the biggest of God's creation," Adam said, his gaze moving over the beast's mammoth size. "Not even the hippos or crocodiles or largest elephants come close to her size. Even her young are bigger than they are at birth."

"Let's look at them under the water." She stepped into the water, held her breath to duck beneath the surface, and swam closer, but not too close. She turned back when the water churned. The beast had moved one foot and stirred the silt at the bottom of the river, making it impossible to see.

The woman rose to the surface and made her way to Adam. She sat on his lap and leaned her head against his shoulder while they studied the giant and her young. "She almost blends into her surroundings." She tilted her head to gaze into Adam's face.

Adam seemed to ponder her words. "She does. When I named her, she came up out of the water and let me stroke her neck. Bearing young has made her shy, I think."

"I wonder if I will feel like she does." She stood and ran her fingers through her hair. "I find it fascinating to see the different ways in which the animals treat their young."

"They are all unique," he said. "God intended it that way."

She reached for his hand to help him up, thinking about his words.

"We will be late again to our meeting with Adonai," Adam said, turning back toward the center of the garden.

She slipped her arm through his and skipped beside him. "Today was fun," she said, leaning up to kiss his cheek.

He looked at her, that ardent affection for her evident in his blue-black eyes. "Tonight we will see if Adonai will give you that baby you long for." He stopped to kiss her soundly, leaving her breathless, but then hurried on, with the promise of their love to come. Besides, she could have Adam anytime. Adonai came only in the evening, and she didn't want to miss Him.

3

A cool breeze lifted some of the strands of hair about the woman's face as she sat in the grass at Adonai Elohim's feet.

"The kingdom of God is like this mustard seed," He said, holding out the tiniest seed she had ever seen and then dropping it into her hand. He pointed to a large bush nearby. "Yet it grows into a plant large enough for the birds of the air to nest in."

She looked up at the birds in the trees, each one dressed in an assorted array of colors, from the tiny sparrow to the larger doves and jays and other birds she could not name, each trilling a different melody.

"But isn't the kingdom of God where God lives, in the highest heavens above us with the angels that we sometimes see?" Adam asked Him. "I know there are thrones and powers and dominions there, but how is it like a tree?"

She looked into Adam's puzzled gaze and then searched Adonai Elohim's kind eyes.

"The kingdom of God is about righteousness and peace and joy," He said. "It is a place of rest where God is worshiped."

"It sounds like here," she said, leaning against Adam's side, content in Adonai's presence. "Is it much like Eden?"

By His approving smile she sensed it was, though somehow not quite. Could humans inhabit the kingdom when they lived on earth and the Creator's abode was so far above them? Though He came to them and made His home with them each evening, He did not remain in Eden. They could see Him only at night when the breezes blew, and He walked with them or told them about things they struggled to understand. That He loved them and wanted to be with them was clear. Love from Adonai was perfect and complete, not the same as what she received from Adam.

Pure. That was what she felt in His presence. Pure love that would give all for her. She couldn't imagine what more He could possibly give them than this beautiful life that was already theirs, but she sensed that He possessed even more to give them one day. They would participate in something more grand and magnificent than she could possibly imagine.

What is it? She held His gaze, searching, longing, but she did not possess the ability to understand His thoughts. Of course, she was simply His creation, not His equal. He knew her thoughts, and she sensed in her spirit that what she asked of Him was not for her to know. She sighed, tilting her head to catch the last of the sun's rays on her skin.

And in that moment He disappeared from their sight.

"I wish we could understand Him better," she said, turning to sit cross-legged and face Adam. "I wish He stayed with us always."

"He wants us to create a life without His constant presence, to multiply and subdue the earth as He commanded. Yet I doubt He ever really leaves us." Adam took her hands in his.

"So He is still with us now, just not so we can see Him? Doesn't He go back to His kingdom in the highest heavens?" She lifted a brow, confused.

"I have a feeling He is everywhere at once. We can never escape Him, nor would we want to." He pulled her to her feet and walked with her toward one of the fruit trees. They plucked some of the ripe figs and fed each other, laughing as they attempted to eat at the same time.

"I never want to be away from Him," she said, still feeling the sense of Adonai's love like the warmth of Adam's arms.

"We never have to as long as we obey Him." Adam pointed to the Tree of Knowledge of Good and Evil in the center of the garden. "We must not even touch it lest we die. Then we will lose Him. We will lose ourselves."

She shuddered, sobering. "I won't even go near it." Even the Tree of Life seemed too close unless Adonai was there. To eat from it was allowed, but the risk was too great because of its nearness to the forbidden tree. God had told Adam they must not eat from that tree, and she determined she would do as Adam said.

Lucifer sat pensively in the council of the Ancient of Days. He looked down from his seat on earth's mountain at the garden he was to guard. Why did the Creator want him to guard a place that was beneath him? And to watch over the humans, a lesser race who held no power, was offensive to his higher sensibilities.

What did Adonai Elohim see in them? He talked with the *adams* every evening, and the woman sat at His feet looking up at Him with such adoration, Lucifer felt disgust curl inside him. The feeling was not new to him as he walked about the earth, watching the *adams* play with the creatures and frolic in the water. He'd even assumed the form of a few of the animals and spoke with the woman once. She had not even discerned that the animals could not talk, acting as though it was completely normal when he spoke to her from the body of a giant serpent. Of course, he had allowed some of his glory to shine through, so perhaps she thought him one of the angels she had met. She was much too simpleminded and so completely *innocent*. By comparison he was so much wiser.

Irritation spiked, and Lucifer examined his thoughts, glancing quickly at the Ancient of Days, whose fiery gaze was also watching the Son converse with the humans. The Spirit hovered in the earth's atmosphere, though God could seem to be in one place and actually be everywhere at once. Why was He the only one who could do such an amazing thing? Why not give His creations, especially one as wise as Lucifer, the ability to do the same?

He could do a lot with such power.

He checked himself. Such thoughts would do him no good. He was the delight of God and certainly cared for above the humans. There was no need to desire greater power.

But it *would* be a delight to have the woman look at *him* with such adoration. Her skin probably felt supple and soft to the touch too. If he were her master, there were so many things he would command of her. He almost smiled but caught himself again when he sensed the Almighty's gaze on him.

He feigned interest in the council's discussion and listened intently as the seraphim cried out "holy, holy, holy" over and over again.

He grew so weary of the praise to the Almighty. The never-ending words played like an unwanted refrain in his thoughts. What was so amazing about God that He deserved so much attention and affection? If that praise were aimed at *him* . . .

A new thought formed in his mind, instantly replacing all others and all sounds around him. He needed to leave. Needed to think. But where could he go that the Almighty would not see him?

He glanced about the large room filled with various colors and types of angels, all seemingly in awe of the Almighty. Then he caught the gaze of one angel, then another, the slightest frown here, a hint of a scowl there. He sensed the same jealousy rising in his fellow angelic beings. They who were higher than the humans should command more attention and respect from the one seated on the throne.

He swiveled his gaze back to the central throne, but to his relief, the Ancient of Days still watched the Son talking with the humans. He was safe in his observations and nearly rebellious thoughts. He must be careful though. He would have to find a way to discuss these irritating actions of God with his fellow angels when he could find somewhere to be alone.

But where?

His mind whirled with the brilliant idea of the exact place to go. If enough of the angels supported him, he could receive the adoration he only dreamed of now.

His thoughts silently screamed at him, his heart jubilant. *That's it! I will ascend to heaven and set my throne above God's stars. I will preside on the mount of the assembly far away in the north. I will climb to the highest heavens and be like the Most High.*

He glanced once more at the center throne, then rose slowly so as to not create a stir. With his wings lifting him up, he floated above the floor, his tail sweeping in little movements. *Slowly. Don't draw attention.* He was near the door now and moved to leave the chamber as other angels had done in the past. It wasn't like they were not free to come and go.

Without warning, his wings failed to hold him, and he felt himself falling, falling, spiraling out of control far from the glorious lights of the kingdom of heaven.

Downward. The earth passed him in a blur as he flailed, trying to somehow right himself, to *fly* upward! Then the earth disappeared from his view, along with the stars above it. Darkness so deep, deeper than that which had once covered the earth in chaos, closed over him. He landed in a heap. All of the brilliant colors that had once flashed in his gemstone-laden body were snuffed out. He saw nothing but darkness.

In the distance, he heard a consistent thump of something hitting the hard surface where he now sat stunned.

The voice of the Ancient of Days bellowed in the darkness. "How you are fallen from heaven, O shining star, son of the morning. You have been thrown down to the earth. For you said to yourself, 'I will ascend to heaven and set my throne above God's stars. I will preside on the mount of the assembly far away in the north. I will climb to the highest heavens and be like the Most High.' Instead, you will be brought down to the place of the dead, down to its lowest depths."

Somewhere beyond him, Lucifer heard the cries of other beings who had landed with him here. Were they the angels who had met his gaze with the same jealousy and angry thoughts?

This was what God meant when He told humankind not to eat from the Tree of Knowledge of Good and Evil or they would die. Was this death?

Then why could he still feel? Still think? Was death a place or a loss of all he had known before? Surely he could leave this place. He must!

The whimpering coming from behind him aroused his ire, and he wanted to whip sense into all of them. There had to be a way to regain God's favor.

God's favor. Did he truly care what God thought? Why should he go groveling and beg for the Almighty's forgiveness? There was no forgiveness for one who went against His will. He knew it was true, though he had never tested the thought. And if there was no way back into heaven's realm, there had to be a way to get out of here and make God pay for this.

But how did one go after the Almighty One, who could see everywhere and knew everything, even the thoughts and intents of the heart? How did one hurt God?

He pondered the ways, considered discussing a plan with the others who had apparently suffered his fate. But he was Lucifer, son of the morning, guardian of the garden of God! He didn't need the advice of lesser angels.

He moved about slowly, creating a path in a small circle. His sight would not adjust to the dark. The dark had overcome it. But if he could get out of here and be free to roam the earth, he knew exactly what he would do to repay God. He would entice the humans. He would go after the woman, and she would convince the man to eat the fruit.

A gleeful feeling rose up within him, and he let out a cackling laugh that he didn't recognize. But it felt good to release it. It felt so very good to think he could do harm to the Creator. If he would not be allowed the chance to return to the council and have all forgiven, he would go after the apple of God's eye. The humans whom He loved.

That would hurt Him more than anything.

4

The first rays of the sun kissed the woman's face, and the birds twittered their greetings as she rose from beside Adam among the soft grasses. She raised her arms to the heavens and yawned, the joy of being alive filling her. She turned at a touch on her arm and found herself encased in her husband's embrace. He kissed her softly.

"And how is my bride this fine day?" He brushed the hair behind her ear and kissed her earlobe. "Beautiful as always."

She giggled and pulled slightly away. "You say the same to me every morning."

He tilted his head, his gaze capturing hers. "Not every morning."

She took his hand and pulled him toward the apricot tree. She plucked the fruit from the branch and handed it to him, then took one for herself. "I'm hungrier than usual," she said. When had she begun to have this constant hunger? In the past, the food she ate always satisfied, but now she could not seem to get enough.

Adam bit into the ripe fruit, the juice spilling over his hand. He tossed the pit to the ground, then bent to brush the stickiness into the grass. "Let us walk to the spring."

She didn't object, for her thirst needed quenching and she

longed to dip her body into the water and let the warming sun dry her skin. As they walked hand in hand, she stumbled slightly.

He held her upright. "Did you trip on something?"

She shook her head. "Did you not feel that?"

Adam stopped to listen and swung his head to search the area. "I don't see anything."

"It wasn't something to see. I felt a strange shift in the atmosphere, like something has changed." A shudder worked through her. She glanced at her belly and noticed that even it seemed larger than before. Was she eating too much? She touched her skin, and Adam's hand covered hers.

"I wonder if it is you who is changing," he said, his voice filled with awe.

She met his gaze. "What are you saying?"

"I don't know. Maybe your body is changing, so you sensed a shift there, not in the atmosphere."

His hand on her middle made her blush, and she sensed his desire. But it was too early to share their love. They had work the Creator had given them to do.

She intertwined their fingers and continued walking toward the spring. "Come, my dear husband. Let us care for the garden first. Perhaps you are right. The shift could be inside of me, as my body does seem different than it was. It may not have been in the atmosphere at all."

"Maybe Adonai Elohim has finally given you what you desire and you will bear fruit like the animals do." Adam smiled down at her, and her eyes widened at the thought. How would she know for sure? Hunger and a swelling belly could be anything.

She shoved the idea aside, unable to believe she could conceive after they had been together nearly a year with no offspring to call their own. "If you are right, we will know in time."

He laughed. "Yes, we will. Perhaps you should ask Adonai tonight."

The idea filled her with shyness. She had never asked the Creator for anything. Not even to give her a child in their likeness, as she longed for. No, Adam was mistaken. But even if he wasn't, she could not ask Adonai. Her whole body heated at the thought. He had made them to procreate, but that didn't mean she felt comfortable talking with Him about such things.

"I should ask Him about the shift in the atmosphere," she said.

"And He would tell you it was nothing." Adam seemed so sure of himself that she could only nod.

They reached the spring, and while he washed his hands, she sat in the water, letting the cool liquid flow over her. She leaned her head back, her hair floating behind her, her face warmed by the sun. What would it be like to bear a child in their image? Would he or she also be like the Creator? Would every human bear the image of the Almighty One?

She longed to feel comfortable enough to ask such questions.

She rose and began the work for the day, feeding the lambs that came to her with sunflower seeds she found among the plants, a treat she often offered them in addition to the grass they ate in abundance. She touched their soft wool and bent to look into their round, dark eyes. She tweaked their noses and watched them bound away to play, then turned to prune another of the fruit trees that had grown too tall. Adam worked near her on a different tree, and she nibbled more fruit as she worked. If only she could stop feeling so hungry!

She stopped abruptly at the sight of one of the shining ones. His upper body glittered like clear jewels while his lower body and scaly tail gleamed bronze. His face was not like hers or Adam's but like one of the angels'. The shape of his head was like that of Behemoth or one of the dragons, but with a thicker forehead and smoother, rounder eyes and mouth. His wings did not move behind him, and he stood watching her. He leaned against the Tree of Knowledge of Good and Evil, and the brightness of his gaze beckoned her.

What was he doing here? Had Adonai Elohim sent him with a

message for them? But Adonai always spoke to them directly. Why would He send one of His angelic beings?

She looked behind her, catching Adam's eye, and nodded toward the creature. Adam lifted a dark brow, his expression showing apprehension and surprise. No doubt he, too, wondered why one of God's angels would appear to them in the middle of the day near the tree they were supposed to avoid.

But as she looked again at the creature's beauty, she found herself slowly moving closer to him. His power to draw her near seemed impossible to resist, and her curiosity over his presence won over any thought to wait and ask Adonai who he was. What could it hurt to speak with one of Adonai's council? One of His chosen angels?

Her heart pounded as the tree came into clearer view. She should not be here. She had promised herself she would not even come near enough to touch the forbidden tree, but she also knew the moment she stepped onto the soil at its base that she would not turn back. She did not even turn to look at Adam. There was no need, for she sensed his presence behind her.

Lucifer forced himself not to flick his tongue or bare his teeth as the woman walked toward him. He had the sudden urge to devour her like prey, but the Almighty One would surely stop him from harming His beloved humans. No, she must choose as he had. God would have no choice then but to destroy these *adams* He had made.

He tamped down the desire to laugh. Not yet. First he must convince her and that overprotective husband of hers to eat the fruit.

His confidence grew with each moment. She couldn't take her eyes off him. He would find a way. If the Ancient of Days gave His angels one chance to obey or rebel, He would surely do the same for the humans. If Lucifer could get them to choose death, they would never be free of him, never be able to lavish their adoration on the Son. They would worship *him* forever! And he already had in mind the things he would do with her.

She stood only a few paces from him now, her wide eyes taking in his beauty. Good. Let her admire him. At least the Creator had not taken away his ability to shine brightly when he wanted to, though since the change, he found himself wanting to take on different forms. The kind that might frighten the humans.

"You are here," he said when she stopped short of touching the tree where he now leaned. He flicked his gaze to Adam. *As are you.*

"Why are you here?" she asked, as though surprised to see him.

"Surely you remember we have met in the council many times."

"I have seen you now and then," she admitted. "But never outside of the council. Why are you here now?"

He looked her up and down, noting the slight swelling of her belly. So, she carried human offspring. Unfortunate. Did she know it yet?

He swiveled his head from her to the tree. "The fruit is enticing, is it not?"

"It is not for us to know," she said, looking away.

No, don't look away. He changed tactics. "Did God *really* say, 'You must not eat from *any* tree in the garden'?"

She looked puzzled by his question. She would think he should know these things, but he feigned ignorance with a look heavenward.

She cleared her throat and glanced at the fruit. "We may eat fruit from the trees in the garden, but God did say, 'You must not eat fruit from the tree that is in the middle of the garden, and you must not touch it, or you will die.'"

"Die?" He fluttered his wings and curled his body more tightly against the tree. He shook his head, his gaze boring into hers. "You will not certainly die." His voice a mere whisper now, he went on. "God knows that when you eat from it your eyes will be opened, and you will be *like God* . . . knowing good *and* evil." He smiled

38

inwardly at the way he had emphasized just the right words. By her look, he knew he had captured her interest.

She turned her head, her gaze no longer on him but on the tree and its ripe fruit, red and bulging, nearly pulsating with life all its own.

He again resisted the urge to flick his tongue. He was sure he had her now. But there was no use pushing too fast or too far—he could lose her if he said any more. He would wait and let her make the choice he wanted.

The woman gazed at the ripe fruit with its round surface and starlike end hanging from branches with thin green leaves. Beneath its hard skin, what did it taste like? It was pleasing to the eye, so it must be pleasing to the tongue. She tilted her head, examining it. Like some of the other fruit in the garden, she would have to peel it to get to the center. It might take some work, but the color and shape were undeniably appealing.

The knowledge of good and *evil?* She lived every day with the good Adonai Elohim had given to her and Adam, so what more would it benefit them both if they knew evil too? She wasn't even sure what evil was, but the serpent angel seemed to think it was wise to know both.

She hesitated, glancing first at the serpent angel, then at Adam, who now stood beside her. She did not want to disobey Adonai Elohim, but what if this was a way to be more like Him? The serpent angel had said God knew that if they ate the fruit, they would be like Him. What better way to please Him than to be like Him?

A check in her spirit made her pause. Adam had told her that God said not to eat of it. Wouldn't God tell them Himself if He had changed His mind? But what if He had indeed sent this messenger to assure them that all was well, that it was okay now to eat of this tree? Hadn't they obeyed Him for more than a year? Hadn't they done all He had asked of them? Perhaps they had passed whatever test they must pass, and now, according to this messenger, they were free to change the path they had followed for so long.

Her mind whirled even as she could not take her gaze from the appealing fruit. Would it really hurt to taste it? What did it mean to die anyway? If they could gain wisdom and know both good and evil, then they could communicate with God even better! They would be more like Him and be able to better understand Him.

Her hesitancy gone now, she lifted her hand and slowly touched the closest fruit. She still breathed. She had not died from touching the tree. She released a deep sigh. If touching the tree did not bring death, then eating of the fruit must not either.

She plucked one of the round red bulbs from the tree, the scent overpowering her. Then she tore into the flesh, revealing small red seeds beneath the skin. She scooped some of them into her mouth, leaving a freshness and a kind of tanginess on her tongue. She smiled and turned, holding out the broken fruit to Adam.

"It's good." She felt nearly giddy when he took it from her and scooped a handful of the plump seeds into his mouth.

He laughed, then kissed her, their decision mutual and binding them together.

For a moment.

The serpent angel laughed, the sound holding no mirth. They both looked at him, then at each other, and she realized in a moment of stark truth that something had indeed shifted. Not just in the atmosphere, which she could still not explain, but in their view of each other.

"We are naked," she whispered, suddenly ashamed in her husband's presence, and in the presence of the shining one.

The serpent angel laughed again, this time sounding eerily strange. *You will not certainly die*, he had promised them. But something had certainly died at that very moment.

They had died to an innocence they could not define. No longer did she take pride in her bare skin and the body the Creator had made for her. Adam also seemed ashamed to show himself to her as he always had.

She turned and ran off, searching for something with which to cover her exposed skin, Adam close on her heels. Fig leaves. They were bigger than the leaves of the tree they had just eaten from. She would pull vines from the grapes and use the thin tendrils to attach the leaves together as a covering.

"This should help," she said, pulling leaves from one of the fig trees and handing some to Adam.

He nodded. No smile graced his lips now, and all she could feel was pain for having led him to disobey their Creator. And in the distance she could still hear the serpent angel laughing.

5

Adam sat beneath the long branches of a willow tree, fig leaves scratching his skin. He chafed and shifted and glared at his wife, who sat some distance from him, also hidden beneath the tree, huddling forward as if to cover herself with her arms, though the fig leaves already did so.

Why had he listened to her? He knew better than to have taken the fruit from her hand. Hadn't the Creator Himself told him not to eat of it? But he hadn't expected this. How had he never realized that they were naked? The beauty of their bodies had seemed so innocent, something that had evoked pride and desire for each other. Now he could barely look at her.

He glanced up at the slender branches, their long leaves drooping toward the river that moved past them, flowing faster than it had before. Had the river changed? The willow itself seemed to weep, as Adam longed to do, for he knew they could not hide from God forever. It was almost time for Him to walk with them in the cool of the day, but how did he dare show his face to the All-Knowing One?

He glanced again at his wife, no longer pleased with her, no longer desiring her. In the past, one look her way had lifted his spirits, and their coming together had surpassed any joy except for the joy they found in God's presence. But now . . .

A shudder worked through him, and he scratched an itch where the fig leaves irritated him. He didn't want to be near either God or his wife. Perhaps he could find solace among the animals. But as one of the deer came to a small pool the river had formed, it startled when Adam moved. The doe's eyes widened, and it scampered away without drinking.

Adam hung his head. He would find no solace among the animals. They had never fled from him before. They had come and eaten from his hand. He'd held their offspring in his arms, and they had drawn close, seemingly proud of what they had produced, glad he had noticed.

What was to happen to them now? A deep sigh filled his chest. A moment later, he stilled, fear nearly stopping his heart.

That sound. He looked at his wife, who met his gaze with a tearful one of her own.

"Adonai Elohim has come," she said so low he barely heard her above the pounding in his chest.

He nodded. How long could they stay here? Where could they go?

"Adam! Where are you?" God's voice sounded as though it was right behind him, yet when he jerked about to look, he did not see Him. But then, God's voice could split the mountains by its power. He could have whispered and Adam would still have heard Him as clear as birdsong in the morning.

"We have to go to Him," she said, though she did not move. "He already knows where we are."

"No thanks to you," he spat, slowly rising. He did not bother to help her up, and she scrambled to her feet and readjusted the ridiculous covering over her. She could have thought of a better, wider leaf. But it was too late now.

He stepped from beneath the willow's leaves and heard her following. One hesitant step after another, they finally came to the place where Adonai Elohim awaited them.

"I heard You in the garden," Adam said to Adonai, "and I was afraid because I was naked. So I hid."

Adonai Elohim looked from him to the woman, His gaze like nothing she had ever seen before. "Who told you that you were naked? Have you eaten from the tree that I commanded you not to eat from?"

She braced herself, waiting for Adam to spew his wrath at her. It was her fault, after all.

"The woman You put here with me—she gave me some fruit from the tree, and I ate it."

Hadn't she known he would blame her? But the words hurt just the same.

Adonai Elohim's fiery gaze searched Adam's until Adam could not hold it, then He faced her, and His eyes held sorrow. They had wounded Him. By disobeying Him, they had torn something within Him.

"What is this you have done?" He asked, his tone firm yet gentle.

She looked beyond Adonai toward the tree where the serpent angel waited, his expression nearly giddy. He had wanted them to disobey. He was not a messenger sent to tell them something new from God. How had one of God's angels become so deceptive?

She looked again into Adonai's eyes, then focused on her feet, her cheeks heating in shame. "The serpent deceived me, and I ate."

Silence followed her remark for many breaths, and her body felt it would collapse under the weight of her disobedience.

Adonai turned to face the serpent angel. "Because you have done this, cursed are you above all livestock and all wild animals! You will crawl on your belly and you will eat dust all the days of your life."

Instantly, the body of the angel morphed as though shedding

its angelic skin, revealing a dragon-like snake without wings or the ability to stand. The angelic spirit that had inhabited the beast floated above it, though it no longer seemed able to take on the gleaming, jeweled body. The spirit scowled, and a feeling of intense hatred filled the air between the spirit and Adonai.

The woman stared, wondering if they would somehow fight, but Adonai's voice resounded in her ear again.

"I will put enmity between you and the woman, and between your offspring and hers; he will crush your head, and you will strike his heel."

The spirit hissed like the snake it had been. What did Adonai mean? Offspring? So she would live and bear children, and one of them would crush this evil spirit.

This was what God had not wished them to know—that evil could exist. And their disobedience—their choice to do what they wanted instead of asking God for wisdom and keeping His command in mind—had ushered evil into God's perfect world.

She hung her head again as Adonai spoke to her. "I will make your pains in childbearing very severe; with painful labor you will give birth to children. Your desire will be for your husband, and he will rule over you."

Was it any worse than she deserved? Yet her punishment seemed too much to bear. She had never felt pain or given birth to a child, so how severe could it be? And Adam had always been her equal, her partner in every way. They complemented each other. He had never commanded her to do anything. They were to rule and subdue the earth together. What did God mean that her husband would now rule over her? Would she lose her ability to come to God on her own, to be close and listen to His voice with or without Adam?

She barely heard Adonai's words to Adam until He mentioned her. "Because you listened to your wife and ate fruit from the tree about which I commanded you, 'You must not eat from it,' cursed is the ground because of you; through painful toil you will eat food from it all the days of your life. It will produce thorns and thistles for you, and you will eat the plants of the field. By the sweat of your brow you will eat your food until you return to the ground, since from it you were taken; for dust you are and to dust you will return."

So they would die as God had said. The serpent had lied to her, and she had foolishly believed it. But God had held Adam responsible for the majority of their sin. He could have stopped her. He could have refused her. What would have happened to her if he had not also eaten?

He had been given the command directly from God. She had gotten it from Adam. God had expected better from Adam, though she was no less guilty.

Adonai gazed at both of them one more time, then walked away toward the small flock of sheep grazing in the distance.

Adam faced her. "So you will bear children. Therefore, I give you the name Eve, for you will be the mother of all the living."

Now he finally named her? He had named the animals before she was even created. Why had he taken so long to bless her with something so personal? And why at this moment, when they were struggling to understand the consequences of what they had done?

Eve turned her attention to Adonai again. He picked up one of the larger rams and carried it over His shoulders. When He set it near them, it made no attempt to run off. He took stones from the ground nearby and laid one on top of another until a structure stood not far from both the tree they had eaten of and the Tree of Life.

He took the animal and motioned for them to come closer, telling them to place their hands on its head. Eve remembered this ram as one of God's initial creations. How she had loved running her fingers through its wool.

Adonai looked into their eyes, His own bearing a new expression that she could not define. She sensed that what He was about to do was costing Him more than their punishments would cost them.

With their hands on the head of the ram, Adonai slit its throat, blood spilling onto His white robe and splattering onto their bare feet.

"Oh!" The cry escaped her, and tears, a sensation she had never known, slipped down her cheeks. Adam gasped beside her, but she could not look at him.

In slow, deliberate motions, as if He wanted them to repeat what He was showing them, Adonai skinned the animal and made clothes for them to replace the fig leaves, then cut up the body and placed it on the stones. As they watched, fire came down from heaven and consumed the animal.

The blood stained Adonai's robe, and though He said nothing in explanation, Eve knew this was the cost of their sin. The ram's blood meant something she couldn't understand, but her favorite ram having to die just to cover her body and free her from the shame of her nakedness filled her with intense grief.

She and Adam stared at the stone altar, blackened now with the ashes of the ram. Oh, what had they done? What would they do now?

Before she could think of what might come next, God spoke, and it was as if Adonai Elohim and the Spirit and the Ancient of Days all conversed at once. "The man has now become like one of us, knowing good and evil. He must not be allowed to reach out his hand and take also from the Tree of Life and eat and live forever."

She glanced at the Tree of Life. What if they had eaten of it immediately after eating from the other? Now they would never taste its fruit.

Adonai Elohim took them by the hands and walked with them to the outer edge of the garden, where they would live outside of its protection. The ground looked less lush and colorful here, its beauty diminished by half. It felt completely foreign. They had never come this far from the borders of the garden before.

Eve looked at Adam, and together they glanced back at the garden's entrance. Eden was blocked by cherubim with flaming swords that flashed back and forth. God had made sure they would not live forever but would one day indeed die, just as He had promised.

6

Eve stumbled after Adam's long strides, her once sure foot-
ing weighted with anguish. Adam was obviously looking
for a place that might give them shelter for the night. The
Euphrates River meandered by on their left. The sun had already
touched the edge of the western sky, and though the moon gave
light, fear filled her. By the time Adonai Elohim had escorted them
from the garden, the cool of the day had long passed, so Adam
was right to hurry. Would they be safe beneath the trees? Did the
wild animals inhabit the areas outside of the garden?

Adam stopped abruptly at the edge of a forest they had not
known. The river tapered to a stream here, and open grasses would
cushion them as they slept. "This will have to do for tonight,"
he said, finally turning to look at her as she slowly drew closer.
"Tomorrow I will build some type of shelter."

They'd never needed shelter in the garden. They'd never needed
coverings for their bodies either.

She wondered if he would sleep at her side as he always had.
Would she rest securely in his arms or be left on her own? They
could never procreate and fill the earth if he abandoned her. They
would both die and the race of humans would end. But perhaps
that would be a good thing.

"Are you cold?" he asked, drawing her to look into his eyes. She had barely looked up from her feet since God's sentence on her sin. How could she face Adam—or God, should He ever speak to her again?

She clutched her arms about her in a self-protective gesture. "A little," she admitted. "It is not as warm out here."

He opened his arms to her. "Come."

She stepped closer, uncertain. Why was she no longer confident in his love? Was this, too, part of the curse?

His arms came around her, holding her near. His breath was close to her ear, and the night sounds of insects and winged creatures filled the air around them.

"I'm afraid, Adam. And I'm sorry." She didn't know if he would forgive her, for hadn't he been quick to blame her when God confronted them?

He patted her back and rested his head on top of hers. "I'm sorry too. I was the one who heard the direct command from God. I knew better than you did that we were going against God's word when we listened to the beast."

"I still wish I'd walked away from him instead of toward him." A shiver worked through her. "Why didn't we just die on the spot as I thought we would?"

Adam said nothing for a moment, then held her at arm's length. "I think God still has plans for humanity, and we are still part of them. Life will just be different now. Harder."

She touched her middle, wondering again if a child was already growing in her belly. How would she know? A thought struck her.

"Adam?"

He lifted a brow.

"What if a baby is already growing inside of me? Will that child also bear our curse? If he was conceived in the garden, did our sin transfer to him?"

Adam took her hands and found a place for them to lie in the grass and look up at the sky now littered with stars. "Everything now suffers from what we have done. The animals are subject to God's curse. Even the ground. Any child you bear will carry God's image and ours as well, and ours is now broken and sinful. Our children, no matter where they were or are conceived, cannot escape that."

"I wish that were not true," she said, leaning into the crook of his arm. "I want our children to have a pure chance to make their own choices."

He didn't respond immediately but let the night sounds fill the silence. At last he spoke. "Our children will all make their own choices of whether to obey or disobey Adonai. The difference is, they will never know a life of innocence as we did, once they are old enough to understand right from wrong. We knew no wrong. They always will."

She pondered his words, saddened by them. How he knew these things, she was not sure, but in her spirit she was certain he was right.

"I will help you build the shelter tomorrow." She kissed his cheek. "Thank you for not sending me away from you."

"Where would you go, and how would we live without each other?" He seemed almost piqued by her comment. "Like it or not, we have no one but the two of us. I'm not even sure God will visit us as He used to. If we want to survive, we have to stay together."

"So you only stay because of need, not want?" She longed to be wanted by him in that moment.

He shifted onto his side to face her, his gaze softening. "I'm sorry, Eve. I am not used to anger or blame or hating myself or any of these new unhappy emotions I now feel. I cannot promise I will always want you. And you cannot promise me that either. At times we may hate each other. But I will tell you this. I will not abandon you. I will not stop sharing our love. You are my wife, created by God especially for me. I will not despise His gift of you as I despised His command. I will do my best to keep my word."

She offered a tentative smile. "And I promise the same."

He kissed her, but the once-normal coming together as man and wife did not happen. She sensed his hesitance and tension as he lay his head in the grass and pulled her to rest against him. He said he would not leave her, but would their love ever be the same?

The next day Eve rose early, but Adam had already left her side. She looked around, not seeing him, feeling suddenly afraid in this unknown place. She walked to the brook, comforted by the sound of the water, and scooped some into her hand to drink. Bending low, she washed her face.

Footsteps coming from behind made her jump. *Adam?* Why she thought it would be anyone else, she did not know. Her nervousness troubled her. Would the beast appear to them again? Try to hurt them?

She straightened and accepted several pieces of fruit from Adam's hands.

"I found these," he said. "Apparently God planted fruit trees outside of the garden too, so we will have food until I can figure out how to plant the grains that grew up from the ground in Eden."

"I can look for other edible plants as well."

He nodded. "First we must find a way to build a shelter. The animals are no longer friendly toward us. I saw a bear in the woods nearby, and I could not approach it. I'm not sure who was more afraid, the bear or me." He bit into a pear, the juice trickling over his beard.

She took a small bite of hers, looking about them, wondering what they could possibly use to build a shelter that would make them feel safe. If only Adonai had built one for them as He had made their clothing. But the clothing had been costly, and she could not bear to see another animal killed because of her sin.

"Do you have plans for what we need for this shelter?" she asked as he tossed the core of his pear into the woods.

He dipped his hands into the water and rinsed his mouth. "I've given it some thought, and there are a number of possibilities. We could look near the mountains for a cave. If we follow the stream toward the highlands, we will be away from some of the wild animals, though not the wild donkeys and goats. But they shouldn't harm us. Surely there are caves in the sides of the mountains where the night creatures live."

She shuddered. "I'd rather not share our home with bats or owls."

"We will look for one that is vacant, or we will coax them out by removing their nests or resting places." He ran a hand through his thick, dark hair.

"That does seem to be the wisest and quickest thing to do. But will we be too far from the fruit and nut trees or the flatter land where you might cultivate lentils and grains?" She hated the thought of him having to walk a great distance each day while she remained in the cave or went off in a different direction searching for something to eat.

"Eventually we will figure out how to build something else. Perhaps Adonai will come to us and allow us to ask for wisdom." He glanced toward the mountains, Eden nestled in their foothills.

Longing for the only home she had ever known rose within her. Why, oh why had she ever listened to the serpent? Regret settled over her again, but even if she and Adam tried to return, the cherubim would stop them.

The sound of bleating sheep met her ear, and Adam turned with her toward Eden. There, coming toward them as if guided by God Himself, was the small flock that had begun to be fruitful in the garden, minus the ram that had given its life for them. Behind them came more animals—goats and cattle and donkeys, though many went in opposite directions.

"It is as though Adonai has decided to send even the animals out of His home on earth," she said, glancing at Adam. "Why do you think He would do that?"

Adam shrugged and walked toward the sheep. He called each

one by name, and they followed him. She joined him, a small sense of gratitude filling her. God had not sent them off alone. He had given them the animals to care for. Perhaps He would give them seeds as well.

"We will take them with us, along with the small herd of cattle, and settle in the foothills if we can find a cave. Perhaps Adonai will join us again soon." He seemed relieved, and she released a sigh.

"At least not all of the animals fear us. Some will still allow us to care for them." She wondered about the big cats, for she dearly loved the lions, tigers, cheetahs, and panthers. But she would not search for them. Their big paws and sharp claws could turn against her.

She glanced behind her and glimpsed one of the young lionesses bounding away from them into the wild. Apparently their days of hugging the cats and riding upon their backs or running beside them were no more.

7

dam climbed the base of the foothills ahead of Eve, who
followed behind the sheep, goats, donkeys, and cattle
that had left the garden and come at their command. Eve
stopped often to wait for the animals to graze, while Adam forged
ahead, looking for shelter. He supposed there must be a way to
build a shelter out of the trees or the clay that lay in the bottom of
the rivers where the water wasn't deep. But that would take time,
and he wanted a place where they were safe now.

Safe. He had never considered that word before. Or felt the
need for safety. God had put them in a place where they had never
considered evil or harm.

Adam rubbed the back of his neck, feeling the sweat from the
heat of the sun. Why hadn't he told Eve no? If he'd been stronger,
been able to resist the words of the serpent and the look of excitement in her eyes . . .

He sighed. There was no going back now. He glanced behind
him, where Eve seemed small in the distance with the animals surrounding her. He would need to build shelters for them too, to keep
them from predators. How did he know which animals would now
be tame and which would be wild, when they had all been living
in harmony since their creation?

He couldn't answer that, but somehow he understood things he had never considered before, like how to build an enclosure. He would find stones and stack them with an opening. He would have to find a way to block that opening once the animals were inside, but each group—sheep, goats, cattle, and donkeys—would need their own spaces.

He looked in every direction. At least the earth was large enough to hold all that God had made. Even as they filled the earth and the animals birthed more after their kind, even as he and Eve bore sons and daughters after their kind, in the image of God, they would never bear so many that the land could not hold them.

He closed his eyes for a moment, longing for shade against the glare of the sun. Trees dotted the hillside, but he was not near one. He kept climbing, noticing a line of caves cut out of the cliffs, as though God had put them there for the use of the night creatures. They were places the humans were never supposed to have inhabited, of that Adam was sure.

God's plan for them had been Eden forever. Why had He given them a choice? To test their loyalty to Him? Sudden anger filled Adam at the thought. Why give His image-bearers a reason to walk away from Him? The animals had no such chance.

If not for that choice, he wouldn't know this constant sense of grief and the anger that rose up at the slightest inconvenience or if Eve said a wrong word. They'd barely been away from Eden a full day, and yet he couldn't stop the need to blame her, despite their mutual forgiveness of each other. But was it God whom he blamed the most?

He shook the irritating thoughts aside, certain he could no longer think clearly. Why would he want to blame the Creator whom he had loved from the beginning?

Regret dogged his steps, slowing his gait as he drew nearer the caves. How dark they were. Somehow he and Eve would need a way for light to come in or they would never see each other once the sun set. Oh, for the fire God had kindled and taught them to use when the grain ripened. In Eden he had known what to do and where to find what he needed. Was the outside world so different?

Of course it was. God hadn't sent them out with the kindled fire. He would have to figure out how to harness it himself.

He fisted his hands, fighting the bitter taste of this new life. He needed Adonai's help, but he wouldn't ask Him. Couldn't ask.

Sudden movement caught his eye. Had Eve joined him so quickly? He turned, heart pounding, fearing the unseen ones. Fearing the animals who had now gone wild. But there, a short distance away, stood Adonai Elohim. In His hand He held a branch with flames like the sun's rays pouring from the top where leaves should be. The kindled fire.

Dumbstruck and terrified to approach Him, Adam fell to his knees and bowed low. *Forgive me.* He could think of nothing else to say. Why would the Creator give him any notice when He knew Adam's thoughts were against Him? He kept his face to the ground, shaking, but a moment later he felt God's touch. He slowly lifted his head and stood, enveloped in God's peace. He took the branch Adonai Elohim held out to him.

The fire matched the blaze in God's eyes, a sight Adam had long grown used to, only now it seemed different. He studied the branch. Something coated the end of it where the fire burned, like the resin of a plant.

He looked at Adonai, then his gaze skittered away. He was too unworthy to face God's scrutiny again, especially after his bitter thoughts. But his heart thanked Him. God had given him a torch to light his way into the cave. From it he could make more torches or build fires to cook the grains he would harvest.

He looked up at a faint whooshing sound, disappointed that Adonai had left him. Of course He couldn't stay. Adam was no longer purely good. That He had visited at all surprised Adam. Would He bless them with His presence again? Perhaps life in the world outside of Eden wouldn't be impossible if he knew that God would still come to his aid.

He wished Eve had been beside him when Adonai had handed him the fire. He turned to see where she was, but she was still too far from him to have glimpsed God. Perhaps another time. He would have to tell her, for she would ask about the fire. And in that moment he wished all over again that they could walk together with God every evening, sit among His council, and see all that He had made, both easily visible and usually hidden.

He trudged on and headed inside the first cave, carrying the torch. Soon he would find the right shelter. He couldn't think about the rest until he had settled this.

Eve met Adam outside of a large cave, where he stood with a torch in his right hand. She lifted a brow, giving him a curious look. The animals gathered around her, mingling together.

"You found something," she said, looking from his face to the cave and then to the fire. "How did you think to make fire like the flames of God's eyes?" Adonai's eyes had been enough to tell her that God was more than love. In His gaze were passion and fire that she had never understood.

"Yes, I found this," Adam said, interrupting her thoughts. His arm swept in an arc toward the interior of the cave. "It is large enough for us and the animals, until I can build them their own shelters or find caves where I can hem them in. For now, I want them near."

"Where did you get this?" She angled her head toward the torch.

"Adonai Elohim gave it to me." He looked at his feet, then met her gaze with a sense of awe in his expression. "I thought to ask for His help but then decided against it, thinking I could find a way to make fire without Him. I knew I could not see inside the cave to tell whether a wild animal slept in the darkness. I did not want to awaken danger." He ran a hand over his face. "And suddenly He stood there with this." He held the torch out. "I don't know why He came. I do not deserve His kindness."

"Did He speak to you?"

Adam shook his head. "No. But I sensed compassion in the look He gave me. Perhaps living in the world won't be so bad if we can still see Him now and then. If He hears our thoughts and knows our needs, perhaps we can talk to Him, just not face-to-face." There was sadness in his tone, and Eve knew he already missed God's walks with them as much as she did.

"I would like that," she said, coming closer and placing a hand on his arm. "I miss Him too." She kissed his cheek and pointed to the cave. "Shall we get the animals inside and you can show me where we will sleep tonight?"

He nodded. Food was still a problem. Though they had found nuts and fruit as they walked toward the caves, they would have little else. Adam would have to till the ground and learn to grow grains. She could find seeds and heat them over the fire now that God had given it to Adam. But she would need to learn to make something to heat them in. *Oh, Adonai, how much I need Your wisdom.* She had seen stalks growing near the river that could be woven to make things. Perhaps to hold the nuts away from the ground, where animals might find them.

"There is so much to learn," she said as Adam led her into the dark recesses of the cave. "So much I long for Adonai to show me. The garden provided for our needs, and I know how to tend to the plants, but we never needed clothing until now. What about other things?"

"What other things?"

"What if we are cold? How do I make coverings without killing another animal? What if I want to store something out of reach of the rodents and other scurrying animals?" The list in her mind seemed endless and overwhelming.

"We take it one day at a time," he said, taking her hand. "If God helped us this far, He will give us understanding on what else we need to do."

"You sound very sure."

"I'm not at all sure, but I have to believe He will not leave us helpless."

She shook her head. "No. He will not abandon us completely." She knew it deep down, but the unfamiliar that was all around her made this new life something she feared. And she had never known fear until now.

8

The hard ground in the cave woke Eve, though it was still dark out. She rose anyway and left Adam's side, slipped past the sleeping animals, and walked to the cave's entrance. The grasses had provided a much softer cushion. How could she make the hard ground easier to lie upon? Even the sheepskins that covered their bodies were little help, for her legs and head still felt the solid earth.

She lifted her gaze, taking in the brilliant stars and the bright moon against the night sky. Even the sky seemed harsher despite its beauty. How was she ever supposed to make a home here? The flocks were too small to kill the animals for their skins. Leaves were too narrow or stiff to make into something useful. She glanced at the torch Adam had left near the front of the cave to keep predators at bay. It was too dark to wander, and even with the torch, she could not do what was better seen in the daylight.

Discouraged, she returned to the cave and lay again beside Adam, careful not to wake him. But dawn greeted them too soon, so she rose again, exhausted from her fitful night. They ate the leftover nuts in haste and took the animals down the hill to graze in the grasses.

"I need to go to the river," Eve said, touching Adam's arm to get his attention. He had a distant, distracted look.

He turned to face her. "What for? I can't stay with the animals all day. I need to search the fields for grains and a place to plant the seeds."

Eve tilted her head to glance at the sun. "Is it the season for planting? Wouldn't we be better to eat the grains and save seeds from them until the weather is cooler?" She knew little about the seasons, but she knew that God had created the moon to govern them. She'd just never experienced anything but steady temperatures—warm in the day, cool in the evening. The perfect environment.

He looked at her and scratched his beard. They hadn't washed in the river since they'd left the garden, and he probably felt the need for it as much as she did.

"We could take the flocks to the river to drink," Eve said, "and there we could search for the wild stalks that have slender stems and woven heads. I think I could weave them together to make things, if they will dry in the sun once they are formed. I won't know until I try." She gave him a pleading look. "We could wash or swim for a little too. I miss those times."

"It's only been two days," he said, sounding slightly annoyed. "But you are right. The animals need water, and until I can build shelters closer to the river and not so far toward the hills, we will have to take turns leading them to drink. Let's go."

He started out and called to the sheep and goats. The donkeys and cattle fell into line with them, and she followed behind. She would have rather walked with him, but she sensed he was still irritated with her. Better to keep her distance, though she didn't like it. Would they ever have the closeness they once shared?

They passed a field of tall grasses on their walk. She could use those grasses to cushion the earth if she could carry enough of them in her arms. Many trips to the field would be needed, but the thought made her step lighter.

The stream came into view, and the animals hurried to drink. She glanced at Adam, who seemed slightly relieved. He removed his sheepskin and stepped into the water a short distance from the animals, and she did the same.

"You were right. I've missed this. And since the animals need to drink, we can come twice a day if we want to." He offered her a smile.

Relieved to see it, she returned it, then glanced beyond him toward the bank. "Those are the plants I had in mind," she said, pointing to the tall stalks with woven heads. "If I can twist them close together, once they die, they might hold together."

"You could add a layer of clay from the bottom of the river to smooth over them when you finish whatever it is you want to make." He moved deeper into the river, dipped beneath the surface, and came up with a handful of clay.

"Yes, that could help. I want to make something to hold our food and carry water and cart things to the cave. There is so much we need."

He lowered himself beneath the surface again, then stood and stepped out of the river. "You will figure it out in time." He shook his hair of the droplets and donned the sheepskin garments again.

Eve did the same, though she wrung the water from her hair. She used to let it air-dry and it would make her skin tingle as she went about her day, but she didn't want the sheepskin to be drenched. A sigh escaped, and she glanced at Adam, but his gaze was focused on the sheep.

The animals drank from the water, and Eve picked handfuls of the plants until her arms were full. She took the sheep and goats with her, while Adam led the cattle and donkeys in a different direction. She deposited the plants in the cave, then returned to the field, calling the animals to follow her. The sun had reached the high point in the sky before she had gathered enough grasses to cushion the place where they slept. Would it still be comfortable once they dried? It was the life in the grasses that had given them softness, and already she could feel some of them hardening as they dried.

She fought a sense of defeat. Somehow she would figure these things out. But she had no idea how to make clothing or weave objects or find the right plants to make a soft place to lie down. And she had no one to teach her unless Adonai came to talk with her—with them.

A small part of her wanted to cry out for His help. The other part of her wanted to figure out what she could on her own. Hadn't the tree given her the knowledge of good and evil? Wasn't the fruit good for wisdom?

Adam would be proud of her ability. Wouldn't he? And when had she begun to want to prove her worth? The new feeling tasted sour. But after what she had done, she felt as though she had lost her value.

Did Adam still love her? Or was she just needed for his survival?

⁓

Weeks passed, and Adam's desire for her returned, but this time it carried with it an almost anxious intensity. The joy was shorter lived than what she had known since her creation.

A feeling of loss settled over Eve as she nestled beside Adam on their now cushioned sleeping area. Would they ever regain the beauty of Eden between the two of them? Or would Adam simply use her to fulfill his ardent need?

A sigh lifted her chest, and a tear slipped onto the goose down that now cushioned their heads. Somehow she must work harder to please Adam, to make him want her the way he did in the beginning. But how? He seemed to desire her body and the help she could provide. But his laughter and playful teasing had been left in Eden. Now his laughter carried an edge, no longer the innocent delight she had loved so much.

The thought turned over in her mind as she rose, took some of the grain from a crude basket she had made, and left the cave.

Adam had obviously taken the animals out already. She should have risen before he did to make sure food was ready. Why did she oversleep?

A sick feeling settled in the pit of her stomach as she envisioned Adam's testy mood. Would he return to eat, or should she search for him and take him the flatbread when it was ready?

Hurrying now, she gathered some sticks and put them beneath the flat stone they had raised on rocks to bake the bread, then touched the fire to them and sat to grind the grain Adam had found. She poured water from a ram's horn and mixed it with the grain, then poured the batter onto the fire-heated stone. The flatbread had become one of their favorite things to eat with the fruit and nuts they found each day.

She used a stick to turn the bread and felt a sudden fluttering in her middle. Were her nerves so frayed as to cause her to feel jumpy? She placed a hand over the spot, willing her emotions to settle, but the feeling came again. What was this new sensation?

She lifted the hot flatbread from the stone and poured more batter on it, then looked up at Adam's approach.

"So, you are finally up," he said. "Good. Bring me the flatbread and nuts when you are finished. I cannot leave the animals alone." He turned and half ran back toward the flocks and herds.

Eve watched him go, wishing again that she had risen earlier to feed him. In Eden they had always awakened and eaten together. Now, Adam always seemed displeased with her, and despite her attempts to make him happy again, she wondered if she ever would.

She flipped the last of the bread and then stacked the pile onto a stone. She carried it into the cave, grabbed the basket of nuts, and took them to the fields just beyond the rise.

Adam stood beneath the shade of a large oak tree, watching the animals graze. At first he did not notice her, and her heart yearned for him. But as he turned and saw her coming, he did not smile in welcome as she had hoped.

She placed the food on the ground before him and knelt in the grass, looking up at him. He crouched low, snatched several rounds of flatbread in one hand, scooped nuts with the other, and walked off toward the sheep without a word.

"Adam?" She could not bear his silence when all she had done was miss one meal. She hated the anger he could not seem to shake since the garden.

He stopped and swiveled about, his brows drawn low, his lips a frown. "What?"

"Why are you angry with me?" She swallowed at the scowl she received in response, wishing she had not asked.

He drew in a deep breath. "You are supposed to *help* me, Eve, not hinder me. You are supposed to have food ready before I awaken so I am not delayed in taking care of the animals. This is not the first morning I have left and you are still abed."

"I have been tired. I do not oversleep on purpose." Was she carrying a child? Could that be the reason she was so weary? "You could be a little more understanding."

"And you could learn to obey me. If you'd done what I'd said from the start, we would not be having this conversation." He turned again and stalked off, his words like a slap to her face.

Tears fell freely, and she longed to weep aloud. She hiccuped on a sob and swallowed back the emotion. He was right, and she hated that he knew it. God had said that Adam would rule over her, and he didn't seem to have any trouble with his role. She longed for his love. He wanted her unquestioning obedience.

Well, he might want her to submit to his will, but she had her own mind, and he had better change. She rose, gathered the rest of the food, and returned to the cave. He might want to rule over her, but she was not about to let his actions go unquestioned. Her desire for him was not so great that he could treat her with disrespect.

Adam returned with the animals in tow later that evening. He would never get any planting done if he had to care for the flocks and herds every day. Eve should be helping him instead of sitting in the cave making things to carry or to hold food and water. She should know he needed her for far more.

He took the animals into the cave and bedded them down, then returned to the fire where Eve sat, her bearing stiff. He did not see any gladness in her gaze as he sat opposite her.

"They are fed and watered, and I've examined them for thorns and briars." He took the bread she offered him.

Silence fell like a pall between them. She blamed him, no doubt, for growing angry with her. But hadn't God said that she was supposed to obey him, that he would rule over her? Didn't that mean she should do what he asked? How hard could it be to rise early to prepare him food?

"I felt something today," she said. "Earlier, and again just now."

He lifted a brow, chewing his bread.

"I felt it here." She placed her hand over her belly. "There it is again." Her smile grew gentle as she looked at her body, but she did not meet his gaze.

Adam stared at her stomach. "It is probably nothing. It hardly seems possible for you to have conceived so soon."

By her look, he knew he'd hurt her. Tears pooled in her eyes, and he suddenly felt ashamed. Was this really how he was supposed to treat her? God had made them equal, and they had shared such deep, pure love in Eden. Was that all for naught because of sin?

"Though we did share our love in Eden," he said, remembering the passion he'd once felt for her and the unmatched joy they'd both experienced in knowing each other so intimately.

She searched his face, her eyes still wet with unshed tears. "Couldn't I have become pregnant before we left Eden? We suspected it was possible then."

He studied her, longing and hurt mingling within him. "Yes, it is possible. We did not stay long away from each other there."

"Perhaps it is too soon for me to feel life inside of me, if this is in fact what I am feeling. But I have noticed other signs of my body changing, and some of it began months ago. It seems to be why I am so completely weary of late."

He knew it could happen but had pushed the thought aside after they left the garden. Had she already been with child when she ate the fruit?

"We will not know for sure until the child is born," he said. "You will not bear a child easily." At the memory of the curse she'd received, he realized he did not want to cause her pain or see her suffer. What a fool he'd been to treat her so harshly, especially if she was carrying his child.

"I know," she said, looking beyond him. "But we were told to be fruitful and multiply, and if we don't bear children, when we die, the earth will have no one to care for it."

"If you are with child, then we are already multiplying," he said.

"If I conceived in the garden before we ate the fruit, are you certain that our child will carry the knowledge of good and evil that we have?"

Adam gave her a thoughtful look as he took a handful of almonds. "If the earth is cursed, I see no way a child of our mating would not be born with the same nature that we now carry."

"But God did promise that my seed would crush the serpent's head. Only a person who is purely good could do that, couldn't they? Could our child be that person?" She seemed anxious to know, as though she needed this child to be the one God had promised.

"I suppose God could make that happen." He smiled at her. "If it does, we could be freed from the curse. I don't know that it would happen so quickly, but I would be very glad of it." He stood and pulled her to her feet, then took her hands in his. "Let us hope that if this child was conceived before we disobeyed God, he will not inherit our curse as the rest of the earth has. But if he does, then maybe the promise is for a future day. We can only hope it will be in our lifetime."

"I will believe for the best."

He released her, knowing he should tell her he was sorry for having been so harsh with her. But somehow he couldn't bring himself to say so. He watched her pick up the leftover food and carry it into the cave, wishing he could be what she needed, as he used to be.

9

FOUR MONTHS LATER

Eve paced the length of the cave, which was at last free of the animals. Adam had spent weeks carting heavy rocks from the stream and surrounding fields to build pens for each of the small flocks and herds. She had used that time to learn to weave a basket from the plants by the stream and filled it with down to make a soft bed for the coming child. The cave had taken on a more livable look as Adam learned to carve wood and she made more baskets, which held herbs and food they could gather ahead and even some of the grain so she could grind it daily.

A sense of peace that they were creating a pleasant place to live settled over her. Though it would never be Eden and she often missed the garden of God, this was home. She had to accept that now. To her embarrassment, she had tried to return to Eden, but the cherubim still blocked the entrance with their flaming swords. She knew after her second try that God would never allow them in again. Still, a part of her hoped that one day He might change His mind.

The pain in her back intensified as she paced. Where was Adam? If this child was soon to be born, she wanted his help. She had no idea what one did once a child came into the world. But she suspected that if she had to, she could deliver it alone. Didn't the animals do that very thing?

She moved to the entrance of the cave and peered into the fading light of dusk. She had made flatbread earlier in the day but had no desire to eat. Adam would need his strength, but she could not stomach the thought of food.

At last he appeared, striding toward her with one of the lambs on his shoulders. He placed the lamb gently in the pen alongside its mother. "She ran off and I had to find her," he said as he approached Eve. He stopped within arm's length and looked her up and down. "You are in pain."

She nodded. "I think the child is coming soon, but I don't know what to do. I don't know how to deliver it or how to clean it afterward. I can't lick it like the animals do."

"Do we have water from the spring?"

She nodded.

"Is it warm?"

Again she nodded. "Tepid, mostly, for I warmed it some time ago."

He looked about, found the container she had made to hold the water, and set it on the heated stones to stay warm.

"That is a good idea." Why hadn't she thought of that? "I hope the wool I twisted into a covering will be enough to keep the child warm."

"I'm sure he or she will be fine, Eve. You must not fear." He touched her arm, and she leaned her head on his shoulder. They had come to a greater understanding of each other since the day he learned she was pregnant, but he seemed to struggle with the ability to apologize when he hurt her with his words. Still, she needed him, so she accepted what he could give her.

"I have been in agony for much of the afternoon. The pains just began to move from my back to my middle. This child kicks a great deal as well." She drew in a slow breath and released it. "What if I die giving birth? Surely it is possible."

He patted her back in an awkward motion as if he wasn't sure how to comfort her as he once did. "If you die, we will all die. We cannot continue the race of humans without you."

She nodded, a sense of relief filling her. She was to be the mother of all the living. She had to live to create more life so her children could bear offspring for generations.

"There are fresh grasses beside our bed for you to lie on afterward when you feed the child. I'm not exactly sure how you will birth it though," Adam said, confusion in his wide eyes. How would a man know such things? She didn't know herself.

"It is probably similar to the way the ewes give birth. I imagine I will stand, and the child will push its way out of me. But perhaps you should be nearby to catch it so it doesn't hit its head on the ground. I don't know if it will have strong legs to stand on or need more time to grow." She held her breath as another wave of pain overtook her.

He looked rather lost as he glanced from the bed to her, and she wanted to ease his mind and tell him that all would be well. But would it?

"Perhaps you should sit on one of the stones rather than stand," he said, leading her to one of the wide stones where they sat to take their meals.

She shook her head. "I need to walk a little longer." She felt the cramping increase but not a desire to push the child out of her.

Dusk deepened, and Adam brought several torches and set them outside the cave. Eve groaned and cried out, and the pain grew so intense that she vowed never to birth another child. At last the desire to rid her body of this burden overtook her.

"I think he is coming." She looked into Adam's terror-filled eyes. "Help me."

He led her to the stone, and she squatted beside it. Before she knew what more to do, her body did the work for her. She bore down on the pain and pushed the child from her body into Adam's waiting arms.

"There is a cord attached," he said. She had not expected this.

"Take the sharpened flint and cut the cord," she said. "Bind it tight with a string of wool and wash the child." She felt another wave of pain and pushed again once Adam had cut the cord, expelling whatever had kept the child encased inside of her. How strange it all was.

"It's a boy," Adam said as he dipped his hand in the warm water and brushed it over the babe.

"With the help of the Lord I have brought forth a man!" Her whole body was drenched in sweat, and she needed the water as much as the child did. But she glanced heavenward and offered a silent prayer of thanks. God had delivered him safely from her.

Adam showed her the boy, and she longed to hold him. "I need to wash first," she said. "Take the wool I set aside for him and wrap him in it. I am going to the spring."

"Take a torch with you," he said.

She grabbed the long stick he had placed in the ground. She half stumbled her way down the hill to the stream. If only she could see better, but the dark cloaked everything around her. When at last the sound of water grew near, she placed the torch in the ground, stepped into the river, and cleansed her body of blood and birth and sweat. She hurried back, realizing that in her rush she had forgotten the clothing she had discarded during the birth.

At last, exhausted and barely able to reach the cave, she set the torch in its place and stumbled to the clean grass and warm clothing Adam had waiting for her. The baby rested in Adam's arms, but his mouth moved and soft mewling sounds came from him. Adam placed the baby in her arms, and she instinctively held him to her breast. He suckled with a fierceness she did not expect, and she laughed for the joy of it.

"He is Cain," she said, meeting Adam's gaze. "Because I acquired him from the Lord."

Though this child was a product of their love, she knew from her many months in the garden with no pregnancy that each birth was a gift from Adonai. Cain was her first, and with one look in his dark eyes and contented face, she knew he would not be her last. Despite the agony of birth, there would be more. Many more.

Eve marveled at Cain's tiny body and soon realized that she would need far more clothing for him than the twisted wool she had made to keep him swaddled and warm. Why hadn't she considered that a small human would have all of the same bodily needs as she and Adam? She also hadn't expected the bleeding that continued from her body. When would it stop?

Adam had trimmed more wool from a few of the sheep, and she worked furiously to create more garments when Cain slept. There must be a better way. The wool was so thick once Adam had shorn it from the ewe's body, and as she studied it, she realized she could thin it out and make it more like the plants she used to make baskets. The wool was easier to weave too. She spent weeks perfecting a technique to help her, and she at last had a pile of cloths to cover Cain's lower body and more blankets to swaddle him.

She held him in one arm now as he nursed and she flipped flatbread over the heated stone. Adam appeared in the distance, climbing the hill to the cave. He sank onto the stone beside her and helped himself to some pistachios from one of the clay bowls she had made.

"Exhausting day?" she asked as she lifted the flatbread to a stone to cool.

"Always. I have discovered how to make larger flint tools to help me till the ground. It will take time, but I think between the sharper stones and flint, I can build a better place for us to live." He took a bite of the flatbread. "We're going to need more room with better light, especially once more babies come along." He looked with kindness at Cain, a smile touching his lips.

She watched him. Pride in being a father was new to him, and seeing it was new to her. "Do you want to hold him?" she asked. At his nod, she handed Cain to him.

"Is he clean?" His nose wrinkled as he smelled the boy. "Guess so."

She laughed. "I just changed him. He did eat though, so he may not stay that way for long."

He made a face, then settled Cain into the crook of his arm and continued to eat with one hand.

She took a piece of the bread and spread heated mashed fruit over it. She handed it to him, then made some for herself. "I wish I knew when my body would return to the way it was before he was born."

His dark eyes held concern. "Surely the blood will stop soon."

She shrugged. "I hope so." She wondered if other things would change now that she was a mother.

"I'm going to look for metals in the earth tomorrow," he said after they had finished eating. "I know they existed in Eden. Perhaps they exist outside of the garden as well."

"Would there be a purpose for them?" She couldn't imagine what anyone would do with gold like Havilah's.

"I'm sure we could find one. If the metals gleam as brightly as the shining ones whose bodies seemed made of them, perhaps they will have some use for us as well." His eyes lit up, but she wondered what they would do with gemstones unless they were hard or sharp and could be used to make things.

"I want to visit the forests nearby," she said. "I think there are groves of olives and grapevines there. I'm sure there is much I can do with both." She had tasted a few of the fruits on one of her walks before Cain was born but had never taken anything to carry them back with her. Now she could.

"Both contain a juice of some sort. I will find stones to help press them." Adam handed Cain to her and stood. "It's getting dark, and I want to inspect the animals once more. I will join you soon."

She watched him walk away. Their conversations were so basic as they tried to figure out the best ways to live and survive in this world without the benefit of Adonai's wisdom or help. She still longed to speak with Him in the evenings, but she always felt too ashamed to call on Him. She needed to try anyway. Perhaps He could help her learn faster and teach her how to raise Cain to be a man. What did she know about mothering him?

You will learn, she told herself. Of course she would. Still, the faint desire to call on Adonai lingered as she entered the cave and put Cain to bed.

10

Six Months Later

E ve had created a way to carry Cain on her back—strapped to her body with strands made of the fibers of some of the stronger plants. She carried a basket in her arms and walked to the olive grove she had found down the hill and to the west of the cave. She and Adam had tested a handful of both the olives and the grapes and discovered that pressing the olives created an oil that helped cook the flatbread and could be mixed with the grain. It also softened their skin, which seemed drier than it had been in Eden. She wanted to gather enough oil to fill one of the clay containers she had made and hardened over the fire. Hopefully it wouldn't leak.

She came upon the grove and set the basket on the ground beneath one of the ripe olive trees. Taking a fat stick she found nearby, she beat the branches to force the olives to fall off. She could pick them up off the ground far easier than she could pick them off their stems one by one. When the ground was covered in the black olives, she bent and filled her basket.

The weight of Cain and the basket put her slightly off balance, but she righted herself and headed back to the cave. Adam had found rounded, cuplike stones that she could use to crush the olives once she removed the pits. If only they could cut stone into large circles to help in the pressing, but they did not have strong enough tools yet for that.

Oh, Adonai, I wish You would help us as You did in Eden. The prayer surprised her, coming from a place inside that would not let her forget the many times she had sunk onto the grass at the feet of Adonai Elohim and listened to Him speak of God's kingdom. She had not always understood what He meant, but just to hear His voice was melody to her ears. She missed His voice, His nearness.

She trudged on while Cain began fussing. He would need to nurse soon, and suddenly she was weary of it all. She was stronger than this. She had taken easily to meeting Cain's needs and loved him dearly. Why did she feel so weak today?

Thankful when the camp came into view, she set the basket down beside the trough of rocks Adam had built and sealed with clay. Cain was crying now, so she sat nearby to keep watch over the olives while she nursed Cain. She didn't like the fear that dogged her now that the animals were both afraid of them and dangerous to them. She should cover the olives but had no cloth handy. One more thing to make for next time.

She shuddered. Why was she so tired? She suddenly wanted to simply curl up and sleep on the cushions they had made of down and wool. But it was barely past midday. She had food to prepare and the olives to press and Cain to put in the bed he was outgrowing. She must make him another soon.

A sound in the distance startled her. The cry of a wild animal? Was Adam hurt? To run to him was her first instinct, but she couldn't leave Cain or stop him from nursing lest his wail add to the commotion.

She tilted her head to listen, and her heart pounded. *Come to me, Adam. Show me you are all right.*

But he didn't come, so she continued to nurse Cain. Then, tired as she was, she found something to cover the olives, strapped Cain to her back once more, and went off in the direction of the sound.

She must know what had happened. What on earth would she do
if Adam was hurt?

~

Out of the corner of his eye, Adam saw the lion crouching low
among the brush, watching the flock. He recognized the cat and
had an instant desire to call its name and step closer, talk to it as
he had in Eden. But he tensed as he watched the cat's narrowed
eyes and predatory stance.

"Arye," Adam called. But the lion did not look in Adam's direction. Its gaze was focused on one of the smaller lambs, one that
had strayed a short distance from its mother.

How was he supposed to scare the cat away if it would not even
look in his direction or recognize its name? He moved closer, hand
on his flint knife. There must be a better way. He picked up a stone
and threw it toward the animal, but it barely noticed.

He silently cursed his own inability as he watched the lion move
from a crouch to a fluid pounce. In a heartbeat, it had grabbed the
lamb between its thick jaws.

"No!" Adam sprinted toward the animal and chased it, barely
able to keep up. When a copse of trees stood before them, the cat
paused, and Adam caught it between the brush and the line of
trees. He grabbed its mane, heard it scream before he killed it with
the knife, and rescued the lamb from its mouth.

Sweat poured down his back, and his breath came hard. He
cradled the lamb a moment, then turned and took it back to its
mother, still panting from the exertion. He looked about, making
sure no other predators were near, then returned to the dead lion.

"Arye," he said softly, wishing he could have rescued the lamb
without killing the animal. But Arye was no longer the lion he had
been in Eden, and no doubt he would have returned at a later time.

He stood over the body of the lion, its full mane beautiful even
in death. *Why, Adonai?* But he knew. The animals suffered from
the same curse that he had brought upon the world. This was his

fault. Grief filled him, but he couldn't have allowed one of the sheep to be taken. The flock was still too young, and his family needed the milk and wool to live.

Please, Adonai, let this male have sired a cub to take its place. He couldn't know the population of the wild animals anymore. Until today, he had not come upon one so close, as they usually kept their distance. How he hated the loss of such a beautiful male of a species he had come to love in Eden. Eve used to ride on Arye's back and had laughed with joy. What would she say when she discovered this loss?

Even as Adam stared at the body, his mind churned with uses for it. They could skin it and scrape it to use the hide for a covering or for something to lie upon. Or perhaps some of the skin could be sewn with the tendons to make containers to hold goats' milk or sheep's milk or the olive oil Eve was supposed to press today.

He pulled the bigger flint knife from the belt at his waist, stepped to the carcass, and began the grisly work of removing the skin from the flesh. Perhaps the bones could be dried and used as weapons or other objects they might need. The head was large, and if it was hard enough, they could use it to hold things—food, perhaps, when Eve cooked. They would need to gather animal dung to build a bigger fire so they could boil the parts to clean them. Even the bladder and stomach might be used to carry water or hold milk once he rinsed them clean in the river.

A new need popped up for them almost daily. He would use every part of this animal as best he could. They could not afford to waste anything, even in death.

Eve caught the scent of death the closer she got to the flocks. Her stomach revolted at the smell, and fear filled her. "Adam!" Her cry echoed in the hills surrounding her.

The sheep came into view, and she hurried forward. Adam lifted his head and motioned her forward.

"Oh!" Her hand covered her mouth, but she could not stifle a cry. She remembered this animal. She had played with him and ridden on his back in the garden, and he'd allowed her to lie next to him and rest her head on his body. "What happened?" she asked, turning away. Her stomach roiled, and she lost her morning meal in the grasses nearby.

Adam stood and placed a hand on her shoulder, then patted Cain's head. "He had a lamb in his mouth. I couldn't let him take her. I actually called his name, but he wouldn't look my way. I tried to scare him off, but he ignored the stone I threw at him. The animals no longer understand us, and he intended to kill and eat the lamb. They used to eat the grasses, but obviously no longer. We must be more careful and watch Cain. Don't let him wander once he begins to walk."

Her eyes grew wide as she slowly turned to stare at the creature she had once considered a friend. She had done this. If she had not listened to the serpent, none of this would have happened. Would she ever be free of this constant grief?

"What are you doing with him?" She sank onto the grass nearby and pulled Cain from his wrappings to hold him in her arms. Fierce protectiveness filled her, and she felt safer holding him closer to her heart.

"I'm cutting the skin away and will scrape it, and we can soak it in the oils from the lion itself or from some of the plants around us. We will need a way to keep it clean and soft. Once I finish with this, I will use every part of the carcass in any way I can. I have some ideas, but you can help give me more." He looked at her, his expression showing concern. "You don't look well."

"Seeing him dead doesn't help. But I know you had no choice." She really didn't feel well and had little desire to help him with purposing this animal for their use, but he needed her. She must push herself despite the exhaustion she felt. "How did you kill him?"

"I ran after him, caught his mane, and used my knife to slit his throat as Adonai did when He killed the ram on our behalf. I am grateful God made me strong enough to keep a hold on him." He ran a hand through the grasses in an attempt to remove the blood. "It is hard work. When I get to the inner parts, you can help me with the smaller things. Why don't you rest with Cain for now? You can stay here among the shade of the trees."

She nodded. "Thank you. I am terribly tired, though I don't know why."

He gave her a curious look. "Don't you?" He turned back to the lion and began cutting the skin away again.

What did he mean by that? She rested her head in the grass and pulled Cain to her, allowing him to nurse at her side. She was simply weary of all she had been doing since Cain's birth. Every day the work grew. Nothing was as easy as it had been in the garden, and guilt filled her every step of her days. Surely God remained angry with her, or at the very least He did not look on her with the love she'd felt from Him in Eden. Even Adam didn't love her as he once did.

But it was Adonai she missed. The truth struck her hard, and she longed for Him to appear in that moment.

Then another thought hit her. Since Cain's birth she had begun to bleed with each cycle of the moon, something she had not experienced in the garden. But at the last moon's cycle, she had not bled. Cain was only six months old, but Adam had returned to her after the boy's second month of life. Could she already be carrying another child? So soon?

Her body was not ready to go through birth again. And since she did not know when she'd conceived Cain, she had no idea how long her body would carry a child before birth.

Oh, Adonai, what am I going to do? How can I care for Cain and help Adam and bear the burden of another child so soon?

Was this God's blessing? Yet pain in childbirth was part of His curse. Was He displeased with her, to put her through this again before she had recovered from the first birth?

She realized that except for the occasional desperate feeling, she had purposely avoided calling upon Him. She did need Him, but she'd been doing all that she could on her own or with Adam's help. As if they wanted to prove they didn't need God. But they did. And she needed Him now more than ever.

Please forgive me, Adonai. Please come to us again. Show us how to live, how to survive this world, how to care for children, how to please You outside of Eden. I miss You.

She drew in a slow breath, the joy of Cain's small body pulling on hers giving her a sense of peace. But it was more than that. She sensed that God had heard her prayer. Perhaps soon He would visit them again. And answer her many questions.

11

ONE MONTH LATER

Eve looked about their small cave, a sense of satisfaction filling her. Adam had done well figuring out how to soften the hide of the lion, and she had used some of the smaller bones to thread the sinews to create a cape for both of them to wear in the evenings or when the days grew cooler. Cain had a warmer covering as well, all taken from the animal's skin.

She checked on Cain, who still slept, though he no longer took two naps in the day. She walked to the front of the cave to finish the stew she had begun over the fire. Adam had found her a large rock in the shape of a bowl, and she heated water in it and added herbs and grains. They would eat lettuces and leeks with some of the olive oil she had pressed and the flatbread she had made earlier. She bent low, added rosemary and basil, and stirred the stew with a long bone taken from the lion's back leg.

The leaves rustled in the nearby trees, and she heard Adam's feet crunching stones along the path. She stood at his approach. "You are earlier than I expected, but the food is almost ready."

He nodded, then went into the cave to check on Cain. Eve again heard rustling in the trees, and light suddenly streamed their direction, bright light that caused her to blink and hold her hand up against the glare.

Adam emerged from the cave and joined her. "It is Adonai Elohim," he whispered, and together they fell to their faces before Him.

He bid them to sit at His feet as they had done in the garden. Eve's heart pounded with a mixture of longing and terror. The splendor of His countenance dimmed as they sat, and Eve lowered her hand, able to see Him at last.

And all of the questions she had whispered in her heart, He answered in her thoughts.

They conversed for a time. Adam received wisdom on how to find iron in the earth and how better to tan a hide or make weapons, and she was given wisdom for spinning and weaving plant fibers and wool.

"An altar of earth you shall make for Me and sacrifice on it your burnt offerings and your peace offerings, your sheep and your oxen," Adonai Elohim said. "In every place where I cause My name to be remembered, I will come to you and bless you. If you make Me an altar of stone, you shall not build it of hewn stones, for if you wield your tool on it, you profane it. And you shall not go up by steps to My altar, that your nakedness be not exposed on it."

"How often should we sacrifice sheep and oxen to You?" Adam asked.

Adonai Elohim did not reply, but they both knew that the offerings were for their sins to be forgiven. They could not sacrifice often at first or all the animals would die, but as the flocks grew, they could come as often as they needed to feel God's forgiveness. For now, they would bring their gift to the altar twice a year, especially on the anniversary of the day they had first learned that death must come to a lamb to clothe them, to cover their sins.

Adonai Elohim left them then, and Adam took Eve's hand and searched her face. "Do you know what tomorrow is?"

She thought back to how long they had been away from Adonai's garden home. "It has been a year since the day we sinned and God killed the lamb on our behalf." Sorrow filled her again at the memory.

"Yes. So tomorrow I will build an altar of earth and we will sacrifice one of the lambs. I will search for a perfect male, and we will place our hands on it as we did that day when God killed the first lamb to cover us and our sin."

"Will we always have to kill a lamb to pay for our sin? Surely God cannot want to see so many animals die." She had seen the sadness in His gaze when He gave His command.

"We will do so as long as He commands it. We have no other way to cover the sins we still commit." He sat near the food, and she scooped stew into wooden bowls he had carved.

"I wish we had never sinned. I wish we could stop." She looked at him, half-fearful that he would blame her for their plight, but he simply nodded.

"We are both guilty before Him. Until He makes a better way, there is nothing else we can do but what He says." Adam bit into his flatbread, and they continued to eat in silence.

Eve missed Adonai's presence. If only the altar wasn't necessary. Disobedience had already cost them so much. How much more could they take?

Adam went to the river with the flocks and herds. While keeping one eye on them, he filled buckets Eve had made, carried them up the hill, and led the animals back to their pens.

An altar of earth, Adonai had said. Adam wasn't exactly sure what that should look like, but it would have to be big enough to hold an animal's body. He set the water on the ground and dug into the clay and dirt in the side of the hill until he had a mound nearly as tall as he was. He poured water over it and smoothed it down until it was longer than it was wide. A lamb's body could rest atop it once he piled wood to burn there.

The altar, crude as it was, ought to have brought him a sense of satisfaction that he had done as Adonai had commanded, but he didn't feel a bit of it. All he could think of was having to search the small flock for a perfect male lamb and kill it for their sins. A sick feeling hit him in the gut.

How he wished he'd never had doubts about God's goodness. If he had simply believed that God wanted only good for him, they would not be in this place. They would not be worrying about the wild animals or having to kill the other animals they cared for.

He looked once more at the altar, knowing he needed to gather wood and go to the flocks, but he couldn't bear to continue. He walked toward the woods, needing to think of anything but this. He couldn't share his emotions with Eve. He would only end up blaming her all over again.

Eve caught a glimpse of Adam walking toward the woods. She had just strapped Cain to her back and had intended to begin grinding the grains she had gathered the day before. Instead, she walked toward Adam, curious as to where he was going. He was supposed to be building an altar. Was he gathering wood for the top of it?

She should help him, but as she drew closer, she heard him cursing himself, and then the sound of him weeping echoed in the trees.

He would not want her to see him in such a state. What could she say to comfort him? She knew what was coming, and she wanted to break down and weep too. But her tears would just upset Cain, and she couldn't allow that.

She turned and headed toward where Adam said he would build the altar. She stopped some distance from it. He had done a good job. The sides were straight and smooth, and the measurements seemed exact. But what pain had he felt as he built it? It represented everything they had done wrong, and she knew, strong as he was, that he could not bear it.

She walked toward the sheep pens and looked at each one. They had grown, but the flock was still not as large as it one day would be. Had Adam already chosen the animal? She looked at each innocent face, tears streaming down her cheeks.

She walked away, back toward their camp, just as Adam emerged from the woods carrying an armful of wood. He met her gaze, and she could still see the stain of tears on his tanned face.

"I'm going to choose the lamb," he said, his voice cracking. "Bring Cain, grab a bowl and a torch, and come with me."

She decided not tell him she had just been there. She simply nodded and followed in silence, dreading every step.

Adam placed the wood on the altar and walked to the pen where he had already set aside the perfect one-year-old male. This lamb could have grown to help increase the flock, but there was no changing what God had told them to do. To choose a different, less perfect specimen would not be pleasing to the Creator. They had already disappointed and separated themselves from Him by their previous actions. Today was a stark reminder of all they once had that was good and all they had lost since then.

He felt Eve's presence behind him and heard Cain's chattering at her back. He left them outside of the pen as he opened the gate he had fashioned out of branches and tied with plant twine, and walked resolutely toward the lamb.

His hands shook as he inspected the lamb one more time. Finding it as perfect as it had been that morning, he lifted it in his arms, unable to hold back the tears. He walked to the gate, which Eve opened for him, and carried the silent lamb to the earthen altar. He set the animal on the ground, and he and Eve placed their hands on its head, both of them weeping now.

Forgive me, he prayed, wondering if he would ever be free of the guilt and sorrow. *Forgive Eve too.*

He glanced up and noticed she still bowed her head, but a moment later she lifted her gaze to his. She placed the bowl beneath the lamb's neck, and Adam quickly slit its throat, catching the blood in the bowl. When the lamb had bled out, he cut out the fat portions and laid them across the wood, poured out the blood on the altar, and lit the wood with the fire from the torch.

Sparks and smoke plumed upward toward the heavens, and the scent of cooking flesh filled Adam's nostrils. He glanced from the altar to Eve, wondering if the smell turned her stomach because of the babe she carried. But she gave no sign of discomfort other than the tears she continually shed in silence.

Adam focused again on the offering, and then a bright, glorious light parted the clouds and shone down on them. For a single moment he sensed Adonai's acceptance and forgiveness and pleasure.

He had done what God required. Joy filled him despite his sadness. He looked at Eve. "He forgives us."

She nodded, smiling, swiping away her tears. "He accepts us again."

Adam put his arm around her and held her close. To be close to Adonai again would bring such pleasure. But the cost was so great. How long would this joy remain?

12

Adam spent his evenings creating a plow from a forked branch. He fitted the longer teeth of the lion to the ends of the branch so they would drag along the ground. After wedging them in place and making a type of sling with the tendons, he pulled on them.

"They look secure," Eve said. She took wool from the lamb that had been slain, tied it to a short branch, and twisted it until it spun into thread.

"I think they will hold. The ground is moist once the mist rises from the earth." He rubbed a hand along the back of his neck. "The soil is still not what it was in Eden though. The thorns and thistles are a constant frustration we never had to deal with there."

She continued to spin, her smile sympathetic. "I wish things were easier for you."

Adam stared at her, the old anger flaring that the ground was cursed because they'd eaten the fruit. He looked away.

She sat in silence beside him, and he knew she regretted her words. But that did not help his anger. He tried to tamp it down, but it heated his face, his neck. He tossed the plow aside and stood. "It *would* be easier if we still lived in the garden. The ground is cursed because of you!" He stalked off, not caring about the shocked look on her face.

How could he have yelled at her so soon after the sacrifice? Had the lamb lost his life for nothing? Could not the blood of bulls and goats and lambs keep him from falling back into the same sinful thoughts and words and actions?

He paced away from the camp toward the trees. *Oh, Adonai, forgive me.* They couldn't sacrifice an animal every time they lashed out at each other. They would be forever killing their animals.

He sensed God's presence and love the moment he prayed. And God had spoken to him in a dream, telling him that now was the time to plant caraway and cumin and barley and spelt. He needed to focus on doing the things he had to do if he was going to keep his family alive. They needed him and he needed them. He needed Eve. God had created her for him because He declared that it was not good for him to be alone. Though he had the animals and God, he still needed another human, made in God's image, made to complete him as he was to complete her.

And without God's constant presence, they needed each other more than ever. There were no other humans to help them, and Cain was far too young to be of any use other than to be loved and cared for. That thought brought another sense of fear to his heart. He needed to protect his family, for not even the shining ones came to their aid here, and he would not trust another one of them after what the serpent had done. How would he be able to tell if they were sent from God or from the serpent? Were there more of them who were now evil?

If not for the occasional instructions from Adonai Elohim, they would be truly lost in a foreign and now hostile world.

He walked back to the camp, humbler now. He must apologize to Eve. She didn't deserve his wrath. He longed to see her as he had in the beginning when she seemed perfect for him. But perfect was something she would never be again.

A sick feeling settled in Eve's middle as she watched Adam stalk off toward the trees, his place to be alone. How could he still blame her after all this time? And so soon after they had been forgiven by God?

Tears threatened, but she blinked them back. Thankfully, Cain slept in the cave while she still sat by the fire, spinning the wool. The babe moved, making her aware of the good that would come from having another child. If only she hadn't conceived so soon. *Let it be a girl*, she prayed, longing for someone like her to share life with. Too many men would only make her life harder. Would Cain be like his father with his varying moods and bouts of silence?

She stared at the fire, then glanced at the spindle, trying to think of a better design so the wool wouldn't catch on the wood. She should have smoothed it better with her flint knife.

The rustle and crunch of footfalls filled her ears, and she turned to see Adam walking toward her. He sat beside her. "I'm sorry," he said, looking contrite. "Sometimes the work is so hard and the ground so full of weeds that need pulling. At least I won't have to water the plants, for the mist does that well. I just have to keep the weeds from choking them out." He paused and took her hand. "Still . . . every time I feel the sweat on my brow, I'm reminded of how easy it was to care for the fertile soil of Eden."

She nodded. "And every time I have to figure out how to make something we never needed before, I wish I had built a fence around that awful tree and never gone near it. I can't even blame the serpent angel because he only told me what I secretly wanted to hear. I had been curious about the tree since you told me we could not touch it."

Adam folded his hands in his lap. The unfinished plow sat on the ground where he had left it. "I had the same curiosity from the day God told me not to eat of it. I told you not to touch it because

I wanted to protect you. To protect us both from the temptation I already felt."

She met his gaze, grateful for his honesty. "Thank you for saying that." She glanced behind her to the cave. "I have the seeds in baskets, waiting to be tossed on the plowed fields when you are ready for them. And if I can help—"

He held up a hand. "No. Tilling the ground is up to me. You have enough work here." He waved a hand over the encampment. "And soon there will be another mouth to feed."

She placed a hand on her middle and felt that same motherly protectiveness she'd had with Cain. "Yes. But there is still time." How much time, she could not say, for she had yet to determine the number of months it took a human child to form within her. Longer than it took the sheep, for she was nearly four months along and her belly was not nearly as large as it would be—as it had been with Cain.

"At least Adonai has not left us without instructions," Adam said, interrupting her musings. "I had a dream where He told me how to beat caraway and cumin lightly with a stick. We've already ground some of the grain, but I didn't understand how to thresh it at first. Now we can gather so much more grain once the crops ripen. I understand better after He showed me in the dream."

Eve looked into his intense gaze. This was the first he had spoken of any dreams to her. "I am glad Adonai spoke to you. We need His help, or it will take us far longer to create what He could make with a word, as He did when He made the world." What must that have been like?

"Except us," Adam said. "God formed us. He didn't speak us into being as He did everything else."

"Except us," Eve repeated. "I never thought of that before. He made us differently, just as we are different yet the same species. He made you from the dust and me from your rib. We have God's personal imprint on our bodies." She looked again at the place where the babe grew. "I wonder if He also fashions the children I will bear. Is He knitting them together as He did us, except they are not fully formed adults when they are born?"

"They bear His image as we do," Adam said. "I can't imagine that He is not involved in their creation."

She smiled. "But He brings both parts of us together to create them. So the child is infused with the dust and the rib and somehow becomes male or female in the process." She pondered the thought. How it all worked she would never know, but the realization that God had formed her, not just spoken her into existence, gave her a warm feeling all through her body. God had touched her right from the beginning and crafted her to fit perfectly with Adam, and he with her.

"It's rather amazing, isn't it?" he asked. "He imprinted us with His image from the very first touch of dust and flesh and bone."

She nodded, suddenly overcome, wondering what this second child would be like. A new appreciation for her body and its uniqueness filled her. There was still so much about God she did not understand, but at least He had not left them without hope. He had not abandoned them to themselves or left them without His comfort and wisdom.

"I will begin at once to make larger baskets with lids to protect the grains once they are harvested," she said, no longer wanting to dwell on all she didn't understand. Better to think of needful things and helping Adam keep their family fed and safe.

Adam picked up the plow again and tightened the tendons with a few more knots. "There," he said at last, holding up the new plow to her. "I will test it in the field just below us tomorrow. You will have to care for the animals if I am going to plow the entire field." He brushed the wood shavings from his legs.

She nodded. She loved the animals, but sometimes the work of feeding and watching the flocks, as well as caring for Cain and making baskets and clothing, overwhelmed her. Not to mention the added weariness she felt with this new child growing within her.

But Adam couldn't do everything at once, and at least she could weave while she sat with Cain in the fields as the animals grazed. They would just have less time to graze than they had with Adam.

She could do this. She had no choice.

13

Six Months Later

Adam left camp immediately after he had broken his fast, leaving Eve alone with Cain and their new daughter, Achima. She set about cleaning up the leftover food, especially that which Cain refused to eat, and then lifted Achima into her arms. Cain toddled away from the cave toward the sheep pens, but Eve was not yet ready to go to them. The goats needed milking, but Achima needed to nurse, and by her insistent cries, Eve knew she could not put her off much longer.

"Cain, come back," she called, carrying Achima. She ran after the tottering thirteen-month-old and caught his arm as he stumbled to the dirt. He flailed his arms for her to let go, but she scooped him up with her other arm and walked back to the cave.

Cain squirmed and whined, making Achima cry harder. Eve marched to the camp, checked the food to make sure all was put safely out of reach of rodents, and set Cain on the ground inside the cave. "Stay here," she said, her tone stern. She watched him as she deftly tied Achima in front of her and opened her clothing to let her nurse. "All right, come with me," she said to Cain, who would not stay still. She took his hand and walked slowly with him to the sheep pens, grabbing a wooden bucket along the way.

When they reached the pens, she let Cain inside with the animals, praying he would not get underfoot, then went to the first ewe and sat to milk her.

She patted the ewe's back when she finished. "Thank you," she said to the animal, which looked at her with what could almost be an affectionate expression. Did the animals remember Eden? Did they remember caring for one another and never fearing being eaten by wild animals?

Her task at last finished, she switched Achima to the other breast and called Cain to come again. She found him sitting near one of the lambs, stroking its wool. The sight made her heart swell. He would make a fine shepherd one day. "Come," she said, offering him her hand.

He hesitated, so she walked closer and took hold of him. He stood and walked at her side as she carried the bucket back to the cave, set it on a high shelf Adam had built, and took another to milk the goats.

By the time she had finished milking the animals, she knew she needed to put the milk in goatskin sacks to make it easier to drink and for Adam to carry with him. But exhaustion overtook her. Achima was only a month old, and Eve was barely over healing from giving birth.

She looked at the milk and decided to go to the river instead. She would take the animals to drink and let them graze along the way since Adam would not have time after he harvested the barley. Some things just had to wait.

Cain began to whine and rub his eyes after she offered him a small bite of leftover flatbread and some curds she had learned to make from the milk. Achima slept against her chest, so Eve shifted the sling to her back and lifted Cain into her arms. "I'm sorry, Son. We have to feed the animals now and take them to the river. You can nap in the shade by the water."

He made noises she didn't understand, but he did not fight her hold on him. Instead he rested his head against her chest and fell asleep, making him heavier to carry. A sigh escaped her. She needed a way to pull him along without having to carry him everywhere when he grew too weary to walk.

She trudged on and reached the animals again, then opened each gate and called them to follow her. They came as they were used to doing now, and she led them to a field away from the areas where Adam was harvesting and other crops were growing. The sound of the river drew near, but she let the animals graze first. Sinking to the ground, she released a heavy breath, relieved for the slight break.

Cain still slept, so Eve laid him in the grasses and moved the now fussing Achima to her breast to nurse again. Eve couldn't remember if she had bothered to eat when she fed Cain. But by her growling stomach she knew if she had, it hadn't been enough.

She closed her eyes for a moment, then jerked them open again to check on Cain and the animals. She dared not sleep, despite how tired she felt. If only Adam could help her. But the barley would not wait, and she could not ask it of him.

Achima finally slept again, and Cain awoke. He turned and pointed toward the river. Eve laughed. "Yes, I suppose it is time to water the animals." She stood, took his hand, and called the animals to follow her.

Reeds and papyrus and trees lined the bank, but Eve found an open area where she could allow the animals to drink in a shallow spot. Swans and geese and ducks floated elegantly in the center and near the edges of the river. Waterfowl and other birds lived here in abundance, and the colorful winged creatures soared effortlessly above the trees.

Peace settled over Eve, and she sat with Cain and Achima near the water. She set Cain among the grasses. "Stay here," she told him, though she wondered if he even understood her at his age.

She turned slightly to watch the animals and untie Achima from her sling. She laid the infant on the sling among the soft grasses and smiled at her. A daughter, as she had hoped. *He will establish.*

That was what Achima's name meant, according to Adam, who had named every animal. Yes, God would establish their future, their dynasty. He would give them enough children to begin to populate the earth, wouldn't He?

But the thought of having another child made her shudder. She was tempted to keep Adam from her until she regained her strength. He had an insatiable need for her, but she did not think her body could carry another child soon. Maybe in a year or more, after Achima was Cain's age or older. Yet she could not keep Adam away that long.

Movement and the sounds of a scream and a splash filled her ears. She jerked her head around to look for Cain. He was not where she had told him to stay. Her back had been turned to him only a moment!

She glanced at Achima, who was still sleeping, and ran toward the river's edge. The water rippled where something or someone had made a splash.

"Cain!" Had he thrown a stone in? Or had he fallen in?

She made a quick, frantic search around her, and then she jumped into the water and ducked her head under, searching for him. The water was murky from stirring up the silt at the bottom, but a moment later, she saw his small body not far from her. She swam quickly to reach him and scooped him into her arms.

As she raised him out of the water, her heart nearly stopped. He wasn't breathing! She crawled out of the water, screaming, "Cain! Cain!" She turned him over and pounded on his back. If he had swallowed the river water, perhaps she could make it come out of him.

She continued to pound his back and scream his name. *No! No! No!* She could not lose him.

Please, Adonai, don't let him die. The very thought made her blood run cold. She pounded his back again, and at last he coughed and water gushed from his mouth.

She rolled him onto his back, and he began to cry. She pulled him into her arms, tears streaming down her face. "Cain. Oh, Cain!" *I could have lost you.* She could not bear the thought. And she must not tell Adam. He would grow angry, and she could not take one more bad thing happening today.

She glanced at Achima, who was awake now but thankfully unable to crawl away. She moved closer to her daughter, still clinging to her son. The animals came near. The ewe she had first milked rested her head against the top of Eve's, as if she understood.

She gave the animal a grateful look, for lack of a free hand to stroke her. She would do so later when Adam had the children or they slept safely in their beds.

Shaking and not sure her legs would hold her, Eve finally stood and called the animals to follow her, quickly counting each one to make sure she had not also lost one of them.

I can't do this, Adonai. It is too much. If only there were other humans to help or the children could grow faster. But she knew her prayer had no answer, for Cain had grown slowly and was a long way from being able to help his father. She simply must do better.

Adam entered the camp as the sun was beginning its descent. He looked about for Eve and found her in the cave tending to Achima. Cain sat in a corner playing with pieces of wood Adam had carved for him in the evenings. "I've brought the barley," he said, setting a large basket on the ground. "I need to go get the other one. I need your help to put it into smaller baskets with lids once you are finished with Achima."

Eve's gaze shifted from him to the barley. Weariness lined her face, and he wondered what caused her to look so exhausted. She had been so strong in the garden. Had motherhood weakened her? Or was it all of the work that did not come easy to either of them that wore her down?

She nodded. "I will begin to scoop this barley into the waiting baskets while you gather the other," she said, wiping sweat from her brow.

He gave her a grateful smile and left again for the field. If they could make sacks out of some type of strong material, he could more easily carry the grain to the cave. They could even sew the sacks shut temporarily until they had time to move them to the baskets. The baskets were good and tight, but Adam wondered if they were the best way to store the grain.

Yet he could not ask Eve to add more work to her load. Besides, he needed to find a plant that could produce a stronger fiber than the flax-like plants she used in basket weaving. Wool could not be used for sacks, and they could not kill animals for their skins every time they needed a better way to do things. Perhaps if he asked, Adonai would give him wisdom.

He pondered the thought as he picked up the second large basket and returned to the cave. Eve had already begun to use a wooden scoop he had carved to fill the waiting baskets. Cain had moved to another area and was digging at the stones in the floor, while Achima lay on her back stretching her arms and legs.

"How was your day?" Adam asked as Eve continued scooping. He took up a cup he had carved and used it to help her.

She glanced at him but seemed reluctant to talk. At last she spoke. "It was busy. I took the animals to the river after they grazed, but watching them and the children is exhausting." She paused, and he thought he saw the beginning of tears in her eyes.

"Did something happen?"

She shook her head. "Nothing that proved serious, but I cannot keep up with it all." She met his gaze, and they both paused in their work. "It's too much trying to make things, keep us fed and clothed, and watch the animals as well as Cain, who moves away from me too easily. I fear . . . I fear something bad will happen."

He studied her, not certain what to say. "I can't harvest the grain *and* watch the animals."

"And I can't weave and search for food and milk the sheep and goats and take them to pasture and watch the children. It is too much." She sank onto the ground and covered her face with her hands.

He knelt beside her. He'd never seen her so broken. He took her hands in his. "Tell me what really happened today that wasn't serious."

Tears streamed down her face, and she glanced at Cain as if wanting to be sure he was still there. "I almost lost him today," she finally admitted. "Do not be angry with me. I only turned to look at the sheep a moment, then I heard a splash and Cain was nowhere in sight. He had either fallen or jumped into the water. Adam, he couldn't swim! Since we could swim the moment we were made, I thought he might be able to as well, but he couldn't. I jumped in and found him, but I had to pound his back to get the water out of him. I didn't want to tell you, but there it is." She was truly crying now.

He pulled her into his arms, alarmed at her confession. They needed help to do all of this. How were they supposed to survive, just the two of them? *Oh, Adonai, help us.*

He held Eve close as she wept, keeping an eye on the children. "I will do what I can to help you," he said at last. "Perhaps I can strap Cain to my back as I harvest the grain. You shouldn't have to watch them both plus everything else."

"He's no longer an infant."

"I'm strong enough, I think." He stroked her hair.

"Thank you," she whispered against his chest. She dried her tears and leaned away from him. "I suppose we should finish this work before we eat."

He smiled. "Agreed."

14

Eve pulled Hasia and Abel in a cart Adam had fashioned for her, with her newest daughter, Chania, strapped to her back. She followed Achima as she skipped ahead toward the river. Cain spent his days with Adam now, and Achima helped her with the household chores. Even Hasia, at four, was able to play with Abel and tidy her sleeping area.

The house of hewn stone that Adam had built them had taken two years to complete, but at least now they lived closer to the river and the pens where they kept the animals. They had learned much with every year that passed, not only about how to care for their growing family but also about creating tools—everything from the cart to smelted metals that allowed Adam to cut and carve wood, stone, animal hides, and so much more.

Chania stirred in the pouch Eve had strapped her in, and Achima stopped at a bush with colorful berries. She turned and called to Eve, "Ima, do these have seeds?"

Eve drew closer, though she already knew the answer. She knelt beside her oldest daughter. "Can you see seeds inside these small berries or around the outside of them?"

Achima studied the red berries and touched the smooth surface.

"I do not see anything," she said, her mouth drawing down in a frown. "I'm hungry, Ima. Will it hurt to taste one?"

Eve pulled one of the berries from the branch and broke it open with a fingernail. "Look closely, my daughter. Do you see any seeds?"

Achima shook her head.

"And do you see any on the smooth surface of the berry?"

"No," she said. "And we are not to eat anything without seeds."

"That's right." Eve stood and patted Achima's head. "You are a good girl to ask me. If the fruit does not have seeds, it could hurt us. Poison us, even, and make us very sick."

Achima's dark eyes widened. "That would not be good."

Eve nodded. "You are right. It would be very bad for us. This is how we test what is good to eat. We eat only what God has given us that bears seeds."

Achima took three steps back from the plant and took Eve's hand. "I don't want to get sick, Ima. I would rather feel hungry."

Eve squeezed Achima's hand as Hasia and Abel begged to get out of the cart and run through the grasses. "In a moment," Eve told them. "Be still a little longer."

They obeyed her, to her surprise, and she continued to pull them in the cart while holding Achima's hand. If only she had always obeyed God's directions when it came to what she ate. The fruit of the Tree of Knowledge of Good and Evil had borne seeds, but God had still told them not to eat of it. Just as He had told them to eat only seed-bearing plants.

It was always for our protection, she realized as the river came into view. "There is a pear tree near the river," she said to Achima. "You may choose any of the fruit there."

Achima's face brightened, and she let go of Eve's hand and ran toward the tree. "Bring enough for all of us," Eve called after her, though she would have to use her skirt to hold them all.

Achima waved, an acknowledgment that she had heard Eve's words.

Eve lifted Hasia and Abel from the cart and set them down. "Don't go near the river's edge."

"We won't, Ima," Hasia called, pulling Abel by the hand and running after Achima. Eve had fed them earlier that morning, but it amazed her how hungry they always seemed. Perhaps it was simply because the food Adonai had given to them tasted so good.

She pulled Chania from her pouch to nurse and sank onto the grass to watch her children. How quickly they had grown. When there were only two, she couldn't imagine having more, but now she couldn't imagine life without any of them. How many more would God give them? How long would she be able to bear children?

I suppose it depends on how long we live. The thought came unbidden. Death was something that was never far from her thoughts, as it frequently happened all around them. And God did promise that if they ate the fruit of the Tree of Knowledge of Good and Evil, they would die. When? How long did life last in a fallen world?

Part of her wanted to know, to understand how long she would live in a world that no longer held perfection. But another part of her did not want to think about it at all. What did it matter if she knew how long? Perhaps she would have many more children and live hundreds of years. Or maybe God would return her to dust much sooner than she expected.

She watched Achima hand pears to Hasia and Abel, then head in her direction, arms full of fruit. Eve smiled, grateful for the time that was now. There was no need to fear tomorrow. Each day God gave them breath, she would be thankful.

Adam walked the rows of plowed ground, bag slung over his shoulder, and tossed seed into each row. Cain walked beside him several rows over and did the same. The child had a knack for understanding the earth and had taken to plowing and sowing quickly for one so young.

Eve had taken the other children to the fields with the animals to let them graze. Cain's help, though somewhat slower, would allow Adam to relieve her soon. Only two more rows.

His son seemed so intent on making sure the seed fell exactly in each row the correct distance apart. Adam reached the end before Cain did and started on the next row. He glanced at the sky, watching the sun slowly descend past the midpoint. There was still time.

"How are you doing, Son?" he asked, turning back to where Cain lagged behind.

"I'm doing it like you asked, Abba." He gave Adam a toothy grin. "I'm not as fast as you though."

Adam chuckled. "That's fine. I don't expect you to work like a man fully grown. You're doing very well."

His son beamed at the praise. He must remember to praise all of the children when given the chance. Truth be told, he was proudest of Cain, but he was the firstborn, and the others were not old enough to help yet. In time.

They came to the edge of the field and turned as one to look at their work. "We did good, didn't we, Abba?" Cain asked, feeling his empty sack, satisfaction settling over his expression.

"Yes, we did, my son." He patted Cain's head. "Now let us go and get the animals from Ima and take them to drink at the river."

Cain's mouth formed a small pout. "I don't like the animals as much as I do working with you here," he said as he fell into step with Adam's slow strides.

"The animals give us milk and other food and wool for clothing. You used to love the sheep."

"They're smelly," Cain said, wrinkling his nose. "I like them well enough, I guess, but I like working in the dirt more."

"Perhaps you will be a cultivator of food from the earth."

Each of his children would surely do different things. They couldn't all be shepherds or keepers of herds. Adam knew all too well how hard it was to do everything. If Cain grew to love the earth and tending the food that came from it, Adam would have one less chore to handle alone.

"Yes," Cain said, interrupting his thoughts. "That's what I will be." He offered Adam a big smile and ran ahead as the flocks and his siblings came into view.

Adam saw Eve moving among the sheep, goats, donkeys, and cattle while the children played near the lambs. Despite five children, they still had a long way to go before there would be anyone who could really help them. Sometimes the load felt far too heavy, almost too much to bear. But bear it he must.

The Unseen Realm

The throne room of heaven filled with radiant light coming from the Almighty Ancient of Days, Adonai Elohim, and the Spirit of God, who floated in iridescent color in the air about them. The council of God's chosen angels took their places around His throne.

The archangel Michael stood near the Almighty, close to the seraphim. Each seraphim had six wings: with two wings they covered their faces, with two wings they covered their feet, and with two wings they flew. They called out to one another, saying, "Holy, holy, holy is the Lord of Hosts. The whole earth is filled with His glory."

Michael listened to their melodic chorus as the Godhead spoke to one another, the Three in One majestic and glorious to behold. The words were thunderous and yet mere whisper.

Michael glanced beyond the Three in One to his fellow archangel Gabriel and saw in his gaze the same awe he felt. Fire emanated from the throne, drawing Michael's attention again to the Creator. A golden bowl stood before the Almighty, which held the prayers of the humans on earth below. Every sacrifice of praise and offering seeking forgiveness was recorded in God's book, and the Book of Life stood open on a table of clear gold overlaid in shimmering jewels.

Adonai Elohim's gaze shifted to Michael, who felt His fiery eyes penetrating deep into his thoughts. God knew he had questions, and by His look, Adonai was inviting him to ask them.

Michael straightened, laying his wings flat behind him. "The humans have populated the earth well so far," he said. "Adam and Eve now have thirty children, and they are following Your decrees and keeping Your sacrifices. Are You pleased with them, my God?"

Adonai Elohim looked at him for a long moment, and Michael wondered if he had asked the wrong question. Then in a heartbeat, he sensed the answer. God was keeping records of each person—their deeds, their faith, their prayers, their repentance. And each one was recorded in His Book of Life. But would their names remain there?

A shift is coming, he heard in his heart. He could almost feel the shaking coming from the earth below the clear, glassy floor of heaven's throne room. He looked down on the humans, who were like grasshoppers in the eyes of those who lived in God's heavenly realm. No longer did the council of heaven interact with them. After nearly one hundred years of separation, they still survived, and often the Almighty sent Adonai Elohim to give them instructions or wisdom. Sometimes He dispatched one of the angels to whisper instructions in their ears.

They had grown, even thrived. Eve especially seemed to care about the Creator and taught her children the things she knew of Him. Adam spent time alone with God, praying. Together they were doing all they could to keep their sons and daughters from repeating their sins.

But what shift was coming? The devil had already caused the greatest shift heaven had known. What could possibly happen to bring about another change for life on the earth?

Michael looked again into the fiery gaze of Adonai Elohim, but no more answers were given to him.

The Three in One spoke again to one another, and Michael sensed sadness in their tone. Though he longed to understand, some things were beyond his understanding. None but God knew what they spoke between them.

Michael looked again at the earth and then clearly heard the Almighty speak, dispatching him to earth to watch over the children of Adam and Eve.

What am I to look for? he asked.

But the answer did not come.

⁓

He should be used to the darkness by now, but every time he moved in this place without the ability to see anything, he cursed. The Almighty had stripped him of everything, even his name when He cast him from His radiant light. *Devil*, they called him now. *Evil One*.

The Tree of Knowledge of Good and Evil was to blame for this. If God had not created the tree, no one would have wanted to eat from it. Even the shining ones in the heavens had been tempted with a desire for such knowledge once they knew it existed.

Lucifer cursed God aloud and shook a fist above his head. "I will destroy You for this," he shouted.

A flutter of wings moved near him, and the voices of the fallen ones—*demons*, as their former "angel friends" now called them—filled his ears, echoing his words like a grand chorus.

"What would you have us do, my lord?" one of his underlings asked him.

He straightened, fluffed his wings, and rose to his full height, squinting, cursing the lack of sight to know who spoke with him. "As you know, the Almighty has forced us here, below the earth, to punish us. But He did not take away our ability to leave from time to time and roam the land. Or stop us from coming into contact with the humans."

"We move among them often," one of them said. "They are devoted to God, even after nearly one hundred years away from Him."

"What else have you seen? I assume you are obeying me and

causing discord between the siblings of the *adams*?" Lucifer scratched an itch near his forehead. The humans were a constant thorn in his side because the Almighty had given them a second chance. Why were they so special? And this one who was to come and crush his head? Who would it be? One of Eve's children?

He was almost ready to tell all the demons to meet on the earth, where they could hide in the shadows invisible to the world. But then the shining ones who had not followed him might hear his words, and he could not take that chance.

"Which one of Eve's sons is most devoted to God?" he asked.

"Abel, my lord. He is one of the older sons, newly married to the first daughter, but has no children yet. He is a shepherd and often gives special offerings to God out of his devotion." The demon spat.

"Watch what you're doing. You just spit on me!" another demon shouted.

Fighting broke out among the ranks until Lucifer could take no more.

"Stop your foolishness! Listen to me. We need to destroy Abel. You are sure he is the most devoted son of Adam?" He scratched in another place, suddenly wondering if God had sent something to crawl on him here.

"Yes," said another. "Cain is too self-possessed to be pleasing to God. He is in the right place, I would say." Cackling laughter followed his remark, and Lucifer smiled.

"I am aware of Cain," he said in a low growl, causing silence to descend. Good. They needed to listen to him. "He is going to be our target. Since he is already bent on rebellion, it should be quite easy to prompt him to rid the earth of Abel." If Abel was the one meant to crush his head, that would soon no longer be possible. He would crush Abel first and use his brother to do it.

"How are we going to do that?"

"Are you so foolish like the shining ones? You will whisper discontent into his thoughts. You will make him weary of going to his brother or father for lambs to sacrifice. Figure it out! I expect you to make Cain hate Abel by the time of the next sacrifice. Just do it!"

Yes, it was a good plan.

"I *will* defeat the Almighty one day," he whispered. "I *will* rule the earth and the humans God *loves*." The word tasted like ash on his tongue. Love. What a witless notion. But . . . if he could convince the humans that love was physical, nothing more, then they could be so easily controlled. They could "love" each other and think that was all that mattered. They would forget all about God loving them.

Giddy with the thought, Lucifer shot upward and left the pit to roam the earth unseen.

15

The morning sun kissed Eve's face as she made her way to the river to gather water. If only the blessing of the sun could pull her from the anger she tried to ignore. After all of her years on the earth, she still fought with Adam and sometimes with her own children.

"I told you we were leaving before dawn, Eve. Couldn't you have kept Illiya quiet in the night? You know how much her cries irritate me." Adam's quiet words, spoken close to her ear that morning, had held a bitter edge.

She took a step back and crossed her arms over her chest, keeping her voice low lest they wake the child. "I should be so privileged as to be able to lie abed when our child is hungry."

"Since you are the only one who can feed her, what do you expect? We've been through this for years, Eve." His brows knit in a deep frown.

Why wasn't he backing down? In the past he had been understanding of her exhaustion, even helped with the children as often as he could.

"Why are you being so spiteful? I was up half the night with her." She walked toward the door of the house, away from Illiya.

"You could show a little compassion." She glared at him, too tired to deal with his moods.

"It's your place to do what I ask, not the other way around, remember?" he snapped.

She clamped her lips tight when she caught a glimpse of some of their adult children emerging from their homes, then whispered, "God didn't mean for you to act like you own me. I am your wife, not your donkey! If we don't get along and work together, what will our children think? What will they learn from us about how to treat each other?" Her breath came hard, and her heart pounded from anger. He'd never struck her, but sometimes she wondered if he wanted to.

Adam had stalked off. *Typical. Be silent then.*

Now she adjusted the straps of the water skins and stepped lightly over the worn path, which led from the house Adam had built to the bubbling waters. Swans floated effortlessly in the middle of the river, and ducks with their ducklings swam near the edge of the bank. Condors, cranes, and birds she could not identify soared above her head, while smaller thrushes landed in the trees, their morning songs a sweet trilling sound.

She attempted to find comfort in the beauty around her, but living with the man God had given her was a mixture of pleasure and frustration. They should be used to evil emotions by now and know how to keep them in check. But they always seemed to get the best of her, and Adam had still not learned how to easily forgive. He punished her with his silence and struggled to admit he was wrong.

Why, Adonai? Why is Adam so irritating?

She bent to dip her goatskin sacks into the river, waited for each one to fill, then lugged them out and tied them tight with flaxen string. She'd given up on trying to carry the heavy clay jars years ago, but now she wondered if they would hold more if she shaped them differently.

The thought lifted her spirits as the idea of working with clay took form again. How much she had learned in the years she had lived on the earth. Even with her frustrations with Adam and the children, she found solace in creating new things.

But if she were honest, it was the children she enjoyed the most. *Thank You for them*, she prayed. They brought distraction from Adam when he grew upset with her. Sometimes there was no pleasing him, and other times he was a most ardent and attentive lover. Would all of her sons grow to be like him?

She hefted the bags onto each end of a long stick and carried it across her shoulders. She did desire Adam, but what *had* God meant when He said her husband would rule over her? He insisted on making decisions but normally accepted her advice along the way. They'd been a team until their sons had grown up.

Now she felt like she was no longer his companion and one he should protect but the one on which he could take out his anger. He could not keep doing that! If he wanted her to give in to his physical need of her, he needed to treat her with respect and understand when she couldn't do what he'd requested. And stop walking off in silence when they fought.

She looked up at the sound of footfalls and crunching foliage. Achima met her on the path coming toward the river.

"Ima, you always make it here before I do. I had hoped to talk with you."

Eve shoved her thoughts of Adam aside, grateful for the interruption to her intense musings. She looked at her firstborn daughter and stood in awe of her immense beauty. Achima had been crafted and sculpted as Eve had been, as if the Creator had deigned to make her just like her mother, though He began with an infant instead of an adult. Achima had captured Abel's eye as soon as he was old enough to long for a wife.

"What is on your mind, my daughter?" Eve stopped and set the skins on the ground.

"I have heard rumblings of discontent between some of my sisters, particularly with Hasia. She claims Cain has grown weary of going to Father or Abel for a lamb for the sacrifices. But why would he tire of such a thing? He provides us with fruit and vegetables, and they supply him with the perfect lambs God requires. We've been doing this since the days when the boys grew to men and began to provide from their own resources, not just Father's." Achima's oval face showed lines along her brow, her dark eyes filled with worry.

"Hasia tends to complain, Achima. You know this. And Cain has always been independent and a bit stubborn." Eve twisted a strand of her long hair behind her ear. Normally she tied it behind her with a piece of wool string, but as soon as Chania had arrived to watch the younger children, she had hurried away from Adam's stinging words to the river and not taken the time.

"But where else will they get the lambs they need? It's not like many of our other brothers are shepherds like Father and Abel. Everyone knows that they are the providers of the sacrifices." Achima held her empty sack close to her chest, and Eve wondered why a few complaints troubled her so.

"Their complaints will die away, Achima. They always do. Cain knows he has nowhere else to go. Perhaps he had a fight with Abel and is just moody because of it. Has Abel said anything to you to cause you such concern?" Achima's worries could be overblown, but if she knew something she wasn't telling . . .

Achima looked at her feet. "Abel does not get along well with Cain, at least not these past few years. They tolerate each other, but it is clear that Abel is devoted to God and Cain is devoted to himself. They clash when it comes to keeping the laws Adonai Elohim has given to us. The laws are not so many that they are impossible to keep. But the time of the yearly sacrifice is coming again, and Abel says that Cain has not come to him yet. Normally he comes a month in advance. Has he gone to Father?"

Eve searched her mind, but with all the things Adam spoke to her about and the fight so fresh in her mind, she could not think. He had said nothing of Cain. Then again, would he have told her? "It is possible that Cain has already worked everything out with him but your father simply hasn't told me. I can't answer your question."

"Can you ask Abba then?" Achima's lips pursed in a thin line.

Eve looked beyond her, a slightly sick feeling in her middle. At last she met her daughter's gaze. "When I have an opportunity, I will ask."

Achima studied her, and Eve turned away, suddenly wanting to go off by herself as Adam had done.

"The truth is, your father and I argued about something else this morning, and I need to calm down before I can speak to him." She looked into Achima's dark eyes. "I know you are aware when we fight, so there is no sense in keeping it from you."

"I wish you wouldn't fight," Achima said slowly. "Abel and I so rarely disagree."

The words stung, as though her children were better partners than their parents. "I'm happy for you," Eve said, squashing her feelings. "Your father and I have been together a long time, and sin never quite leaves us. It never will."

Achima nodded. "Instead of Abba then, would you talk to Hasia or Cain? Maybe they will tell you why Cain is so upset with Abel." Worry filled her expression, and Eve realized her concern was more than her normal older-sister anxiety.

"I will try," she said, "but they are grown. They don't listen to their mother like they did when they were young." How well she knew it and often wished it were not so. She missed the days when they confided in her, but that was long ago.

"Thank you, Ima." Achima kissed her cheek. "I will gather the water and wait to hear what you discover."

Eve lifted the skins and started walking toward the house again. "Don't worry, Achima. God will take care of us."

How easy it was to say such things. But He would, wouldn't He? He had always done so, even out of Eden.

Still, these rifts between her and Adam and now between Cain and Abel—were they simple misunderstandings? Or something worse?

~

Eve entered their large compound and set the water skins in a hole in the ground. She really did need to create a sturdier container that would hold the water, not be too heavy, and not leak. Perhaps today she would gather some of her girls and see what they could make.

But her first goal was to do as Achima had asked—find Hasia and talk. Her stomach fluttered at the thought of confronting this child. She checked on her younger children first and found them happily playing with Chania. "I'm going to be gone for a few minutes. I should be back soon."

"That's fine, Ima," Chania said. "They already ate some flatbread and goat cheese. Illiya may need to nurse soon, but I'll watch them while you are gone."

Eve looked with affection at her twin toddlers, Kaelee and Kalix. Even after giving birth to twenty-seven other children, birthing twins had taken a toll on her. And to have another girl so soon afterward had drained her physically and emotionally. Couldn't Adam see that?

She stuffed her irritation. "I'm going to find Hasia," she said as she headed toward the door of the house. "Have you seen her?"

Chania shook her head. "She's probably in the house she shares with Cain, unless she went for water."

Eve nodded her thanks and stepped again into the sunshine. Cain lived across the large compound. Each of Eve's adult sons had married one of their sisters and had built homes of their own in a circle spreading out from hers and Adam's. Cain had chosen to build a larger home farthest from the group.

She walked slowly toward his house, her heart beating a little faster. What was it about these children that troubled her? Hasia had not been an overly difficult daughter, but Cain had been a challenge from the day he was born. She had thought he might be the son of the promise and would save them, but he had quickly proved her wrong. He was too bent on rebellion to be a savior to anyone. Abel seemed a better possibility with his love for Adonai, but even he had his faults. The thought saddened her, for she dearly longed for the Promised One who would crush the serpent's head to come soon. Though she had not seen the shining serpent since that awful day, she sensed that he prowled about the earth. God would not have simply killed him, would He? Could angels, even fallen ones, die?

She drew close to the house, noting the tall door and the way Cain had carved the wood to stand out from the other homes. Hasia had changed after she married him, and not in a way that pleased Eve. What was she supposed to say to this child? Both Hasia and Cain complained often, and the family had more peace when they left the communal gathering. But she could never tell them that.

Sighing came too often of late, but she released the pent-up breath just the same. She knocked and waited. Cain had even put wooden planks above the dirt. Perhaps working in the earth with the plants caused him to no longer want to step in the dust when he walked into the house.

Footsteps came from behind the door. It opened, and Hasia stood looking at her. "Ima. Welcome!" She moved back, inviting Eve inside. "This is a surprise. I expected you to be caring for the twins and the baby."

"Chania is watching them, but I will have to leave soon." Eve settled onto a wooden chair that Hasia offered her, and Hasia took a seat opposite her.

"You don't usually visit in the day, so there must be a need. What can I do for you?" Hasia clasped her hands over her stomach, and Eve wondered if her daughter held a secret there. Was she pregnant? Could that be why she was more irritable? It would make perfect sense. And since Achima had yet to conceive, she would not be able to share that experience.

"Achima came to me today, concerned that there are problems between Cain and Abel. She heard complaints about the animals for sacrifice. Has something come between your brothers?" She searched her daughter's face, looking for any hint of a problem.

Hasia lowered her gaze, her dark lashes brushing her cheeks. The girl had beautiful, large, dark eyes and had caught Cain's attention far sooner than Eve had expected. But Cain often wanted what he saw, and Hasia was no exception.

Eve waited until Hasia looked up at her again. "Cain doesn't like Abel, Ima. He is too 'good' for the rest of us. And he flaunts it to Cain. Cain is tired of going to him to beg for a perfect lamb to feed the lust of God."

A little gasp escaped Eve's lips. "Be careful what you say, my daughter. You sound bitter against our Creator. That will do you no good, and you know it."

Hasia's cheeks darkened, but her eyes flashed with a sense of her own rightness. "Well, why else are we required to kill lambs every year and sometimes more often? Why can't we just bring Him a different gift and apologize for our failings? Why does it always require blood sacrifice?"

"We have explained that to you since you were small. Adonai Elohim told us, 'Without the shedding of blood, there is no forgiveness.'" Eve felt an inner shaking she could not stop. What could have possibly made her daughter so against the God who had made her? Undoubtedly Cain felt the same.

"But why? Just because you needed clothing and God killed a ram to make it for you, should that mean that we have to keep killing lambs each year to be forgiven? Why wasn't one enough and we could just pray to be forgiven for the rest? I've never understood that, Ima." Hasia's gaze softened, and her look took on a pleading quality.

How to explain it to her? Eve had already taught her all she knew. "There is no better way to say it other than that God Himself told us this is what He requires of us. If we don't come to Him

120

and repent with the blood of an innocent, perfect, spotless lamb, He can't cover our sin. The blood is our covering. How or why, He has never explained to us."

"Well, Cain thinks it's wrong and I agree with him." Hasia pulled her arms tighter around herself.

"What if Cain is wrong? Will you still go along with him?"

But what choice did her daughter have? Cain was her husband. He ruled over Hasia just as Adam did her, though Eve had learned many ways to control Adam through the years. Apparently Hasia had not been married long enough to learn to counter Cain's choices.

"I have to, Ima. I'm carrying his child. I can't leave him and marry a different brother. That would not be right, would it?" Her expression now held a challenge.

So Eve had been right about the babe. "No, that would not be right. God would not approve of that at all. But you are pregnant. How wonderful!" A first grandchild—a child she didn't have to bear!

Hasia smiled for the first time. "Yes. We are excited, though we have not told anyone yet. Cain wanted to tell Father first. And I you."

"I'm glad that you did." How long would it have taken her if Eve had not shown up at her door today?

Eve stood, realizing that the conversation would not improve if her son and daughter had such animosity toward the Creator. No wonder Cain did not like Abel. Abel worshiped God with all his heart. He and Cain were almost like light and darkness trying to mix. Oh, that Cain would embrace the Creator as well!

"I hope you can work things out with Achima and Abel," Eve said as she opened the door to leave. "I don't like to see my children at odds with each other."

"Then Abel should stop acting so self-righteous. Perhaps then Cain could put up with him better."

"Try to do your part as well. Women have great influence with men, whether our men think so or not." Eve kissed Hasia's cheek. "I look forward to meeting my first grandchild." She walked away, her mind spinning with troubled thoughts.

Oh, God, please help my children to see that You are the one who made them. They need to obey You and not end up like Adam and I have since we chose our own path. Please let them choose Your path.

She could not stop praying, though it brought no peace. There was nothing she could do to make her children believe in the God who made them. How could they think He did not deserve their obedience?

But then, she had once walked with Him every night, and she chose her own path too. Why had she ever thought her children would be better?

16

Cain pushed open the door of his house, his bearing stiff and straight, sweat dripping down his back. He loved working with the plants in the soil, but not today. His nostrils flared and his breath came fast as Hasia greeted him.

"Something troubles you, my husband," she said, leaning up on tiptoe to kiss his cheek. "Come, eat and drink of the food I have prepared for you." She took his hand, but he shook her off.

"I'm not hungry." He was in fact ravenous, but anger filled his belly, and he paced the large room, spewing curses.

Hasia backed away from him. He hated the way she reacted, hated that his anger caused her fear, but she knew better than to try to appease him when he'd had a fight with Abel.

He paced away from her, seeing again Abel's insolent smirk and haughty expression. "God wants us to sacrifice a lamb, not our crops," Abel had said. The words still stung. As if he knew better than Cain did what would please God.

"Won't you tell me what is troubling you?" Hasia leaned against the post that led to the room where they slept. One of many rooms he had made to show he could build a better house than any of his siblings or his parents. "Please, Cain. You will wear a path in the floor." She stepped closer, and he faced her and stopped, arms crossed over his broad chest.

"Abel has done it again," he said, knowing she would understand.

"He has said something to upset you."

"Doesn't he always? I was in the fields, tending the fruits and vegetables that grow close to the earth, and Abel passed by with his flocks. I told him to keep his filthy animals out of my gardens."

"Were they eating the produce?" Hasia's beautiful eyes widened.

Cain shook his head. "No. They were just within my sight, and you know what I think of Abel's flocks. If it were not for our need for wool and the food they provide, I would have nothing to do with them. But Father provides for so many of the others, we can't all go to him."

"Perhaps we should get a few of our own sheep so we could be done with needing Abel for anything." Hasia searched his face.

He frowned down at her. "Absolutely not! I want nothing to do with the smelly beasts." He whirled about and sank onto a wooden chair, splaying his hairy legs out in front of him.

"Not even a goat to keep for the coming babe? You know we will need to keep a few animals, unless you don't mind sharing with our family. We can't live on fruits and vegetables alone. Not even nuts and grains give the milk we need. Or the wool or the skins for—"

He held up a hand. "Stop! Don't you think I know all of that? It is Abel that irritates me. I told him today that I would take my own offering to God at the sacrifice, and he asked if I wanted one of his lambs. I told him no. So he asked if I was getting one from Father. Again I said no. But would he leave it at that? Of course not! He wanted to know where I was going to get a lamb for the sacrifice, and I told him I would do things my own way and to stay out of my business!" The words came out in a rush, and then he heaved a deep sigh.

Hasia stared at him as though he had lost his senses. She was supposed to be on his side. What was wrong with her?

"What? Do you agree with Abel now over your own husband?" He fisted his hands until his knuckles whitened.

She shook her head. "No, of course not. I was simply wondering what you planned to offer God as a sacrifice in place of the lamb, that's all. It's not that I don't agree with you." She clasped shaking hands in front of her, and he knew he should not take his anger out on her. Especially in her condition.

He stood and walked closer, taking her in his arms. "I'm sorry, my love. I am not frustrated with you. I just feel as though every time Abel offers me a lamb, he is looking down on me for not wanting to be a shepherd like he is. He acts like he knows what God wants and that I don't. It feels like he thinks he is better than I am. But you know this."

She held him close, silent. He rested his chin on her head, letting his breathing calm. Abel was not better than he was, and he did not know God better than anyone else did. Keeping flocks did not make him closer to the Creator. Hadn't God provided them with food from the land as well?

Cain *would* offer God a sacrifice, but it would be one of his own choosing. He could not bear to continue to offer the blood of lambs and goats. Animals should not have to die every year simply to appease a Creator who had made everything. He would offer Him something better.

<hr />

Three weeks later, Cain stood with the entire family as they gathered in the central courtyard and then walked together toward the place where his father had made the original earthen altar. They had considered making one of stone in its place, but his father had insisted that this one marked their first offerings to God, and they would use it as long as they could.

His father walked ahead, carrying a year-old lamb in his arms, while his mother kept pace beside him. Their younger children followed, while each of Cain's married siblings came with a lamb for their individual households. Cain trailed with Hasia at the back, a basket of fruit and vegetables, some of his best, in his arms.

"Are you sure you won't reconsider?" Hasia had asked him that morning, despite her original assurance that she agreed with him.

His blood pumped faster and anger rushed to the surface. "I told you no. Stop asking me, woman!"

She'd grown silent after that, but Cain did not care. Head held high, he trailed his family to the clearing not far from their encampment. The bleating of lambs met his ear, and he felt a sense of gladness that this year he would not be among those putting one of them to death. He and Hasia would miss out on using the skins or other parts of the animal, but they would find other provisions. At least this time Abel would not be able to think Cain dependent on him.

The earthen altar came into view, and his father turned and spoke to the group. "As we have done every year, we will do so again. Each family must place their hands on the head of the animal, then kill it, catch the blood in the bowls you have brought, and pour the blood out over the altar. We will burn the fat portions on the fire one at a time."

Cain watched as his father, Abel, and every other married brother put their hands on the lambs, bowed their heads, and one by one confessed their sins to God. He fidgeted as he listened to their earnest cries for forgiveness. Why did the lamb have to pay for their sins? He would never understand.

He turned to Hasia. "Place your hands on the fruit. We will confess as well."

She stared at him for a lengthy breath, then did as he asked. She spoke first, asking God to forgive her for complaining, for her frustration with Him, for not being the wife she should be.

Cain waited and finally whispered, "Forgive me for my anger. I will try to do better." It was the best he could offer.

The lambs' bleating quickly stopped as each man slit the throats of the animals. His father had already piled the wood on the altar, and one by one they brought their offerings and placed the fat portions on the wood. His father leaned forward to light them with the torch and jumped back as fire from heaven consumed the sacrifices. Smoke rose in a pleasing aroma to the heavens.

Each son came forward, with the same result. God accepted each offering, including Abel's, which caused Cain's jaw to clench.

When the fire died and only ashes remained, Cain stepped to the altar and placed his basket on top of it. His father looked at his offering, his brow knit in confusion—or was it displeasure?

Cain waited for the same fire to devour his gift, but nothing came. Perhaps his father would have to use the torch for his. "Light mine too, Father," he said.

"You want me to burn the fruit? That's not how it's done, my son." His father stepped away from the altar. "If you want to burn it, you will have to bring your own fire and do it yourself. I'll not have a part in this."

His father turned, took his mother's hand, and headed home. Each of his brothers moved toward their homes as well, leaving Cain alone with Hasia. Anger rose so fast within his heart that his cheeks heated, and he felt as though his blood might boil.

"Go home," he told Hasia.

She did not argue with him but hurried to catch up with their parents. Not even his wife supported him. And God obviously favored Abel over him as well.

He waited until he was alone, then staggered toward a thicket of trees. A voice thundered in the air above him and blinding light filled the space around him, stopping him in his tracks.

"Why are you angry? Why is your face downcast?"

Cain knew immediately that God was speaking to him. Fear snaked down his spine, and he gripped a tree to hold himself steady.

"If you do what is right, will you not be accepted? But if you do not do what is right, sin is crouching at your door. It desires to have you, but you must rule over it."

As quickly as the light and the voice came, they disappeared, leaving the small forest eerily quiet. The words terrified him, but the more he pondered them, the more other thoughts entered his mind as though also spoken to him. Only he knew they weren't. His thoughts were his own.

I did nothing wrong. Why wasn't I accepted? Because I didn't want to kill a lamb? I was showing compassion to the animal. What could be wrong with that?

"Sin is crouching at your door," God had said. What sin? Because he chose a different type of offering? How could sin have him anyway? He was master of his actions and emotions. Sin wouldn't rule over him. He simply disagreed with God. Hadn't his parents done the same thing? The serpent had told them, "You will not die," and they hadn't. His mother missed Eden and a life that was easier, but she still lived. God had not spoken the truth to them. The only death that had come since that day was from God's insistence that they kill the lambs as a sacrifice for their sins.

He still couldn't see how eating one piece of fruit could have such consequences. It seemed as though God had been completely unfair to his parents and was being the same to him now.

Sin wasn't crouching at his door. He was just fine the way he was.

Feeling better, he left the copse of trees and lifted his chin, walking steadily toward his home. He did not need God telling him what to do. He would make his own way.

17

Hasia watched Cain storm out of their house, relieved when he finally left. He'd been angry since the sacrifice and often took it out on her. He hadn't struck her—yet—but she feared him now more than she ever had.

She sighed. Had the visit from God after the sacrifice changed him so? But Cain would not tell her what God had said, only that he'd heard His voice and seen a blinding light.

A knock sounded on her door, and she moved from the food storage area to answer it. "Achima!" She looked beyond her, but Achima was alone. "Do you want to come in?"

Achima nodded. "I wanted to speak to you about our husbands."

A sense of foreboding swept through Hasia, but she allowed her sister to enter. They moved to a large sitting area with a few hand-hewn wooden chairs. She had managed to weave rugs out of wool they'd gotten from Abel, but Cain always took a chair, as though he needed to be above his brothers when they visited and sat on the floor. Not that they came often. How many of her siblings actually enjoyed Cain's company? A shiver worked through her, but she smiled at Achima and indicated where she should sit.

Achima took the chair Hasia normally used, and Hasia perched on the edge of Cain's, which was taller and harder to sit on. "Speak plainly," Hasia said, meeting her sister's gaze. "We are alone."

"I know. I waited for Abel to leave, then watched for Cain to do the same. I do not want either of them to know we talked."

"Perhaps we should have left the camp then. Anyone could have seen you come here." Though she doubted her sisters would care that they met. Only Cain had trouble with Abel, and no one really understood why.

"I don't mind if others know. I just don't plan to tell Abel unless he asks." Achima smiled, and Hasia's nerves settled a little. "I wondered if you think there might be a way to get our husbands to find something in common. To break this silent feud that you and I both know they've had since childhood." Achima clasped her long fingers, and Hasia looked down at her own.

"Since we've known them most of their lives, wouldn't a solution have presented itself by now?" Hasia found Achima's question strange. A person couldn't change another. They could only hope the other person would eventually want to change.

"Things seem worse than they were then. I remember when they played together. Even though things have felt tense of late, since the sacrifice it feels as though there is a chill that hovers over us every time the men meet. Don't you feel it too?" Achima lifted pleading eyes to Hasia.

Heat crawled up Hasia's cheeks as she wavered between agreeing with her sister and defending her husband. Hadn't she also thought Abel's pious attitude suffocating at times? Most of his life he had seemed overly interested in God and His ways. Though Achima might agree with him, many of their siblings didn't spend as much time talking about God or going off and talking to Him—if Abel could even see Him. Even Cain had not seen God. He had seen only His blinding light and heard His thunderous voice.

Hasia and Cain had often laughed about having a conversation with an unseen one. Their parents may have seen God and the rest of the unseen world, but they hadn't. A voice with a bright light wasn't the same. How did she know it was even God who had spoken to her husband? But if it was, why was Cain still angry with Abel?

"You have to admit, Abel is part of the problem," Hasia said at last. "Cain feels as though Abel looks down upon him because he does not worship God in the same way, and he has no desire to be a shepherd." She held Achima's gaze, daring her sister to disagree.

"Cain is the only one who does not follow the guidelines Adonai Elohim gave to us. Doesn't that concern you? He risks angering God Almighty! What will Cain do if that happens?"

"Have you never questioned Adonai Elohim? What if we are not even hearing from God but another of the unseen ones who we only think is Adonai Elohim? What if we are wrong and we've been killing lambs for years for nothing?" Hasia heard the words come from her mouth but was stunned that she had spoken them. She had been the one to change her mind and ask Cain to follow the laws of God, and here she was parroting Cain's words.

Achima stared at her. "Ima and Abba know the Creator. They've met the unseen ones, even the evil one. They can tell the difference." She stood, visibly shaken by Hasia's words. "Do you really believe what you said?"

Hasia looked down, unable to hold Achima's gaze. Deafening silence followed. At last she looked up. "I don't know. I've never met Adonai Elohim, so I only have Ima's and Abba's word to go on." Her voice dropped to just above a whisper. "I asked Cain to offer a lamb."

Achima sat again. "You did?"

Hasia nodded. "He's been angry with me ever since our failed offering."

Achima knelt at Hasia's side, touching her knee. "I'm sorry. I will talk to Abel. We can surely talk less of God to Cain, and if Cain will offer a lamb next time, he can take the best of the flock. Father would say the same, I'm sure."

Hasia offered a small smile, but tears rimmed her lashes. "He's been taking his anger out on me. Since God spoke to him, he has grown bitter. I can barely talk to him."

Achima stood and pulled Hasia into a warm embrace. Hasia clung to her, forcing back the urge to weep. She had married Cain and understood him better than anyone. She had to stay strong for their coming child. But Achima was right, and she loved her sister too. She would accept the comfort.

"I will speak to Abel tonight. Perhaps that alone will fix things. Don't say anything to Cain. I don't want you to suffer for my request." Achima kissed Hasia's cheek and walked with her to the door. "Things will get better," she said as she stood in the archway. "Surely Cain's mood will improve soon."

"I hope so," Hasia said as she watched Achima walk away. But knowing Cain, she doubted it.

Cain paced from one end of his fields to another, bending to pick weeds here and there, fuming. He glimpsed Abel leading the sheep to pasture but turned away from him. He could not bear the thought of even speaking to his brother.

Had he always felt this way? Was Abel really so awful as to cause him such hatred? But every time Cain considered treating him well or patching things up between them, he came up empty. He had done nothing to deserve Abel's disdain, and yet he felt it, that looking down on him every time he asked for a lamb for sacrifice. Every time he chose one that didn't meet Abel's standards.

He yanked a thick weed from the edge of a barley field and turned about, unable to focus his thoughts on his work. Could it be that his anger was the problem? Was Abel really as innocent as the others seemed to think? In his mind's eye he saw the looks of approval his brothers and sisters directed at Abel, while few ever gave Cain the same affection or attention.

No. The problem was Abel, not him. Maybe it was everyone,

as they all seemed to be against him. He must do something about it, for he simply could not continue to live in the same camp as Abel.

But if Abel died . . .

The thought startled him. Where had that come from? He looked quickly about him. His parents claimed the unseen ones could whisper evil thoughts in the air around them. But he'd never seen the shining ones. And though his parents seemed to know that the serpent had taken many shining ones with him and they were now servants of evil, how could he know?

Surely the thought was not his. He didn't want Abel dead.

Did he?

He bent down again and settled on a patch in a field where the cucumbers grew. He weeded carefully, forcing his movements to slow. As he worked, the appalling thought would not leave.

Perhaps he should just talk with Abel. After his brother returned the flocks to the pens, Cain would invite him to walk with him in the field away from the camp. They could discuss their differences.

And you could kill him.

No! He would simply talk to the man. Hasia would never forgive him if he harmed Abel, nor would his parents.

Hasia. He must be kinder to her. His anger was not good.

But it still simmered beneath the surface, and he began attacking the weeds as though he were trying to beat the rage from his mind. He had to calm down. Abel wouldn't go with him if he showed his anger. He must speak with him in a better way. He must be kinder. If he could.

Hours later, the sun began its slow descent into the west, and Cain tossed the weeds into a pile he would later burn. He drew in a calming breath and forced his gait to slow as he headed toward the sheep pens to wait for Abel.

His brother was coming just over the rise, leading the sheep, whistling a tune that the animals readily followed. A smile broke out on his dark face as he met Cain walking toward him.

"How good it is to see you, my brother," Abel said as he opened the door to the pen and inspected each sheep as it entered. "How are you today?"

Cain held back a grunt. "I am well. Let me help you inspect the sheep." He stepped closer, and Abel allowed him to enter the pen.

"Thank you for helping me." Abel patted the last ewe's flank, and when Cain left the pen, Abel closed the gate behind him. "The work is always easier with two."

"Perhaps you should encourage one of our brothers to help you. I will never see what you find enjoyable in caring for these creatures." Cain ran a hand through his long, unruly hair and walked slowly toward a distant field. "Let's go out to the field."

Abel matched his strides. "Is there a need? Achima is expecting me home."

"Achima and Hasia can wait. We need to talk." Cain marched ahead, and Abel hastened to catch up.

They walked in silence until they were a good distance from the camp, at a field that had yet to be plowed for sowing. The family rarely came this way, for the caves that lined the field were home to some of the more unfriendly animals, though they usually did not roam until the sun had fully set. Cain glanced at the sky. Dusk had fallen.

"What did you want to talk about?" Abel faced him, arms crossed over his chest in a protective gesture.

"Your attitude."

"My attitude?" Abel lifted a brow, and Cain felt his ire rise. As if Abel didn't know how he sounded to everyone but Achima.

"Yes. You can't pretend you do not see your pride. Just because we see things differently does not make you better than me." Cain glared at his brother. "I think it's time you explained yourself, little brother. Why do you think you are so righteous and I'm not?"

Abel looked at Cain, confusion in his gaze. Was his brother

really so naive to think Cain didn't notice his pride? His arrogance?

"I never thought of myself as better than you, Cain," Abel said. "I am just a shepherd. You make things grow from the earth that I never could. I am not more righteous than anyone else."

Cain detected pity in his brother's expression. Did he think himself empathetic? Compassionate?

Abel was a fool!

"I can see that I should have treated you better though. Brothers should not be at odds with each other. What can I do to change things?" Abel placed a hand on Cain's shoulder, but Cain shook it off.

"How dare you act as if you could ever make this right! It is not up to you to tell me how brothers should feel toward each other. You've been a thorn in my side since you were born!" He whirled about and stalked a short distance away.

Abel followed him. "I truly am sorry, Cain. I never meant to cause you grief. I want to help—"

Turning around suddenly, Cain stuck the iron blade he used to cut weeds into Abel's belly. Abel's eyes widened, his face contorted with pain. But his pain only hardened Cain's resolve. He twisted the knife until he could feel Abel's lifeblood spill over his sandals. He dropped his brother to the dirt as Abel's eyes rolled back and a blank stare replaced the pleading one he'd had moments earlier.

Abel was dead.

And you killed him.

He sank to the earth, stunned at his actions. What had he done? What would Hasia say, or Achima or his parents? How could he face them again?

He placed his head in his hands and moaned, longing to undo the past few moments. How had his anger grown so strong? Abel did not deserve this. Did he?

Of course he did. It was what you wanted to do for years—to be rid of him. You did nothing wrong.

The voice in his head merely whispered, but he wanted to scream to drown it out. He let out a howl like that of a wounded animal. The sound echoed in the hills around him.

The sun blazed orange as it set over the horizon, waking Cain from his half stupor.

He had to hide the body. If he put it in one of the caves with the wild animals, they would surely devour it, leaving no trace. He could tell anyone who asked that he had no idea what happened to Abel. He'd helped Abel count the sheep and then watched him head toward home.

Yes. That was what he would do.

No one would know. It would be the truth because he would make it so. He'd done nothing wrong. He'd simply done what had to be done to rid the camp of a nemesis. Abel had not deserved to live.

He drew in a deep breath and walked to Abel's body, staring at it one last time. He hefted his brother into his arms and carried him to the cave where lions were known to live. Then he rushed to the river to wash the blood from his clothing and sandals.

No one need ever know.

18

Hasia heard the door and hurried to greet Cain. The sun had long since set, and she had worried that something had happened to him. "What took so long? I feared you'd been eaten by a lion." She rushed into his arms, felt his wet clothing, and pulled back. "Were you in the river?"

Cain nodded, his profile dim in the light of a small clay lamp that stood in the main room. "I grew sweaty working in the heat and decided to wash off."

"With your clothes on? The skins will take forever to dry." She searched his face. It was not like him to get the lambskin wet just to dip in the river.

He bent to remove his sandals. Even they squeaked with water, which dripped onto the wood floor.

"Your sandals too?"

Cain frowned at her. "I didn't feel like stripping to the bone. I'm home now and everything will dry by morning. Don't fret about it."

He sounded testy, so she backed farther away, not wanting to rouse his anger. She'd put up with too much of that of late. "I kept the stew warm." She had stirred the pot over the fire until she wondered if all the water would boil out, but thankfully, it seemed to still be the consistency he liked.

"Good. I'm going to change into something dry. Bring it inside."

He left her for their sleeping quarters, where an extra set of clothing and his night tunic hung on pegs. She hurried to dish the stew into wooden bowls and placed flatbread beside it on wooden plates. She poured him a skin of barley beer, his favored drink.

Cain returned to the room just as a knock sounded on their door. Hasia hurried to open it, finding a distraught Achima standing there.

"Have you seen Abel? Is Cain home? Abel should have been home long before now, but he isn't here!" Achima's voice rose in pitch and wobbled. She sounded on the verge of tears. "I'm calling on our brothers to search for him. Will Cain join us?"

Hasia's heart fell like a stone in her middle. She turned toward Cain, who was now behind her, tying on his wet sandals. "I'm coming," he said, grabbing the torch from outside the door.

"Do you want to come inside?" Hasia asked Achima.

Achima looked into the house, then outside. Their sisters and mother were all hurrying toward Achima's house. "I better go home," she said, "but you are welcome to join us."

Hasia did not hesitate, despite the fear rising within her. Cain's hatred for Abel was no secret. And why were his garments so wet? Had he done something to harm Abel?

She followed Achima to her home, where the women had gathered, and kept her thoughts to herself. It would do no good to speak of what she did not know. Perhaps Abel had simply gone after a wayward lamb, and it had taken longer than usual.

But something inside her did not think so. Still, she wanted to believe it, and as the women all came to that conclusion, she decided she would believe it. Nothing else made sense—at least any sense that she dared to think.

The night waned, and Eve looked at her daughters in the dim light of Achima's home, her fear rising. The men would have to return soon and wait until daylight. They risked their own safety if they strayed too far from the camp. Lions roamed the hills, and bears were often about, looking for food. A man could get caught off guard and become one of their prey.

Abel, where are you? The moment the question left her mind, her heart pounded with a sense of impending dread. Until that moment, she had hoped he was simply caught in the dark rescuing a lamb. He would not have wandered far from camp without a good reason. Abel was an excellent shepherd, and he'd been known to go to great lengths to find a lamb that was lost.

But she wondered if her dear son was the one who was lost or if something far worse had happened to him. She rose from one of the few chairs in Achima's home, offering it to Hasia, who seemed particularly uncomfortable. Perhaps from the pregnancy.

Eve paced about the room slowly, looking from one daughter to the next, as if their expressions could tell her something she should know. But none of them revealed anything other than fear, especially Achima.

She came up beside Achima and wrapped her in her arms. Her daughter burst into tears, and Eve longed to join her, but she patted her back and held her close.

"There, there," she soothed. "We can't fear the worst until we know. It may be that he took shelter in a cave with a lost lamb and the men won't be able to look for him until the morning."

Achima slowly calmed. "You're right. It would be like him to wait it out if he could not see." She hiccuped on a sob. "But he would have allowed the moon to guide him home. He wouldn't stay away once he found the lamb."

"Would he stay out if he didn't?" Eve asked, feeling again that sinking sensation. Something was truly wrong, but she dared not try to guess what.

Achima shook her head. "He would have returned to search in

daylight. He would not have gone out and not returned to cause me worry. At least he never has before."

Eve nodded. A commotion in the yard caused the women to jump up and hurry outside.

"Did you find him?" Achima rushed up to her father, arms clutching his. "Where is my Abel?"

Adam shook his head, defeat in his gaze. "We looked everywhere, but we could not find him. He would not have gone to the higher caves where the lions and other big cats have their dens. We will have to wait until dawn." He pulled Achima to him, and her tears wet his tunic. "We will rise early and not stop until we find him. Don't worry, my daughter. God will surely lead us to wherever he is."

Achima quieted at his words. "I will pray," she said softly, turning to push past the women and enter her house.

No one followed her, and Eve wondered, given the feeling in her heart, whether she should join her daughter. She accompanied Adam as he began the walk to their larger house at the end of the compound. Their sons and daughters dispersed to their homes, though hopefully Chania had the twins and the baby asleep in their beds.

When they were alone close to their house, Eve took Adam's hand. "Do you think you will find him? I have a bad feeling about it all and wasn't sure I should join Achima in prayer to Adonai. Do you think we should?"

Adam faced her, taking her hands in his. "It never hurts to pray," he said slowly. "I don't know whether we will hear from Him though."

"Do you have the same bad feeling I do?" she asked.

He shrugged. "I am not one to trust my feelings. I think anything is possible. But perhaps you are right. Let us join Achima to pray for Abel. Perhaps Adonai will tell us where he is."

"I will tell Chania that we will be late," Eve said, hurrying into the house to check on her children.

A moment later, she followed Adam as he turned from their home and returned to their daughter's house. All they had was prayer, and while they couldn't walk with God as they once did, perhaps He would hear and give them wisdom. Perhaps He would even ease the nagging worry that she simply could not shake.

Cain rose before dawn. He glanced at Hasia, who was still sleeping, and slipped out of the house. Darkness shrouded the compound. He ought to take a torch, but the light from the early rays of the sun would come soon, and right now the moon still shone brightly enough for him to see.

The cave was a good distance from the campsite, and the lions could still be about, but they would soon return to their dens and sleep. He would watch and wait. But he had to know if Abel's body had been devoured by them or if it still lay inside the crevice of their lair.

Guilt nudged him as he picked his way through the field toward the caves. Achima needed to know her husband was dead. His parents needed the finality to give them peace so they would stop searching for Abel.

But he couldn't simply tell them what he'd done and lead them to the body. His father needed to find it. What was left of it. But then they would know that Abel had been stabbed, and how could Cain get around telling them the truth then?

He raked a hand through his hair, his breath coming fast. He quickened his steps as the first gray light of morn gave him a better view of the ground. There was no use in denying what he'd done, was there? Could he keep his secret from his family? Surely there must be a way to convince them a lion had gotten Abel.

The cave came into view, and he slowed his pace. He glanced quickly about. Nothing stirred, and the night sounds had disappeared.

He approached the cave, hoping he had the right one, and poked his head inside. Darkness caused him to stand a moment and adjust his eyes. He drew closer to the corner where he'd left Abel's body and saw a mound covered in sheepskin clothing. He did not need to roll the body over to know it was Abel. But he stepped closer just the same.

Crouching low, he examined Abel's prone form. Was this not the lions' den? Yet they had not touched him!

Cain stood and prodded the body with his foot. The blood had dried on Abel's clothing, but his body was simply gray from decay.

A shiver worked down Cain's spine. How was this possible? The animals had to have caught Abel's scent, yet they had left him alone? Cain looked about, fearing that God Himself had protected Abel's body.

The shock of that thought reverberated through him. He must move the body or the others would never find him, for no one would think Abel would go into a lions' den in the dark of night.

His chest lifted in a deep sigh as he bent to grab Abel's ankles and dragged him into the clearing. He pulled him to an area where the trees were thick, kicked dead leaves over him, and left him facing away from him. He'd done what he could. His family would easily find him in daylight and would no doubt be rising soon to head out and do that very thing.

Cain headed to his fields to work, to rid his mind of the disturbing thought that Abel, though dead, was unharmed by animals.

⁂

The sun rose higher in the sky, and in the distance, Cain heard his father and brothers calling Abel's name. When he joined them, he would tell them he'd been looking since dawn in another area. They would accept that.

He gripped a particularly difficult weed, dug around it with his knife, and yanked it from the soil. He didn't need these annoying weeds crowding out his plants. He took solace in the fields and among the groves of fruit trees, one of the few places where he felt satisfied.

He lifted his head and stood, admiring the work of his hands, when the blinding light of God filled the space surrounding him. His heart skipped a beat and then raced as though he were running the length of the field. Sweat beaded his brow and trickled down his back, though the sun was not yet warm. He turned about, searching for the source of the light, dread coursing through him.

"Where is your brother Abel?" Adonai's voice called from the light in the trees.

Cain's stomach flipped, and bile rose in his throat. Surely God knew. But if He did, why ask Cain? "I don't know," he said at last. "Am I my brother's keeper?"

Silence followed his remark for several lengthy breaths until the voice spoke again. "What have you done?"

The question cut to the core of his being, and he fought the curdling sickness in his gut. He stood mute, his gaze fixed on his feet, unable to look into the brightness of God.

"Listen!" God said. "Your brother's blood cries out to Me from the ground. Now you are under a curse and driven from the ground, which opened its mouth to receive your brother's blood from your hand. When you work the ground, it will no longer yield its crops for you. You will be a restless wanderer on the earth."

Dumbstruck, Cain covered his face with both hands. He loved the soil and the work of his hands. How would he feed his family if the ground no longer yielded food for him? What would he do?

"My punishment is more than I can bear!" His strangled cry met with God's silence. Surely there must be something he could do to change God's mind, to make things better for himself, for Hasia. "Today You are driving me from the land, and I will be hidden from Your presence. I will be a restless wanderer on the earth, and whoever finds me will kill me."

Would he actually miss God's scrutinizing presence? Yet how could he bear to leave everything he held dear?

"Not so," God spoke into the tense silence. "Anyone who kills Cain will suffer vengeance seven times over."

A moment later, Cain felt the light move closer to him, and a gentle pressure, a touch, marked his forehead. In that instant, Cain felt such sorrow and love mingled together that it made him weep uncontrollably. But Adonai had already left him.

19

Before dawn, Adam rose with Eve, and together they left the house, where the twins and Illiya still slept.

"I'm going to look again," Adam said. "I'm going to the ridge where the caves are. When the others awaken, send them in that direction."

"Did God give you wisdom in the night to look there?" Eve touched his shoulder, and he could feel her trembling. Neither one of them had slept well, and Adam knew that they both feared the worst.

"I didn't have a dream as I've had in the past," he said, meeting her worried gaze. "But I have a sense in my spirit that it is where I should begin."

"Where?" Mahaz asked, drawing close to the fire where Adam and Eve now stood. He was one of several sons born after Abel.

"I'm heading toward the ridge where the line of caves is. Perhaps Abel found refuge in one of them when it got too dark to come home." Adam said this to leave Eve with something to hope for, but his own heart held hope by a mere thread. He nodded to her and followed the path out of the camp toward the ridge, Mahaz at his side.

Eve would tell the others, and soon there would be many sons spreading out searching again. But would they find Abel? Had he fallen into a pit or gotten caught in a lair of wild beasts? Had a snake bitten him and the poison kept him from getting home?

As Adam passed the sheep pens, noting that the animals were all still resting, waiting for Abel to call them to pasture, he knew something was terribly wrong. Abel would not have put the animals to bed and then not gone home. Something drew him away after he'd finished his work for the day. The question was, what?

<center>~~~</center>

Eve sat before the fire, sending her sons off to search in the direction their father had taken. While Chania had agreed to care again for her younger siblings, several of Eve's other daughters—Tehila, Pessel, Naava, and Achima—had joined her, but none of them seemed able to rouse themselves to grind grain for the men to eat when they returned.

The girls talked softly among themselves, trying to engage Achima in easy conversation, but Achima's eyes still filmed with tears, and she did not speak.

Eve moved closer and placed an arm around her first daughter. "We must trust," she whispered, despite the feeling that there was nothing left for them to trust in. Except God, of course, but trusting Him didn't mean all would be well. She and Adam had brought death to the world, and though the animals died in sacrifice or fighting in the wild, not one human had yet perished. The very thought made her ill.

Achima looked at her, dark eyes wide and hurting. "What if he doesn't come home? What will I do?"

Eve had thought of that more times than she could count. Her daughter couldn't remain alone. But to suggest she marry again so soon . . . she could not even begin to broach the subject.

"Right now, you will help us prepare food for the men. They left without eating, and they won't be able to endure that for long." Eve roused herself out of her own stupor, went to the house for grain, and returned with the sack. The other women gathered the

146

millstones and sieves and took turns grinding the grain, sifting it, and mixing it with olive oil. Eve cooked flatbread for those who were still in the camp, then made stacks of them to have waiting for the men.

A solemn air settled over them as they worked, and few of them spoke until Kaelee, Kalix, and Chania, holding Illiya, emerged from the house. The children were not nearly as quiet as the adults had been, and their innocent energy helped lighten everyone else's mood. Eve gave them each a hug as she fed them, took Illiya to nurse, and glanced toward the place where the men had left to search.

A moment later a guttural cry pierced the air, the sound coming closer to the camp.

Eve stilled, her heart pounding, her limbs weak like water. She lifted Illiya over her shoulder and looked toward the sound. Adam, surrounded by the sons who had followed him, walked toward the fire, carrying a body. He wept as he placed it gently in the dirt near the center of the camp. Her strong husband, who had never weakened in the many years she had known him, crumpled to the earth, head in his hands, body shaking.

"Abel, Abel! My son, my son!" His cries carried the tone of a wounded animal, and Eve's own voice broke with sobs, the baby's cries mingling with hers.

Achima rushed to her husband's side and fell nearly on top of him, then jolted away. "He's so cold." She hurried to their home, returned with a woolen blanket she had woven, and covered him with it.

Eve wanted to tell her she would ruin the blanket with the aura and scent of death, but she couldn't bear to stop her. *Abel!* She handed Illiya to Chania as her heart screamed Abel's name. How she longed to pull him close and hold him like she had when he was a child. She wanted to rock him and tell him everything would be all right. But one look into his colorless face and lifeless eyes and she knew she would never comfort him in this life again.

She knelt at his side, opposite Adam, while Achima clutched his feet. Eve's gaze lifted to meet Adam's, and in that moment, she read in his face the exact feeling that lived within her. This was their fault. And it wasn't supposed to be this way. They should have died the moment they sinned. Death shouldn't come to children before it came to parents. How could this have happened?

"There are no obvious animal markings on him. He wasn't killed by a lion or bear or any other predator. Not even a snakebite," Adam said once his tears were spent.

"Then how did he die?" Achima cried, appearing unable to speak in a normal tone.

"Someone killed him," Adam said, pointing to the blade marks in the sheepskin Abel was wearing. "One of us, as this is definitely the work of a man."

Or woman? Which of her daughters had anything against Abel or was bitter enough to hurt him? Abel wasn't built like Cain or a few of his other brothers, but he was strong. Had been strong.

Cain did this. The thought assaulted her, and she nearly lost her balance even though she was sitting in the dirt. She looked about the camp but saw no sign of Cain. Hasia stood at the outskirts, her wide eyes filled with dread. She knew something.

Eve stood and walked over to her daughter. "What do you know of this, Hasia?" She searched her daughter's beautiful face, the familiar wrenching feeling settling in her gut.

"Cain and I are leaving," Hasia said loud enough for all to hear. "God has sent Cain away from His presence for killing Abel. I've packed our things, and we will leave your camp and go to the land of Nod, east of here."

Eve stared at her, and Adam rose to join her. "But how will you survive, just the two of you, and with you expecting a child?" she asked.

Hasia's lips trembled. "I suppose the same way you and Abba did before any of us were born." She lowered her voice. "I do hope you will visit sometime."

Eve nodded, but Adam's face had hardened. "If Cain did this to Abel, it is best you go," he said. "He is no longer welcome here."

Eve wanted to say, "He is our son too," but she couldn't. If God had sent Cain away, this was His punishment to Cain. Yet her mother heart ached so badly she thought something inside of her might burst in her grief. Oh, for the days when she'd held her sons as little boys. Tender children who would never have imagined something so awful as this.

But they were children no longer, and now one of them had gone the way of all the earth.

Adam turned to his other sons and asked for their help to build something to encase Abel's body, then find an empty cave they could cover to bury him. The first tomb on the earth.

Eve was certain she would never get past this day.

20

Eve woke the next morning, her mind a blur until every detail of the past few days came into sudden focus. She sat upright, grief hitting her like a thousand tiny stab wounds. If only she had died in place of Abel. This living death of such great loss made her long to cry out or to curl into a ball and never rise again. But her younger children still slept nearby, and she didn't want to awaken them with her cries.

She glanced at the pallet beside her, but Adam had already risen, no doubt to go off to his place among the trees to do his own grieving. He was far angrier than she had ever seen him.

She felt only guilt. If she had been a better mother, had taught Cain how to handle his anger, had warned her children, had been a better example to them . . . but the memory of Eden and her own sin just kept coming back to haunt her. She couldn't blame Cain when she had started the rebellion against the Creator in the first place. If only she had not eaten the fruit!

She forced her limbs to rise, limbs that felt leaden and aged despite her apparent youth. Though she had lived nearly one hundred years, until now her body had felt as youthful as the day of her creation. She'd had no hint that death could be near. Had barely imagined it coming to a human, only to the animals. A thousand lifetimes would never erase the fact that now she knew. And her whole body rebelled at the thought.

A sob rose, and she hurried from the house. The pink light of morn greeted her, but she saw no beauty in it as she usually did. How had this even happened? She walked past the central fire where she should begin to grind the grain and headed toward the river. Nothing would ever be right again. She had not only lost Abel, but now Cain and Hasia along with their first child were out of her reach.

Would Adam travel to Nod, so far from Eden, just to see this wayward son and their daughter, who had no choice but to go with him? Did Hasia agree with Cain's behavior? Had she hated Abel as much as Cain did?

But no. Achima and Hasia had been friends. Or at least they had attempted to be friends. She couldn't imagine that Hasia had been happy to leave, especially after the way she had clung to Eve before Cain led their loaded donkeys and a few young goats Adam had allowed them to take away from the camp.

So little had been said. There was just packing and Eve pushing past her grief to make sure Hasia had all she would need for the baby. Everyone else had kept their distance, watching in silence. She'd seen the looks on the faces of some of her sons and wondered what went through their minds. Did they despise Cain? Sympathize with him?

Sin was insidious—of that, she knew too well—and once dabbled into, it could cause a person to behave in ways that they never thought possible. Is that what had happened to Cain? Had Cain ever truly worshiped God?

Memories of the last sacrifice tormented Eve as she picked her way in the breaking light toward the river. The slow-moving sounds of the water lapping the shore and the musical voices of the waterfowl greeted her, offering a small sense of peace to her troubled soul.

She sat beside the bank, watching the swans and geese and

ducks floating and diving for food, wishing she could join them and hold them as she had so long ago. So many years had passed since they'd been forced out of Eden. The garden remained hidden by a circle of forest, and the cherubim still stood guard, blocking the way in.

A sigh escaped her, but her memories were interrupted by the sound of weeping. She looked up to see Achima farther upstream, face buried in her hands. Eve's heart constricted again.

Achima's cries grew louder as Eve approached her. She knelt at her oldest daughter's side and placed a hand on her shoulder. "Achima." Her voice was low, barely above a whisper.

Achima turned to her and fell into Eve's embrace. "Oh, Ima! He's gone. How will I live without him?" She wept until the fabric on Eve's shoulder was damp.

"I don't know," Eve said when Achima's tears finally dried, though the sheen of them still glistened in her dark eyes. "We will live one day at a time, as we always have, and ask the Creator to help us. Surely He knows our sorrow and is not blind to what has happened. The enemy no doubt had a hand in tempting Cain's anger until Cain could no longer control it. I know too well how cunning he is, and who knows how often he whispered in Cain's ear?"

Achima pulled back and looked into her mother's eyes. "Do you think Cain saw the serpent?" She visibly shivered.

"I don't know," Eve admitted, brushing the hair from Achima's eyes like she used to do when she was a child. "The serpent is cunning, and many of the unseen angels followed him in his rebellion. Perhaps one became acquainted with Cain or whispered things that Cain wanted to hear. Sin always follows when we think what we want to do is best and leave God out of our plans."

Achima nodded but said nothing. Eve had shared these things with her children over and over during the years, and perhaps her daughter was tired of hearing them. She released a long-held breath, fighting the feeling of defeat. For all her pleading and telling them the truth, her son was still dead at the hand of his brother, and she did not know how to comfort her daughter. She didn't even know how to comfort herself.

"I suppose I will live alone all my days and die childless," Achima said at last, her tone resigned. She stood and turned to walk back the way they had come, but Eve's hand restrained her.

"No. You must marry another brother who has no wife yet. Jabril would make a good husband. He believes as Abel did." Eve stood and placed a hand on Achima's back. "You will bear him children and live a long life. You must not allow Cain to steal your life as he did Abel's."

Achima walked with her in silence toward the camp, and Eve wondered if she had spoken too soon. But it was important that they continue to be fruitful and multiply on the earth, as the Lord had told them. Achima would become too lonely and a burden if she did not have her own home to care for.

As they neared the camp, Achima finally spoke. "It is too soon, but perhaps in a week or two, I will marry Jabril. If he agrees."

With so few of them on the earth, Adam and Eve chose their children's spouses. Jabril was a good son. He would agree.

Hasia followed the donkeys, preferring to walk after hours of riding. The land of Nod came into view, and Cain turned to her and smiled. "We're here at last." He walked faster, but Hasia stayed with the pace of the donkeys.

Her heart dipped at the sight. It was so barren in comparison to where they had lived all of their lives. They were so completely alone except for the few animals. How would they survive? Had God sent them here to die?

She missed her family. Why had she ever agreed to marry Cain? She should have known his temper would be his undoing. But he had been energetic and charismatic, and she'd liked his rebellious streak. How foolish she had been. Why had her parents chosen her to be his wife? Because he'd asked for her?

The thoughts had often tormented her on the long walk here. And the babe within her brought her quickly to exhaustion when coupled with the pain of so much loss. Would she feel better if some of her brothers and sisters had joined them? But why would they join a murderer?

The valley spread out before them, and a few lush fields blanketed the area between the hills. "We will set up camp here," Cain said when he returned to her. He'd hurried ahead and walked the valley's length and breadth by the time she had reached the center of the green, flowering fields.

"What about shelter?" They'd slept under the stars for so long. She never felt safe. They needed to be inside a cave at least until Cain could build a house for them.

Cain looked at her, then again at the surrounding area. "I will search the hills for a dry, empty cave. You can follow or wait here."

She glanced about her, not sure she felt safe even in an open field. "I'll follow you." She took the reins of one of the donkeys, and the other donkeys and goats fell in behind them.

By nightfall, Cain had finally found a small cave that seemed to be free of night creatures. She took small comfort in the rock walls. At least they weren't so exposed. But her heart felt totally unprotected. She had no words to explain how empty she felt. She simply knew that if she could leave Cain and return home, she would.

~

Eve watched her sons leave the central fire after the morning meal, missing Abel's smile all over again. Even a month after they had buried him, the sting of his death still hit her at odd times, and always, always with the acute agony of loss. She blinked back the ever-present tears and caught Chania watching her.

"Are you all right, Ima?" Chania knelt at Eve's side and touched her shoulder. "I know you still grieve."

Eve glanced at Illiya asleep in a basket at her side and nodded, unable to speak for the emotion clogging her throat. She shook herself and looked away a moment. She needed to work. A new project would give her solace.

She looked at Tehila, who was among the many daughters working with her. "Will you watch the young ones?"

Tehila nodded. "Of course, Ima."

Eve turned to Chania. "Come. I cannot sit and weep all day, so let's go to the river."

Chania grabbed a wooden bowl, following Eve's example, and together they walked the dirt path to the river. They stepped into the water and bent low to scoop clay from the bottom. Shells and fragments of seaweed came with it.

"Leave the shells and rocks with the clay," Eve said. "Perhaps we can use all of it to help form the container I have in mind."

"What type of container, Ima? We already have so many, though I suppose we can always use more," Chania said as they walked with full bowls back toward the fire pit.

Eve shrugged. "I am not sure. I simply need to work with my hands at something new. Perhaps a different style of lamp or a jar covered in gemstones, if we have enough of them in the house to use." Something beautiful and useful would please her.

"I will go and look for the gemstones," Chania said, leaving the fire.

She returned as Eve's other daughters gathered around, watching while Eve began to form the clay. She dipped her hands into a bowl of water and worked the clay, continually keeping it wet, not sure what she wanted to make of it. She looked up for a moment at the interested faces, then formed the clay into a long-necked jar with a flat bottom. She fitted some of the gemstones around its neck and made the mouth wider than the neck, with the base wider than both.

"Now let's add dung and wood and whatever else we can find to make the fire hot," Eve said. "We will see if the jewels hold while it heats."

Chania lifted the jar with care and set it on the fire, while the rest of Eve's daughters gathered the dung and wood they needed. Soon the fire blazed around the urn, and they watched in silence.

As the fire died down, Eve added more dung. "I don't know how long to let it stay in the fire. But it looks different now, doesn't it?" She glanced at Chania, then the rest of her daughters. How strange it was in that moment to not see Hasia among them.

"I think it looks hardened enough," Chania said, interrupting her thoughts. She used a thick piece of goatskin and a stick to gently lift the jar out of the fire.

"What will you use it for, Ima? It's too pretty for everyday use," Achima said, her eyes still dull with the ache of loss despite her recent marriage to Jabril.

"I think it should be used to hold wildflowers to brighten one of our homes." Eve looked at Achima. "I want you to have it."

Achima looked at her feet, then studied the cooling urn. The jewels shone along the rim, and Eve felt a sense of gratitude that for a moment her daughter was able to focus on something other than her great loss.

"Thank you, Ima," Achima said.

"Let it remind you of beauty to come." Eve met Achima's gaze, sensing the approval of the other daughters who surrounded them.

"I will try," Achima said after a lengthy pause.

Eve knew what her daughter couldn't say—that nothing they made or did or said would erase the pain of losing Abel. But she could hope. And they could pray.

21

Thirty Years Later

Eve groaned with the last of the birth pangs, grateful that after she had borne so many children, birthing wasn't as hard as it used to be. She had honestly thought that after having thirty children over one hundred years, she had finally stopped bearing. And for a time after Abel's death, she had. But at one hundred thirty years, her womb had quickened again, and now she waited with an anxious heart to see if God had given her a girl or a boy.

Another pain seized her, and Achima leaned close. "Let me see how you are coming," she said. Chania and Tehila stood at Eve's back, holding her upright while she knelt on stones above the dirt floor.

Achima looked beneath her skirt. "I see the head, Ima." Excitement filled her voice. "Another push or two and that should be it."

Eve bore down, unable to resist the urge to do so, and let out a cry as the babe slipped from her and into Achima's waiting hands.

"It's a boy!" Achima's voice held the thrill Eve felt. A son!

She waited as Achima cleaned the baby and Chania and Tehila washed her. Exhaustion filled her as they helped her to her pallet, which was laden with cushions. Achima brought the babe to her just as Adam stepped into the house.

"We have another son," Eve told him as he came closer.

A smile lit his face, filled with a rare joy that reached his eyes. "What will you name him?" He shifted his gaze from the child to her, and for a moment she saw the old adoration that he'd once had for her before they left Eden.

She felt suddenly shy in his presence, a strange new joy filling her. Perhaps this child would bring them together in a way none other had. Perhaps he was the Promised One who would redeem them all from their sins. She slowly smiled. "He shall be named Seth, for God has granted me another child in place of Abel, since Cain killed him."

The moment she mentioned Cain and Abel, she regretted her words. Why, oh why had she brought them up at such a joyous time? The scowl that replaced Adam's smile caused a sick feeling in her middle.

"Don't even speak your son's name to me, Eve. I will never forgive Cain for what he did."

Her son? Cain was as much his son as hers. But Adam still bore a deep grudge against him, whereas her mother heart could not hate him forever no matter what he had done.

Adam cleared his throat. He was no longer looking her way but had fixed his gaze on the babe. "Seth," he said. "Appointed one."

She nodded, but the sting of his words had silenced her. She focused on the babe now suckling at her breast, and she felt the familiar joy of new life even as she grieved Adam's inability to forgive. Would Adonai be pleased with them if Adam kept holding on to his anger?

"Perhaps this child will be the son of the promise," Adam said, breaking the silence.

She looked at him, unable to hold back the sudden emotion pouring through her that he would think the same thing she had. "Perhaps," she whispered.

He kissed her and walked to the door. "I'll be home late."

She simply nodded again, uncertain whether to ask where he might be going. Right now, she was too tired to care. She studied Seth's face, so fresh and new, grateful for another chance to teach a child of the Creator and perhaps instill in him the love for God that Abel had had.

"Who will you be, little Seth? What kind of man will you grow up to be?" *Don't harbor anger like your father does.*

Eating the fruit had given rise to anger, bitterness, and a struggle to forgive in Adam, something she could not fully understand. What good did it do to hate one of their own flesh and blood?

Seth's mewling sounds drew her thoughts back to him. She would pray for Adam later. This child needed her now, and he *would* be different. She would do her best not to make the mistakes she did with Cain.

Please, Adonai, help me to be a good mother to this boy and teach him Your ways. May he follow You all the days of his life.

If only she could know that her prayers would be answered the way she longed for them to be.

Eve held Seth's hand and walked with him toward the pens where Abel once kept his sheep. Four years had passed since his birth, and though he was too young to help much, Eve loved the delight in his dark eyes when he was among the animals or when she took him to the river to see the swans, his favorite water bird.

"Can I go with Jabril to watch the sheep today?" Seth asked as he skipped along.

Eve hurried to keep up with her exuberant son. He had been a quick learner and walked before her other children had. As a toddler he had climbed things she never imagined he could or would want to try.

Now he gave her an easy smile and giggled for the sheer pleasure of laughter. He was too young to make sense of what he found humorous, but Eve didn't bother to understand. She just enjoyed his little-boy happiness.

"Please, Ima," Seth said.

Eve reined in her thoughts and held back a small sigh. "When you are a little older. Perhaps when you are five." She patted his head. "Jabril cannot watch you and the sheep. Let's wait a little longer." She should have said five years from now, but the words had not come out as she intended. It was so hard to deny him.

They reached the pens where Jabril was calling the sheep out to follow him. He looked up at Eve and Seth. "Baby brother!" he said, scooping Seth into his arms. "How are you this fine day?"

"I want to go to the fields with you and the sheep," he said loud enough for Eve to hear.

"And I told him we have to wait a little longer." She saw a hint of determination in his pout. Cain once had that same expression. But then, so did all of her children at one time or another. Why did she think of Cain instead of Jabril?

"I don't mind taking him if you come for him before the sun reaches its midpoint. The boy does love to sit and pet the smallest lambs." Jabril hugged Seth.

Was she being too protective of Seth because she'd not had another child since his birth? Had her womb again grown barren, for good this time?

"Ima, Father took me with him to the fields when I was four," Jabril said. "Seth will listen to me, won't you, Seth?"

He nodded with vigor. "I'll do good, Ima."

Eve stood in indecision but finally relaxed. "I'll be back soon. He can stay for a short while."

Seth squealed and squirmed to be released from Jabril's arms, then headed for the smallest lambs. The boy was nearly the same height as they were, but he was good with animals. Maybe God was preparing him early to take Abel's place. She walked away, thinking about her children.

Voices coming from a distant copse of trees that lined the camp made her pause.

"I've been to see Cain," her son Ravid said to Mahaz. "He's building a city and named it after his son Enoch."

"A whole city? By himself?" Mahaz sounded skeptical.

"It's not a big city, of course," Ravid said. "But as his family grows, I'm sure it will too."

"We have far more family members in our camp, and we don't have a city. What does it look like?"

"Like many buildings made of stone spread out. I have no idea why he needs so many buildings. But Cain always had to prove his things were bigger and better."

"I'd like to see it. Maybe we should consider relocating with him and help him build his city," Mahaz said, sending a stab of fear to Eve's heart. They would leave the land closest to Eden, where their father had built the altar to Adonai? Why would they even think of such a thing?

"Let's plan a time to sneak away, then, and talk to Cain. At least see how he's doing and see what we think of his 'city,'" Ravid said.

Eve stood stunned as they continued to plan a day to leave their duties in the camp and their families to take the long trek to the land of Nod—to see Cain? The one God had sent away?

When her sons' voices went silent, she looked up to see them walking away. They hadn't seen her. Good. But now she had information that she must tell Adam. Were they to just let them go? Or tell them not to? Her sons were adults with wives and children. Would she be able to get them to reconsider? Should she try? One could not force a child, once he was grown, to obey a parent anymore. Her children usually honored her and Adam, but they chafed at some of Adam's requests of them. Yet none had seemed as evil as Cain had shown himself to be. Why visit him?

But a part of her also wanted to see Hasia again, hold Enoch close, meet her other grandchildren, and visit with Cain. How she missed him, despite everything. In a heartbeat she knew Adam

161

would never agree. And even if she told him in just the right way, he would be angry. Wouldn't he? Mahaz had been with him when they found Abel's body. Adam would feel betrayed if Mahaz left them to live with Cain.

How could *any* of her sons consider joining Cain? Was this how it was when some of the unseen ones followed the serpent out of God's presence?

She shivered, though the day was warm. She didn't have to imagine what it was like to be away from God's presence. Nothing was as good as it had been in Eden when God walked with them in the cool of the day and they could talk with Him unashamed. When God banished the devil and his followers for their rebellious choices, was it a foretaste of how their fall would affect every human too? Were any of Adam's descendants going to follow Adonai Elohim instead of going their own way?

She turned to go in search of Adam. Seth could stay with Jabril a little longer. She could not keep this information to herself for long.

Heart heavy, she walked with slow, weighted steps toward the pastures where Adam kept their sheep. *Oh, Adonai, please help him to react well*. She grew weary of his brooding and silences and sudden outbursts. Even though he did not always blame her, she blamed herself. Ever since Eden, she never felt quite accepted by anyone. Or wanted. Or loved. Except by her children when they were small.

And now, with her children talking as if they no longer cared to stay near the God she missed with every fiber of her being, her heart beat with a physical ache.

Please, Adonai, keep my children from following the ways of Cain. If they visit, don't let them want to stay. Keep them near You, not the land where evil surely dwells.

Perhaps the devil and his followers did not actually live in Nod, but Cain's heart had shown no sign of softening or he would have returned and asked the Creator to forgive him. Would that have made a difference? If Cain had repented as she and Adam had learned to do, would he have had to leave? If Adam could forgive their son, would his forgiveness make any difference in Cain's life? Cain would not even know of it unless they saw him again.

Somehow she needed to help Adam see things in a different way. A helpful, forgiving way. If only she knew how.

Adam looked up from pulling brambles from a lamb's soft wool at the sound of footsteps rustling the tall grasses. Eve moved toward him, her expression burdened, the lines along her beautiful mouth tight. He left the lamb and walked toward her.

"What happened?" He touched her arm, meeting her gaze with a concerned one of his own.

She searched his face and cupped his cheek with her soft hand. "I have news. Promise me you will not be angry."

He took a step back and stared at her. Did she honestly think him so quick to lose his temper that she should ask him that? But a stab of guilt told him he did have that tendency.

"Tell me," he said, keeping his voice as gentle as his emotions would allow. He was not an angry man. If he grew upset with anyone or anything, he had good reason.

But you were not this way in the garden. No, he wasn't.

She clasped her hands in front of her and drew in a deep breath. "I took Seth to stay with Jabril. You know how he loves the sheep."

He nodded, wanting to urge her to get to the point.

"After I left, I walked along the tree line toward our house and heard voices. Mahaz and Ravid were talking. I stopped to listen." She paused again, testing his patience.

"Go on." Did he sound irritated? By her look, he knew he did. "I'm sorry, Eve. Do not be afraid to tell me. Please continue."

She nodded. "They were talking about visiting Cain's city. They sounded as though they might like to not only visit but live there."

Adam took another step back, her words feeling like a kick to his gut. Mahaz? Ravid? How could they even consider such a thing? He swallowed hard, tamping down his quickly rising frustration. "Did they say when they were going?"

She shook her head. "No. But it sounds as if they want to sneak away." She moved closer. "Should we speak to them? Offer to go with them? If we were with them, perhaps we could help them to see that Cain's choices are not wise ones."

He looked at her. Such vulnerability in those large, dark eyes. How he had loved her the moment God handed her to him to love and cherish. His perfect mate. But she had learned to fear his moods, and regret filled him in that moment. He had not treated her as he should have. She had lived with the stigma of her choice for so long, and he had not reassured her often enough to help her see that his love and forgiveness were real.

Or were they? So often he couldn't distinguish between his blame for her and blame for himself. When life grew too hard, all he could think of was what they'd lost because of their own foolishness.

"I don't know what to do with this, Eve," he said slowly. "I can't see Mahaz or Ravid wanting to live with Cain, but who really knows the heart of another? If I talk to them, they will know you overheard them or suspect someone else did." He scratched his beard. Why were adult children so hard to reason with sometimes?

"What if we decided to visit Cain and invited them along? Would they suspect something then? I haven't seen Hasia or our grandchildren—I'm sure she has had more since the first—and I long to see them."

Her pleading expression softened his heart, and he pulled her into his arms. "I don't know if I can," he whispered against her ear. "Cain killed our son." He swallowed hard.

"Cain is also our son," she said, matching his tone.

"God rejected Cain."

"God sent Cain away, as He did us. But if Cain could be persuaded to repent . . . might not God yet forgive him as He did us?" She pulled back to look into his eyes.

164

He slowly nodded. In his heart he knew God could forgive any human willing to repent. "He could . . . but Cain has never shown a desire to repent, my love. He would have returned to the altar he shunned and offered a sacrifice if he seriously cared about Adonai."

"Perhaps it is our wrath he fears." Of course, she meant his wrath, for she had forgiven Cain long ago.

"Perhaps." He brushed a strand of hair behind her ear. "I will think on this, and I will pray and ask Adonai for guidance. That is all I can give you."

She offered him a soft smile. "That is all I ask." She took his hand and squeezed it. "Thank you."

He kissed her forehead, and she hesitantly backed away. "I must retrieve Seth from Jabril."

"Yes." His thoughts whirled with all she had said as he watched her go without another word. He could not possibly visit Cain with his sons. Could he?

22

ONE YEAR LATER

Adam woke before dawn, kissed a heavily pregnant Eve goodbye, and left the house. He carried a large sack of grain over one arm and a skin of water in the other. Mahaz, Ravid, and Jabril met him in the center of the courtyard, each of them carrying fruit and nuts their wives had packed in goatskin sacks the night before. He shouldn't be going, as he had no use for Cain or his kin. But after many talks with his sons over the previous months, he had finally agreed that Eve was right. His presence might keep their other sons from following Cain's way. If he didn't go, he was sure to regret his choice.

"Do we have the gift?" Adam asked as the four of them walked toward the pen where they kept a small herd of donkeys. He planned to give the grain to Cain as a peace offering, but his sons were supposed to bring produce from the land Cain once loved.

"I already loaded the sacks of vegetables and skin of olive oil on the donkey," Mahaz said, his long strides reminding Adam of the days of his youth. Adam still felt vigorous, but not quite as young or energetic as his sons appeared to be.

They reached the pen and took two of the donkeys, one to

166

leave with Cain and one to help carry their own food home again. "We're all set, Father," Jabril said, his jaw set as though he was not at all sure this trip was wise.

Adam wondered if Jabril was the right one to accompany them since Cain had killed his wife's first husband. "And all of you are still sure you want to go?" he asked.

"We're sure," Jabril answered.

Adam almost wished Eve could be with them, but her time was too near. Even she admitted the trip would not be wise in the end.

Adam grabbed a stick from the ground and set out toward Nod. It would take them days to arrive, and each man carried various weapons with them in case of wild animals.

As they walked through the winding hills, questions churned in Adam's mind. If God had sent his son away, didn't that mean the rest of the family should break off contact with him? Could God forgive Cain? And if He couldn't or wouldn't, then Adam was justified in feeling as he did. This visit could simply tempt his other sons to want to live where Cain did. To escape the family compound and wander off on their own.

If he were honest, Adam had thought now and then of moving his family to another area of the earth. Farther from Eden. Not because he wanted to leave God or the altar he had built to honor Him but because Eve still longed too much for Eden.

He missed Eden, but to go back only increased the memories of that day. The day they had disappointed the Creator and lost the privilege of His daily presence.

Why would Eve want to return to a place where she could no longer live? Did she hope something would change God's mind and she'd be allowed in? But he knew that wasn't true. More likely, her guilt drove her. She struggled with guilt while anger and frustration constantly dogged his troubled thoughts. Why was it so hard to think as they had in Eden? To think pure, compassionate, loving thoughts?

He shook his head. He couldn't take Eden's nearness from

Eve, not when the babies kept coming and the family camp was firmly established. Yet he might never understand his wife or what made her long for times past. When God made him a helpmate, he hadn't expected her to be so opposite of him in ways that he would never understand.

Eve stirred at the sound of her newest daughter softly crying from her basket at Eve's side. The babe had made her appearance into the world the day after Adam and three of their sons had left to visit Cain. Salema had come quickly, almost before Achima and Chania had arrived to help. Eve reached for her new daughter, quickly changed her wet underthings, and put her to her breast.

She looked into the cherub face and smiled, silently thanking the Creator for healthy children. She vowed to keep this child close and teach her well. Seth would make a good husband for her one day.

She shook herself. It was not like her to consider whom a child would marry so soon after their birth. But somehow she knew Salema would make a great helpmate for Seth. She would encourage him, and he would cherish her.

A deep sigh escaped her as she burped Salema. *Oh, Adonai, God Almighty, please let this child grow to love You. And keep Seth from becoming like the children who do not follow You.* She desperately wanted Abel's replacement to love God as Abel had.

The door opened, letting in the morning light. Chania walked toward her and sat at her side. "How is she?"

Eve smiled. "She is perfect. As you all were."

"Are you suggesting we are no longer perfect?" Chania laughed.

"Most of the time you come close, but we are all self-seeking now and then," Eve said, sitting up. Salema had fallen asleep again, and Eve laid her in the basket before picking it up. Chania rose with her, and together they walked to the fire pit to grind the grain and prepare flatbread for the family. Eve's many daughters joined them, and soon the camp came alive with the voices of adults and children.

"How long do you think it will take the men to return?" Achima asked as she poured the batter onto the hot stones over the fire. "They've been gone nearly a week. Shouldn't they be home soon?"

"I suppose it depends how long they talk with Cain." Eve's heart ached at the angst in Achima's expression. Jabril should not have gone with them. What if Cain killed him too? Achima would never recover.

"I just worry. I never trusted Cain. I wish Jabril hadn't thought he needed to accompany Abba." Achima used a wooden utensil to flip the flatbread. The sizzling sound made Eve's stomach growl. She was always hungrier after the birth of a child. But she couldn't eat before feeding her family.

"I know this is hard for you," Chania said, putting an arm around her sister. "Jabril will be fine. I doubt Cain will ever harm one of us again. He has been punished severely. Surely he will be more careful to obey our God."

Achima gave Chania a skeptical look. "I rather doubt that. He never seemed repentant or sorry for what he'd done. Maybe Hasia has convinced him to change, but from what I knew of Cain, he never listened to anyone. He did what pleased him, not God."

Eve listened in silence as the two women and a few of the others discussed Cain and the grief his actions had caused. Memories of Abel surfaced all over again. The pain was still real, at least for her and for Achima, despite Achima's marriage to Jabril. Were they destined to grieve forever?

Five-year-old Seth emerged from the house and bounded over to her, full of exuberance. He threw his arms about her neck, and she scooped him up. He might be her baby no longer, but he was somehow different, special to her in a way she hadn't felt with her many other births.

May he love You always. It was her constant prayer for all of her children.

The city of Enoch stretched before them, larger than anything Adam had ever seen. Walls were in the process of being built to enclose the buildings. Obviously Cain felt the need for protection. Were the wild animals such a problem here? Or did he fear something more? After thirty-five years, Cain's children, however many he had by now, would be old enough to marry and bear children of their own. Adam wondered how many grandchildren whom he'd never met lived in this city. Grandchildren whom Eve longed to know. But why did he care when thoughts of Cain himself still brought a sour taste to his soul?

Pushing his nagging questions aside, Adam walked toward an open area and led the donkeys toward the center of the town where a large house stood. No doubt Cain's house, for who else would command the largest space but his extravagant son? Jabril, Ravid, and Mahaz followed behind, talking softly among themselves. Adam approached the house and knocked on the door.

Hasia opened it with a babe in her arms, and her eyes widened as if she could not believe they were standing there. "Abba!" She rushed toward him, and he gave her a partial hug, patting the child's back. "It's been so long." She craned her neck to look behind him. "Is Ima with you?"

"No. Ima is about to give birth, if she has not already done so. She wanted to come. We've missed you," he said, kissing her cheek. He did miss Hasia. It was only Cain he did not want to see.

"And I have missed both of you."

Her brothers stepped forward, and she hurried toward them to be held by each one. Adam stepped back to allow the reunion, looking about at the wood and stone structure Cain had built.

"Please, come inside," Hasia said. "You can tie your donkeys to the post there." She pointed to a post some distance from the door. Jabril did as she suggested, and Adam entered with his sons.

170

"And who have we here?" he asked, pointing to the baby in her arms.

"This is Irad, my grandson. Enoch, our firstborn, married his sister, and Irad is now three months old. We have five sons and five daughters. Enough for each to have a mate." Hasia smiled, but Adam noted the strain around her mouth.

"You've been blessed to have so many. Your ima will be sorry she missed meeting them all." Adam searched her face. "And you are well, my daughter?" He looked for the happiness he once saw in her. Her eyes did not shine as they used to, though she attempted a worthy smile.

"I am happy, Abba. You need not worry about me. The children keep me busy, and now I am pleased to help Ashira with Irad." Hasia glanced at her feet, then invited them to sit.

A young woman entered the house, carrying water, and brought it to Hasia.

"This is Ashira, Abba," Hasia said. "Ashira, this is your grandfather, and these are your uncles." She moved her hand in an arc, naming each one. She handed the baby to Ashira, took the water into an adjoining room, and returned with clay cups of water and a tray of fruit and cheese.

Adam accepted her offerings, watching her. "I assume Cain and your sons are out tending flocks or herds or crops?"

Hasia glanced at Ashira, who sat in a corner of the room and nursed the child, before meeting his gaze. "The boys handle the crops, as nothing grows for Cain anymore since God's curse. And as you know, Cain never liked animals, so some of the girls help with that as well. Cain spends his time building." She pursed her lips, seeming unwilling to say more. "I wish you could all visit more often," she said at last. "And if any of you want to live here, I'm sure Cain would enjoy having you."

"He would not enjoy having Achima and me living here," Jabril said, drawing her attention.

Hasia covered her mouth, obviously surprised by his comment.

A moment later, she lowered her hand and nodded. "I'm happy for you," she said stiffly. "Achima deserves a good husband."

She already had a good husband. Adam bit his tongue at the words. Hasia meant well, and undoubtedly she missed her family. But Adam could not imagine even one other child leaving the life they now had to live away from the Lord near Cain.

"I'm sure it's been hard for you, my daughter," Adam said after an awkward silence. He glanced at his sons, alarmed at the interest in Ravid's and Mahaz's eyes. "We brought grain and oil for you. They are tied to our donkeys." He rose to stand. "Let me get it. Ravid, come and help me."

Ravid joined him, and once they were outside, Adam faced him. "You would not seriously think of coming here to live as Hasia suggested."

Ravid shrugged. "Mahaz and I were curious to see Cain's city. I do not know if I would enjoy living apart from you and being under his watchful eye. Perhaps we should build our own city."

Adam held back a sigh. This desire for independence away from the group was not surprising. "Cain would definitely watch you," he said, trying to steer Ravid's thoughts to Cain, away from his obvious general wanderlust.

"I know." Ravid shrugged. "There is nowhere we can go that someone does not see. Especially God."

"His is the only watchfulness we need to care about," Adam said, forcing his tense jaw to relax. He silently prayed that God would give Ravid and Mahaz peace about staying near home. Near him and Eve.

Ravid moved ahead of him into the house, carrying the jars, while Adam put the sacks on the floor where Hasia indicated. "Next time we come—for your mother will insist on meeting your children—we will bring a few mating sheep if you would like." Next time? Why had he said that?

"The goats you gave us when we left have borne many more

already, Abba. And Cain found some wild sheep, which are doing well. You must go and visit the pens when Cain returns."

"We do not know how long we can stay, so we will go in search of Cain now if you can point us in the right direction."

"You will spend a few nights at least, won't you? You can't possibly leave so soon. And we have plenty of room for you to sleep."

Adam nodded. "We will stay at least a few nights. But we are anxious to see Cain as well." He flinched at the lie. The last thing he wanted was to see Cain. But he never felt quite as comfortable with his daughters as he did with his sons. And he couldn't bear the deep longing in his daughter's eyes.

Hasia walked to the door and pointed to the fields and pens behind the house, then indicated the caves in the surrounding hills. Had they lived in the caves at first as he and Eve had been forced to do?

"I will prepare a fine meal for you when you return," Hasia said, her tone earnest.

Adam looked into her eyes. This daughter was hurting, though she hid it fairly well. He hoped to stay long enough to find out why.

What would he do if Cain was harming her? Cain had grown angry at the slightest things when he lived in the family camp. How would anyone ever help Hasia if he was mistreating her? Perhaps her sons were her protection, unless they had inherited Cain's temper. How would the women in this camp fare if all of the men were like their father?

Adam's own anger was Eve's constant frustration with him, and his bitterness toward Cain wouldn't help matters. He must keep his own temper in check, despite the resentment he felt. He kissed Hasia's cheek and headed with his sons toward the hills to find Cain.

They saw him working in a field, where he lifted a heavy rock and carried it toward a section of wall that was not completed. They waved as they approached.

Cain set the rock down, then met them, his expression wary. But a moment later, he offered each one a smile and welcomed them, kissing their cheeks. "Welcome to my city," he said, pride in his voice. "I did not expect to see any of you again." He perused his brothers and then met Adam's gaze. "I truly didn't expect you."

"I didn't expect to come," Adam admitted. "Your mother wanted to be here, but she was too close to giving birth again. We brought you a donkey and grain and oil. We should have brought a few mating sheep as well."

Cain laughed, his tone lacking mirth. "Thank you. But you had no need to bring me anything. I found a ram and a ewe in the wild, and they have mated quite well. The goats are flourishing. They have borne many kids since we arrived here. Soon we will have more in our flocks than you have. So please do not worry. Keep what you have."

Adam nodded. "Are you keeping the sacrifices to our God with the blood of goats or young pigeons?"

Silence followed the question. Even his other sons seemed surprised he would ask such a thing. Why was he suddenly so bold? But some part of him deep inside hoped Eve was right. Perhaps God could forgive Cain. Perhaps Cain had actually repented.

Cain kicked a stone and sent it flying away from them. "Father, I know these things matter to you because you've seen better days than any of us have. But all I see is a Creator who demands too much of us. Why should I kill my animals to please His lust for blood? He didn't like it when I shed my brother's blood, but he wants us to kill the animals?"

"That is far different," Adam said through gritted teeth. How dare he compare Abel's loss to that of a sheep! "The animals are not made in God's image. We are."

"It still seems cruel to me," Cain said. "To answer your question, no. I do not keep the sacrifices, nor do I ever intend to. Did you come here to lecture me?"

Adam fought the urge to argue, noting the anger in Cain's eyes. He had grown harder in the years they'd been apart. "No, my son. I came to see you. I would like to meet my grandchildren. I will say no more about Adonai." Did he sound sincere despite his agonizing desire to know why Cain thought as he did? Why he'd done what he'd done? Could Cain tell that Adam did not want to be here?

Cain grunted, then walked back to the wall and set the stone in place, leaving them standing there. He turned. "Go back to the house. My sons and I will return when we return."

Adam looked from one son to another. Each one shrugged and turned about to head back.

"He hasn't changed for the better," Jabril said when they were out of earshot.

"Not at all," Adam said. But in a place within him that he did not like to visit, he wondered if he had changed for the better either.

23

The return home three days later gave Adam a sense of deep relief, now that he was away from the intensity of Cain's disdain for all things concerning Adonai. None of Cain's sons followed the Creator, and though Hasia privately told Adam she still believed, he doubted how much. How could she worship Him on her own in a land with a husband and children who did not agree with her? Even she had compromised things like the sacrifices, and Jabril had seen a small object in the form of a serpent near the basket where Irad slept. An object their own hands had made. What did they expect it to do that God could not? Adam led the donkey while Jabril, Mahaz, and Ravid followed, talking among themselves.

"I think Cain has done well for himself," Mahaz said, a hint of admiration in his tone. "I wonder what Dalea would think of the place."

"I think Pessel would enjoy being near Hasia again. Think of all we could accomplish if we worked with Cain."

Ravid's words should not have surprised Adam, but after their talk, he had hoped . . . A sick feeling settled in his gut.

"You aren't seriously thinking of moving to Nod." Jabril sounded aghast at the idea. "God sent Cain away from His presence as punishment for killing Abel. You would not leave the camp of God to join the one who murdered, would you?"

Adam stopped walking and turned back to join his sons. "What is this I am hearing? I thought we discussed this. Have you both lost your senses?"

Mahaz lifted his chin, defiance in his eyes. "I didn't say we were going to move there. I just think it might be a nice change, and Hasia seems to miss us. What could it hurt to visit for a time?"

"Visit or stay? One can easily turn into the other," Adam said, crossing his arms over his chest. "Would you really want to live away from the Creator?"

Mahaz gazed at his feet as though ashamed. Ravid spoke in his place. "We've thought about it long before we came this week. We want to branch out, fill the earth as God said to do. What better way to start than to add to Cain's city and expand it beyond his family? There will still be plenty of our brothers and sisters living near the garden of God."

Adam shifted from foot to foot, arms now at his sides. "If you want to move on to fill the earth, why not go and build camps of your own as you suggested a few days ago? There is no need to help Cain. He is obviously doing fine on his own."

"You would not mind if we moved on?" Mahaz met Adam's gaze.

"I would miss you both, but if that is what God is leading you to do, I would not stop you," he said. Eve would hate losing any of her children, and he would as well, if he were honest, but they could not all stay in the same place forever.

"Thank you, Father," Ravid said. "With your blessing, I know it will be easier to convince Pessel."

"And Dalea," Mahaz added.

Adam nodded, trying to appear glad that they were at least considering something different. His pace slowed as he returned to the donkey. The truth was, he was not convinced that he had talked them out of seeking after Cain. Even if they built their own towns, would their hearts yearn after Adonai, or would they go the way of Cain whether they lived near him or not?

⁓

Eve carried Salema in a pouch of soft lambskin she had made years before, which allowed her to nurse and work at the same time. She settled near the central fire, measured grain onto a round stone, and began to beat it with a wooden flail. Mixed with olive oil pressed from nearby trees, the crushed barley could be boiled or baked over the open fire.

She smiled as Pessel, Dalea, Kaelee, and Naava approached her. Adam and their sons had returned from Cain's city several months before, and Eve was grateful that there had been no more talk of Mahaz and Ravid and their families moving away.

"Good day, Ima," Kaelee said, kneeling beside her to work with another flail and stone. Many hands were needed to feed their large, growing families.

"Good day to each of you. How are you this fine day?" She looked from one to the next, studying their faces. Only Kaelee met her gaze.

"We have something to tell you, Ima," Kaelee said, glancing at her sisters. "We want you to be happy for us."

Eve caught the determined gleam in Kaelee's eyes and the rigid set to her jaw. "How can I be happy for you if I don't know what you are about to tell me?" Somehow she knew she would feel the exact opposite.

"We've talked about this for some time now, and we are all in agreement, so we hope you and Abba will understand our desires." Kaelee glanced at her sisters, and they nodded in response. She met Eve's gaze and drew in a deep breath.

Eve's heart pounded, and she was filled with sudden dread.

"Mahaz and Ravid have both told us how much Hasia misses her family, and Cain's city has room for all of us and more. So rather than going off to build a new city of our own, we have decided to join him and strengthen what he has already begun." She lifted her hands in a pleading gesture. "Please understand, Ima. We will miss you, of course, but this is something our husbands want to do."

Eve stared at her, then at each of the others. "And you did nothing to try to persuade them against this?"

Kaelee's eyes widened. "Why would we try to change their minds? We are excited about this new adventure."

"Cain does not follow the ways of the Creator," Eve said, but the expressions on her daughters' faces did not change.

"That doesn't mean we have to agree with him. Ravid thinks Hasia still believes. Cain can't control our thoughts, Ima," Pessel said.

Eve turned to deal with a fussing Salema, putting her to her breast, cupping her head, and avoiding eye contact with these four daughters who had just broken her heart. What could she say to stop them? They did not sound like they would be convinced to change their minds.

"Will you support us, Ima? And help Abba to see that we want this?" Kaelee placed a hand on Eve's arm.

Eve looked up, unable to keep the sorrow from clogging her throat. She swallowed hard, trying to envision life without these families. "I cannot give you what you want, Kaelee. To move to live with Cain, whom God sent away, is a dangerous act of rebellion against the Creator. He would not want you to put yourself in the way of the evil one."

"Cain is not evil, Ima," Dalea said. "He did something wrong, of course. But doing things the way you want to do them doesn't make a person evil. How can you say that about your own son?"

Achima drew close to the fire in that moment, and Eve saw the look of horror in her eyes. "Cain is not evil?" Her voice rose with each word. "Did you really just say that? Because if killing your brother isn't evil, I don't know what is." She glared at her sisters. "You would go to live with him? You will regret it." Achima spat in the dust, turned on her heel, and walked away.

Kaelee and her sisters stood, anger evident in their eyes. "You agree with *her*?" Kaelee said to Eve.

Before Eve could respond, Kaelee, Pessel, Dalea, and Naava stalked off toward the river.

Eve sat with the grinding unfinished, too stunned to continue. Why could her girls not see how wrong this was?

Salema tensed and cried, for Eve's anxiety had stopped the flow of her milk. She drew in a deep breath and forced the unpleasant conversation from her mind. They would come to their senses before it was too late. Adam would talk with his sons and convince them. He'd done it on the trip home, he could do it again.

He had to. She couldn't bear the thought of losing another family member to a city so far from the Creator's dwelling in Eden.

A few days later, Eve walked with Adam in the forest where he liked to pray. Salema was in Achima's care tonight, giving Eve a welcome break from watching her. She slipped her hand into Adam's larger one as the sun began its descent in the west.

"The Creator has painted the sky in glorious colors tonight." She leaned her head on Adam's shoulder as they stopped to admire God's handiwork of swirling yellow, green, pink, purple, and blue.

"I think He enjoys surprising us with different blends of color each evening." Adam squeezed her hand, and silence fell between them.

"You are worried and grieving tonight, my husband," Eve said after a time. "Tell me."

He faced her, taking both of her hands in his. "I attempted to convince Mahaz and Ravid and Lasaro and Kalix to abandon this idea of moving to Enoch in the land of Nod. I used every argument I possessed, but they would not be dissuaded."

She felt the sorrow weighing him down—exactly the way she had felt since Kaelee had broken the news to her. "I can't believe the twins are in agreement with Mahaz and Ravid."

Adam shrugged. "They all get along well, and Mahaz and Ravid are quite persuasive. And wanderlust fills their hearts. Perhaps they will only be gone for a short time, but I fear Cain's influence."

"How can they do this?" She cupped her face with her hand. "There must be something else we can say."

Adam shook his head. "They are already packing and plan to leave at daylight."

She stared at him, disbelieving. "So soon? We have to do something, Adam!" Tears filled her eyes, and she caught the despair in his. "I don't think I can bear to lose all of them. Even one of them."

"What can we do? I've already tried to talk sense to them. They won't hear it." Adam paced a short distance away. He returned a moment later to take her in his arms. "Perhaps after they are there for a time, we will go for a visit and see if they will change their minds. Sometimes children have to experience things before they realize what is good and what is not." Adam ran a hand through his hair. "I wish it were not so, but weren't we the same? If we are denied the ability to do something and God tests us in that, we seem to want it more. Perhaps after they taste Cain's anger and control over all who live near him, they will realize how wrong they are."

"Or they will think Cain is wise and want to be just like him." The thought sickened Eve. Hurt and frustration pulsed through her. "I'm going to talk to Kaelee again. If she will listen, perhaps Kalix will too." Mahaz and Ravid might listen to Kalix, and then perhaps Pessel and Dalea would agree if she asked one more time. They were her daughters, after all.

She turned and hurried toward the camp, Adam following. "It isn't going to change anything," he called to her retreating back. But she had to try to fix this. If she didn't, she would never forgive herself.

⌒~⌒

Eve found Kaelee at her house, packing their things into bundles to tie to the donkey's side. "Kaelee," she said after she was alone with her in the center of the house. "Please listen to me and rethink this decision. You know what Cain did. He cannot be trusted."

"Lasaro thinks the move will be good for us." She pulled out utensils she had made and tied them together, unwilling or unable to look Eve in the eye. Why had this daughter always been so stubborn and strong-willed?

"Kaelee, please. You know that if you said something, Lasaro would reconsider."

Kaelee looked up at last. "Ima, I don't think he is wrong."

The expression on her daughter's face made Eve feel unsteady, as if her legs would no longer hold her. She forced herself to stand firm. "So you won't change your mind."

Kaelee came close and touched Eve's crossed arms. "I don't want to leave you, Ima. But our city is not big enough to hold us all. And didn't God say to fill the earth? Ravid said that Cain's city is large and not nearly full enough. There would be plenty of room to grow there."

Eve felt as though a wall had risen between them, too tall to climb, too wide to get around. What had happened to her loving daughter? "I can't bear to lose you," she said.

"You won't lose me, Ima. You can come to visit us, and surely Lasaro will want to return to visit you." But her words and tone were unconvincing.

"I might never see you again, Kaelee. You know that could happen. Can you live with that?"

Kaelee looked at the pile of belongings and then scuffed her foot along the ground. "I have to go with my husband, Ima." She did not meet Eve's gaze, and Eve knew that there was so much more her daughter would not say.

Silence fell between them for an uncomfortable breath.

"You are right," Eve said softly, forcing back tears. "I will miss you." She turned to leave, and Kaelee did not follow. At the door, Eve turned back. "You are always welcome to return if you change your mind." With that, she left the house, defeated.

Eve hurried home to find Adam waiting for her. "I thought you would be off working somewhere," she said, surprised to see him sitting on a cushion in the dark room.

"I waited to see if you were successful in your talk with Kaelee."

The tears came then, and she could not stop them.

He stood and pulled her into his arms. "It's all right. You can't make them be what you want them to be now that they are adults. They are responsible to God just as we are."

"I told her they are always welcome to return," she said, pulling away and wiping her eyes.

He nodded. "Good. It would be tempting to try to keep them here by telling them they *aren't* welcome to return," he said wryly, "but you are right. We could never shut them out. I would even welcome Cain back if God allowed it and he repented. But that is not my choice."

"So we make the choices that are ours to make and leave the rest to God." It wasn't what she wanted, but after years away from Eden, she knew that what she wanted wasn't always best. She took Adam's hand and squeezed.

"I love you, Eve," Adam said, startling her.

She held his intense gaze. "I don't think you've ever told me that."

He gave her an apologetic look. "I should have. I did in Eden."

She lightly smacked his arm. "And you waited all this time to tell me again?" She smiled, feeling the warmth in his gaze. "I love you too, Adam."

Eve stood beside Adam the next morning and kissed each one of her children and grandchildren who made up a small caravan of people and many animals headed east toward Nod. Would she ever see them again? Would she and Adam really visit Cain's city in the future, and was it even possible that by then they could convince some of these sons and daughters to return home?

Kaelee hugged her tight, and Eve struggled to hold back the tears. "I'll miss you, Ima," she said softly against Eve's ear. Perhaps their talk had softened her daughter in some small way.

Eve held her at arm's length and searched her face. "You know you don't have to go," she said, hoping, longing for a different response.

Kaelee glanced ahead at Lasaro. "Lasaro is convinced we must, Ima. I cannot stay and let him go without me."

"But do you really want to go?" Eve whispered.

Kaelee gave her head a slight shake and lowered her voice. "I had no choice, especially when Kalix agreed with him."

Of course she would go where her twin went. And her husband ruled over her, so like Hasia years ago, she couldn't leave him and stay behind.

Eve sighed. "You are right, Kaelee. Perhaps things will change in the future." She patted Kaelee's hand.

Kaelee slowly turned and joined the group. Moments later, Ravid ordered them to move out. Eve watched until they were no longer visible, feeling as though a part of her heart had gone with them.

24

Eve stood at the river's edge, listening to the lapping of the water against the shore, missing her children. Why she focused on the eight who had left with their families when she had so many more still living with them, she couldn't tell. A few others had also moved away in the ensuing years, but they had gone toward the west to begin new cities of their own. They were keeping God's command to fill the earth.

She missed them all.

"Ima?" Salema called to her, and Eve turned to see her daughter walking toward her, arms full of flowers. "I want to weave these together and put them in my hair before I enter Seth's home tonight."

Eve walked away from the bank and climbed the incline to meet her. "I will be happy to help you. You are a beautiful bride."

Salema beamed. "I can't wait to begin our life together."

Eve returned her daughter's smile. "How well I remember, though it was a long time ago now."

"You had God Himself to give you to Abba! I would love to have had that same experience," Salema said, her tone wistful. "But I am glad that I have you and Abba." She fairly skipped as they walked the path back to the camp.

If only the whole family could be here. Would she and Adam

ever visit Cain's city as Adam had suggested? Or would her children ever return to see them? There had been no word from those living in the land of Nod, and the hope of their permanent return dimmed with each passing year.

"What was it like when you saw Abba for the first time?" Salema asked, interrupting her thoughts. "Did you really wear no clothes?"

Eve looked into her daughter's wide, dark eyes and laughed. "Yes, we really wore no clothes. We did not know we would ever have need of them because our eyes were pure, and our thoughts were only good."

Salema sighed. "I cannot imagine it."

"When we take you to Seth's house tonight, you will understand it better," Eve said, putting an arm around Salema's thin shoulders. How young her daughter seemed, though many years had passed since her birth. Time had a way of slipping by without her notice, and Eden seemed a lifetime ago.

They reached the camp, and Chania and Achima met them near the central fire. "Salema wants to make a wreath of these flowers to place in her hair," Eve told them. "Perhaps we can attach one to her robe as well."

Achima and Chania stepped forward and surrounded Salema. "Let's do this in Ima's house," Achima said. They walked ahead of Eve, who suddenly felt no longer needed. Still, she wanted to be part of every detail of this child's wedding day.

Hours later, Eve helped Salema dress in a new tunic and robe she had woven of lamb's wool and dyed with bright colors made from different roots and flowers. She took the flowers Achima and Chania had woven together and placed them atop Salema's long, silky hair, then threaded one through the fabric of her robe near her heart.

"There, let me look at you." She held Salema at arm's length, gazed at this daughter who had given her new hope since her birth, and smiled, taking Salema's hands in hers. "I knew this day would come when you were born. But I never dreamed the years would go so quickly and you would grow into such a beautiful woman who loves Adonai." She kissed Salema's cheek, then held her close, careful to not crush the flower. "And now you will marry Seth."

Salema gently hugged Eve in return, then straightened her robe and belt. "I wasn't sure about marrying Seth for a long time," she admitted once everything was in place. "He was so full of energy that I could never keep up!" She sat on a chair and bent to pull on her sandals. "I'm glad he slowed down as he matured."

Eve laughed. "How well I remember! Poor Jabril had his hands full watching him when Seth insisted he needed to help with the sheep."

Salema blushed and smiled shyly. "He is a good shepherd now. I think he surpasses all of our brothers in his care for the animals."

Eve walked to a small box Adam had carved for her and returned with a string of beads made from gems her sons had found in the earth and polished in the stream. She draped it over Salema's neck. "I've been saving this for you for this day."

Salema touched the jewels and pressed them against her heart. "Thank you, Ima!" She kissed Eve, and they walked toward the door.

"Your father and I will take you to Seth's house. Then you will be his wife." Eve stopped and touched Salema's shoulder. "Be good to him and respect him, and he will cherish you always."

"Shouldn't he cherish me if he wants my respect?" Salema grinned. "I know, both go together. We've already talked about this, Ima. Seth loves me, and he agrees that we must love each other mutually."

"I guess I should have had this talk with you years ago, then, if my son is already talking about such things to my daughter." They chuckled, and Eve reached for the door. "But I can see that you are ready, so let's go. Your father is waiting—slightly impatiently."

They entered the center area of the camp where their other children had gathered. They had not thought to create a tradition for the mating of their children except to walk the bride to the groom's house.

"You are ready at last?" Adam asked as he stepped forward and took Salema's arm.

"Yes, Abba." Salema's face glowed as her siblings surrounded her and placed flowers in her arms that matched the ones in her hair, something the women had begun to do in recent years. She accepted each colorful bloom and then walked between Adam and Eve to the door of Seth's home.

Seth opened the door to her and welcomed them all inside. He provided food for the entire camp, and after hours of laughter and blessings, Adam and Eve walked away with the rest of their children, leaving Salema in Seth's care.

"She is in good hands," Adam said as he led Eve toward their house, which no longer had young children sleeping there. Eve had borne twenty more children in the past many years, but her youngest had now reached adulthood.

"Yes," she said, leaning against Adam's side. "Seth is a good son. He is God's provision for our future, I think. He is not like Cain, the one I thought God had given to us to be our Redeemer. Seth will lead his brothers and sisters to return to the true faith in the Creator."

Adam nodded. "He does have a love of Adonai I've not seen before. Perhaps you are right." He led her inside and sat on one of the wool cushions she had made long ago.

She retrieved a skin of wine that they saved for special occasions and handed a cup to him, then took one for herself and sat beside him. The sounds of revelry quieted as everyone returned to their homes and crying children were settled into bed.

"God has blessed us despite everything," Adam said, his tone reflective.

"He has. And now I know that it is God who will make a way

with the son He deems best, not the one I thought best. Sometimes I wonder if I will ever truly trust Him as we once did."

"Sin makes it much harder. We will always want our own way." Adam's smile held a mixture of satisfaction and regret.

"I wish it wasn't so," Eve said, her voice low. She sipped from her cup, tasting the tangy fruit of the vine. She didn't always feel as guilty as she once had, but the memory of Eden and what she'd lost, what they'd all lost, never left her. She used to blame herself. Now she just prayed God would soon send the Redeemer. How long must they wait? Would Seth's son be the one?

"I wish it wasn't so too," Adam said.

He rarely spoke of that time, but to know he shared this feeling caused her heart to feel lighter. They carried the same burden for their children and the same burden of their sin. And though the pain of the past remained, she thanked the Creator for giving her someone to share this experience of life with. She would not have survived this far without him.

25

Seth paced in front of his house, waiting. Salema's cries pierced his heart, and though he'd heard the same sounds coming from his mother for years, it was hard to accept them coming from his wife.

"She'll be fine," Jabril said, patting Seth's shoulder. "Come with me to watch the sheep. It could be hours before she delivers."

Seth looked at his older brother who had been caring for the sheep since before he was born. He smiled. "You don't actually need my help, you know."

Jabril grinned. "Of course not. But today you need mine." He wrapped an arm around Seth's shoulders and pulled him toward the pens.

Seth turned quickly back. "Wait." He ducked his head inside, where his sisters scolded him all at once and told him to leave.

"We'll find you when the baby is here," Chania said. "Now go!"

"I'm going to the fields with Jabril. Find me the minute he is born."

Seth pulled the door closed, but not before he heard Tehila yell, "It might be a girl, you know!"

190

Sisters! He hurried to catch up with Jabril. "How did you stand it every time Achima gave birth?"

Jabril laughed. "The first is always the worst, but you get used to it. God meant it when He told us to be fruitful and multiply, though it is not easy on the women. We've all been very fruitful ever since."

Seth matched Jabril's long strides. "Except for Abel."

Jabril stopped and placed a hand on Seth's arm, facing him. "Achima's first child will always be considered Abel's as far as we are concerned. He is still my son, but I am honoring Abel with someone to carry on his name. Though our parents seem to think the one to do that is you."

Seth's cheeks heated. "I know they think that. But who am I to fill the role of a brother I did not even know?"

Jabril turned and continued walking toward the sheep and goat pens. "I think you already do so without knowing it. You preach at all of us every time there is an offering and even around the supper fire to trust in Adonai." He grinned at Seth. "Perhaps you need to trust Him right now and stop worrying about Salema."

Seth untied the cords that held the pen closed. He called the sheep to follow him while Jabril went to gather the goats. The two of them would head to different pastures, but they would be near enough to see each other across the valley.

Was Jabril right? Was he already filling Abel's role to call his brothers and sisters to love their Creator? Or was he supposed to do something different to be like Abel? Maybe he wasn't to fill Abel's place at all. He was unique in his own way.

What do You have for me, Adonai? He'd taken to calling the Almighty "Lord" when he was old enough to understand about the need for the sacrifices and how his parents' sin had cursed them all. He didn't want to sin against his God, though he knew all men and women did. Still, he had a longing and hunger for God that his brothers didn't seem to understand.

He'd seen Mahaz and Ravid and Kalix and the others grow restless and watched the heartache in his parents' eyes when they left to join Cain. Why would they want to forsake the land near Eden and their closeness to the Creator? God had sent Cain away, not the rest of them. But not all of his brothers and sisters believed as he did.

Why not?

He led the sheep toward the closest field so he could be near when Salema finally gave birth.

As he watched over the animals grazing among the lush grasses, he pondered Jabril's words. He did preach a lot. He just couldn't keep quiet when he feared or sensed one of his brothers or sisters growing faithless or faint of heart or just giving in to blatant sins against God. Why did he feel so compelled to speak?

God knew he was no better than they were. He was just as much a sinner and found himself at the foot of the altar, praying, even when it was not time for the sacrifice. Somehow he always knew that God heard him.

Would his family members grow weary of listening to him if he continued to coax them to turn back to the Lord? How he longed for that day when the entire family worshiped the Lord as He wanted them to.

At the bleating of a lamb, Seth hurried to where one of the smaller ewes had gotten caught in some brambles. Sheep were so much like humans. They were always getting caught in one mess or another.

A voice calling in the distance made him turn. One of his sisters ran toward him. "You have a son!" she shouted. "Come!"

Seth began to tremble. A son! He looked across the valley and waved at Jabril, who saw him and jogged closer. "I have a son! Can you watch both my animals and yours while I go to meet him?"

"Go," Jabril said. "They will be fine. Just come back when you are done. I don't want to handle them by myself all day." He laughed, bringing a smile to Seth's lips.

Peace settled in his heart. "Thanks, Brother." Seth turned and ran all the way home.

Eve sat with Salema and her newest grandson, Enosh, on stone benches placed about the central fire. Multiple conversations moved around them, but Eve was caught up in watching Enosh and listening to his baby coos. How she missed those days when she could hold a newborn babe in her arms and nurse him or her.

Seth stood in the center of the group. He towered above both Adam and Eve, and his commanding presence brought respect from the entire clan.

"We need to call on the name of the Lord," he said loudly, drawing Eve's attention from Enosh. "We've drifted from Him for too long. We need to bring sacrifices that please Him and do what is right."

"Seth is right," Jabril said, picking up his youngest daughter and resting her on his knee. "Achima and I both see the need to get to know our Maker better than we do now."

"How do we call on Him?" Tehila asked. "Since we cannot see Him, how do we know whether or not He hears us?"

Seth rubbed a hand over his beard. "I just talk to Him. I find a place to be alone and pray to Him. He does not speak in a voice I can hear, but He often answers in my heart, and I feel peace."

"How do you know it is God giving you peace?" Ruel asked, his tone skeptical. "Perhaps you just felt better for having spoken of what troubled you."

Eve glanced at him. Ever since eight of her children had moved to Nod, Ruel and some of her other sons had questioned many things about the Creator. She had expected him to join some of the others when they left the camp to move west, but he remained, probably because his wife, Tehila, always balked at the thought of leaving.

"Sometimes He comes to us in dreams," Adam said, joining

the conversation. "Sometimes He does speak to us and appears as Adonai Elohim. Even Cain saw His light and heard His voice, as have some of you." He pointed to Jabril and Seth.

"He has spoken to me as well," Eve said. "And Achima and Chania have seen His light."

"So He only comes to the people that He wants to?" Ruel asked. "Why not all of us? Why doesn't He show up at the sacrifices? What is their purpose if we never see Him?"

"He sends fire from heaven to accept the sacrifices," Seth said, his dark eyes sparking like those very flames.

This was his passion, and Eve knew that if he could, he would single-handedly convince everyone to think as he did. He was young yet. What would happen when he discovered he could not help them all?

"We should worship Him because He made us in His image," Seth said. "We should call on His name because that is how we converse with Him. He will answer in His own time and His own way. But if we never call, He won't respond."

Seth moved to sit beside Salema after his last words.

Ruel stood and excused himself. "I'll think about it," he said to Seth as he left. Several other sons and daughters said the same. Some left without a word until only a few of Adam and Eve's children remained with Seth and Salema.

"Do you think they will listen?" Seth asked Adam.

Adam held up his hands in an uncertain gesture. "Only God knows, my son. You are doing well to remind them. Just remember that they have to want God as much as He wants them. It took us a long time to learn that." He glanced at Eve, and she nodded.

It had taken them time to realize that they needed to want God again after they had lost fellowship with Him. They spent years trying to make it on their own before they truly wanted Him, daily wanted Him, in their lives again.

Adam was right, but so was Seth. She looked around at the small

194

group that remained, all talking about Adonai Elohim. How good it was to hear them speak about the Creator in such a respectful way. Perhaps the Redeemer would come sooner than later if these children continued to call on their God. Surely God wanted to set them free from sin as much as they longed for it.

Eve looked at Enosh. Perhaps through him.

The Unseen Realm

The earth turned on its axis as Lucifer stood above the spinning orb, his fellow fallen ones floating aloft, looking down on the world below. From this distance, they could still see the *adams* living in three separate parts of the earth. A smile spread over his face as his gaze narrowed in on the sons and daughters of Cain. The man had taken no time in building his city and multiplying his dynasty. Even some of Adam's other children had joined him. Lucifer laughed. Such a delightful turn of events!

The other unseen ones flew closer to him. "What causes you to laugh, Master?" one asked.

How he loved the sound of that word! All of the angels who had followed him were worthless wimps he'd had no trouble controlling. They adored him and did what he said. Now he just needed to get the humans to do the same. They were far weaker. But they were a stubborn lot.

"We need a plan," he told those now crowding around him. "And I have the perfect one." He looked at each upturned, grotesque face. They had lost their beauty when they followed him, and though they could change their likeness, it was temporary. Unfortunate. Yet the Creator had allowed his beauty to remain.

"What is it?" one of them asked, his beady eyes eager.

"I see that Cain has had many daughters, and several are old enough to mate. I think it is time we took advantage of that." He folded his scaly wings across his body. "I want some of you to transform into the appearance of a shining one, take those young women, and mate with them. Do not give them a choice."

Eager voices erupted around him until the sound grew deafening.

"Enough!" he shouted. He pointed to five of the more obedient demons. "Go at once. Cain will try to refuse you, but once you have taken his daughters, he will accept your offspring as his. We will destroy the *adams* by mixing with their seed. God will never be able to save them once *we* are a part of them."

He laughed again, his whole body shaking with the thrill of it all. He couldn't attain his will by attempting to rise above the Most High, but he could destroy the apple of God's eye—the *adams*.

The five demons flew away like a flash of light and entered earth's atmosphere. Now they would wait. He would follow and watch to make sure they did what he had said.

What kind of beings would come of mixing the two different races? Maybe he would take one of them for himself if things went well. But he was patient. He could give himself time. And wait to see the Creator's anger rise against the humans until He destroyed them all!

⌒↗

Michael flew to the Almighty One's side and bowed low. "You called for me, my King?"

He looked up at the pleased response and listened as the Godhead spoke to one another. When Adonai Elohim spoke to him, he fell at His feet.

"My Spirit will not always strive with men," He said.

Michael offered a quizzical look. But as the three spoke again among themselves, he slowly understood. God was angry with the devil for telling his followers to mate with the daughters of men. By doing so they had ruined humans, who no longer gave birth to offspring made in God's image alone. Those who had been born of such unions had tarnished the perfection and beauty God had made.

Sorrow filled him, and he glanced at the Almighty, who knew every feeling, every thought he possessed. As he felt the King's fiery gaze upon him, he drew in a breath of relief. Seth's line still existed, and others among Adam's race had not gone the way of Cain. The demons had not captured all of the daughters of men. There was still hope for the future and the redemption that he had heard God speak about since before the humans were created.

"So the Redeemer will still come to save them?" Michael asked, knowing the answer but needing the reassurance of the Creator.

Adonai Elohim nodded, but Michael sensed deep, wrenching sorrow in His heart as well—a sorrow greater than he could bear, a sorrow only God could truly understand. But in that one glance he knew. Redemption for the *adams* would cost God far more than it would cost them. The Godhead would not be unaffected by this promise to save them.

What would it take to bring reconciliation between God and the *adams* again? Somehow, though he could not understand it, he sensed a great change coming. And heaven would never be the same when at last that day came.

26

Adam leaned on one elbow and looked into Eve's eyes. Dawn approached, and they must rise whether they wanted to or not.

Eve studied his tired face. "Have you dreamed again? I didn't sleep well, but I sensed you did not either." She stroked his cheek, and he returned the gesture, tucking a strand of loose hair behind her ear.

"Though I am loath to do so, as I cannot accept Cain even now, I'm going to take Seth and visit Cain's city again. I want to see if I can convince any of our other sons to return to us." He rubbed his face. He had tried to forgive, he'd said, but she knew that resentment and bitterness crept into his heart every time he remembered Abel or thought of the children who had followed Cain.

She stroked his forehead as she had her children's when they were afraid or worried. "I want to go with you," she said after a lengthy pause. "I'd like to see our daughters and their children." She missed them every day. Would she ever adjust to the loss of their nearness?

"I'm not sure taking you with us is a good idea," Adam said, interrupting her musing. "I don't think Cain's city is a safe place."

She sat up. "The last time you went, you found it safe, though not entirely pleasant. Why do you say this?"

Adam rose and offered her a hand to help her up. "Rumors filter to us when we are in the fields."

"Rumors? How on earth would you hear something from such a distance? Did the birds tell you?" Her laugh held sarcasm.

He shook his head. "Sometimes one of our sons travels near with herds of his own. We've met now and then."

Eve lifted a brow. "Why didn't you tell me sooner? Who did you see?"

Adam released a deep, defeated sigh. "Kalix. I'm not sure he's entirely happy there. Seth and I are going to try to convince him and Kaelee and their spouses and children to come home. Perhaps we can convince some of the others too."

"I want to help," she said, arms akimbo. "If Kaelee can live there as long as she has, it can't be that bad. I can defend myself."

Adam put both hands on her shoulders and searched her face. "I know you can." He pulled her close. "I just feel a need to protect you, to protect all of our children. Obviously I can't do that anymore. But you are all I have."

She leaned into him, feeling his heartbeat. "I will stay with you and be careful. But please don't deny me this need to see our children."

He held her at arm's length and nodded. "If you are sure."

She smiled. "I'm sure."

"Gather some food, then, and be ready as soon as I've milked the goats. Seth will come for you."

He left the house, and she set about gathering nuts, dried grapes, dates, a small sack of grain, and a skin of oil. Surely Adam would take a donkey to carry it all. She grabbed a lamp with the flame still flickering, added oil to it, and took the sacks outside.

A donkey indeed stood waiting near the fire as Seth drew near. "Ready?"

"I just need to bring the other things that are still in the house. You can get them if you want to." She smiled.

He returned with the other items and placed them over the donkey's back. "We have a torch, Ima. You don't have to bring the lamp."

She shrugged. "The more light, the better." She would feel safer near the light, however small it might be.

The trip to Nod took four days, and Eve reveled in the joy she felt in having Adam and Seth to herself. Such a rare occurrence. They spent time each evening around the fire talking of the Creator and what Adam and Seth planned to say to her other sons and daughters to hopefully return them to their senses. *Please, Adonai, bring them home.*

When they arrived, she stared at the towering city with its walls and gates and glistening jeweled towers. Mahaz greeted them at the gate. She hugged him, though his response was stiffer than it had been in the past.

"Welcome to Enoch, city of Cain," he said, nodding to his father and brother. "Why have you come?"

The question startled her, but Adam didn't seem to pay it any notice. "We came to see our children and grandchildren and speak with them."

He stood aside. "Be sure not to speak of the Creator while you are here. Cain forbids it."

Eve raised her eyebrows at Mahaz as she passed through the gate, wondering if he agreed with Cain's rule. He looked away.

A lump settled in her middle as they walked the stone streets and heard the laughter and music coming from the center of the square. One of her descendants played some type of instrument that gave out a musical sound, and he was singing a song with it.

"Adah and Zillah, listen to me; wives of Lamech, hear my words. I have killed a man for wounding me, a young man for injuring me. If Cain is avenged seven times, then Lamech seventy-seven times."

She glanced at Adam. "What does he mean?"

Adam shrugged. "Nothing good, I am sure."

A shudder worked through her as she looked about. Adam and Seth walked straight ahead of her toward Cain's house, the largest in the city. Eve had never seen this place, but Adam had been to visit a couple of times. He tied the donkey to the post and knocked on the large door.

Footsteps could be heard coming toward them, and then an older Hasia opened the door. "Ima?" She peered around Adam and Seth and, after a brief pause, rushed into Eve's arms. "I'm so glad you came!"

Eve held this long-lost daughter and never wanted to let go. "How I've missed you!" she whispered against Hasia's ear. She finally released her and looked her up and down. "You are still as beautiful as you were when you left."

"And you don't look a day older, Ima." Hasia took her arm and coaxed all of them into the house. "You are best not to be seen outside," she said, closing the door behind Seth.

Eve followed her into a large room with plush furnishings to sit upon. Hasia must have learned many new skills since coming here.

"Please sit while I pour you some cool water." Hasia moved to another room, her resplendent robes trailing behind her.

Eve glanced around, suddenly aware of how wealthy Cain had become. Of course, he would be considered the leader, the patriarch of this community. No one would rank higher.

Hasia returned with golden goblets of cool water. Eve sipped hers, wondering where Cain had found gold and learned to fashion it into such objects.

"Why do you think it is not safe for us outside of your house, Hasia?" Adam asked after accepting the water from her.

"The giants will not like you. The watchers will know you are here and send for them. You should not stay long, though I am sure you will want to see the others." Hasia could not seem to hold Adam's gaze, and a dark flush colored her cheeks.

"Who are the watchers?" Seth asked.

"The unseen ones." Her voice was soft, and they all strained to hear her. "They came some time ago and snatched some of the young virgins from among us. We could not stop them, as they are far larger and even stronger than Cain. When the mothers and fathers complained to Cain, he told them to let it be. There was nothing to be done to stop them. But mothers watch their daughters more closely now."

"What did the unseen ones do with the girls?" Eve asked, though she already guessed the answer.

Hasia looked up, her lashes wet with unshed tears. "They forced them to mate with them, and the girls gave birth to the giants. They call them the Nephilim. They are half demon and half human."

Eve stared at her daughter. How was it even possible? But they knew from Adam's dreams that when the serpent fell from heaven, he had taken many angels with him. These were the unseen ones who had now corrupted the human race.

"Tell us where our other sons and daughters live and we will go directly to each of them. We will stay to the shadows of the streets as much as we can," Adam told Hasia. "Is there a place here where we can spend the night?" The day had just begun, but it could take the men days to try to convince her sons and daughters to return—if they could do so without being overheard.

Hasia did her best to describe the town and where each of her siblings lived. "But you must not speak of the Creator," she whispered. "The watchers will know, and if Cain hears of it, there will be violence against you and anyone who listens to you."

Eve realized that Adam's fear had validity. Neither of them had known just how bad things were here. To not even be allowed to speak of the one in whose image they were made?

But not all bore His image any longer. Not if the demons had created a race that was only half human.

She looked from Adam to Seth. What were they going to do?

They left Hasia's home with Eve clinging one last time to her daughter, knowing she might never see her again. She half ran to keep up with Adam's and Seth's long strides as they hurried the donkey along and went to each home Hasia had indicated. Ravid was not at home but in the fields with the sheep. Pessel assured them she was happy here, though Eve did not see any satisfaction in her expression.

At Kalix's home, they were quickly ushered inside as they had been at Hasia's. Eve hugged her son and Naava, relieved that Kalix had not yet left for the fields.

"Is Lasaro also still about?" Adam asked, releasing Kalix from a fatherly hug.

"We tend the sheep and goats together, and as it is yet early, I was just about to go and get him." Kalix tied a scarf about his neck. "Why have you come, Abba? What is the urgency?"

"Go and get him now and bring Kaelee and all of your children here," Adam said.

Kalix's brow lifted, yet he did not question Adam further. He slipped out the door.

Eve turned to Naava. "Are all of your children with you here?"

Naava nodded. "You are worried, Ima. You suddenly come to visit, and now I see fear in your eyes."

"Hasia told us there are giants, born of demons and the daughters of men. Why are you unafraid, my daughter?"

Naava looked beyond Eve as though she was not sure what to say.

The door burst open, and Kaelee rushed into Eve's embrace. "Ima! I'm so glad you came!"

Eve clung to this daughter who was once so small and vulnerable. Did these children have any idea the danger they were in?

"Why the rush to bring everyone together?" Lasaro asked, setting their youngest child on the floor.

"We have come to ask you to leave this place," Seth said, stepping closer to his older siblings. "When we arrived and heard about the watchers and the Nephilim, we knew God had sent us for you. Will you return with us and escape the evil that is in this place?"

The adults exchanged looks while the children huddled together near them. Eve longed to pick up each grandchild and hold them close, but the urgency of their decision made her pause.

"We have not been happy here," Kalix admitted after a brief silence. "At first it was exciting to see what Cain had built, but then the unseen ones came in the form of men and snatched the older virgin daughters of some of Cain's children, and terror filled our hearts. We have not known what to do. We dare not leave our homes unless we carry weapons. Our wives are prisoners in our homes, and the children . . ." His arm moved in an arc where the children stood. "You can see they are afraid."

"Why did you not simply leave then?" Seth demanded.

"We had built lives here by then," Lasaro said. "To take our livestock and leave would have garnered everyone's attention. Cain would not have allowed it. The watchers would have told him."

"Then you must come with us at once," Adam said, motioning toward the door. "We must leave before the sun climbs any higher in the sky."

"But what of our flocks?" Kalix asked as Naava hurriedly packed their things.

"You can have some of mine," Seth said, his tone urging. "We must go now."

"We must," Kaelee agreed, gripping one child in each hand and glancing about her. "We will make more things and borrow from our sisters until we do. Let Cain have our flocks. I won't risk having our daughters snatched from us." She looked at Lasaro, who nodded his agreement.

Eve's nerves grew taut as she witnessed the fear in her daughters' and sons' gazes.

Kalix looked at his wife. "Would you not rather flee before we are caught? Kaelee is right. We must take the children and go."

Naava looked skeptical, but she dropped her utensils and scooped her youngest child into her arms.

Together at last, they all headed out. Kalix led the way with Seth beside him, the girls and youngest children on the donkey behind, and Adam and Eve at the last. Eve's attention heightened at every sound, and she noticed Adam's eyes shifting in every direction.

At the gate ahead of them stood a man whom Eve did not recognize. She looked up and up. He was nearly as tall as the gate itself, with arms thick as pillars and legs that looked as though they could stomp a person with one heavy step. One of the giants.

Her heart nearly stopped, but Kalix led them around him to a side entrance, and the group raced through the door out of the city. Eve was almost through the door when the thunderous sound of a heavy foot came from behind her.

"Where do you think you are going?" the man boomed.

Adam turned about and shoved Eve behind him. "We only came to visit. We are leaving now."

With that, he turned and grabbed Eve's arm, and together they ran like the wind after their children. But not before Eve caught a glimpse of the giant's glinting silvery eyes. Just like the serpent's. She shivered, feeling as though she had once again looked into the face of the devil.

27

SEVEN GENERATIONS FROM EDEN

Eve rose before dawn, as was her custom, and walked toward the river, her place of peace. She settled among the grasses that lined the shore and placed her bare feet into the cool water. The morning mist still clung to the area surrounding the river, and she watched the light dance like jewels in the fields.

Life had been the same and yet so different for more years than she could count. More children had been born to her children and grandchildren, and generation after generation had grown up around her.

Their compound was no longer what it used to be. Even now she could hear the sounds of work beginning on another wall they were building to surround their ever-expanding city, one of many cities that now stretched east and west of Eden.

She wiggled her toes in the cool water and flicked some of the droplets toward the center of the flowing river. The ducks and swans and beavers and muskrats kept their distance, some diving for food, others carrying twigs in their mouths to build their dens.

Memories of Eden still filled her thoughts when she settled here. Adonai seemed closer somehow, though she could no longer see Him. So much had changed, and every time a child grew ill or an adult child moved away, she felt it deep within as if she carried the weight of them all on her shoulders.

But here . . . here she could give the burdens back to God as she talked to Him. "I miss Achima and Jabril, Adonai. I never thought they would lead their clan to begin another city away from us."

She listened, longing to hear Him respond to her aloud, but only the whisper of wind in the leaves above her answered. And she never could understand the voices in the wind.

Leaves crunched behind her, and she turned to see one of Seth's younger descendants walking toward her. Enoch. Such a kind child. Seth's generations of children had remained with her and Adam in this original camp turned city, but Chania had followed Achima, and the twins had gone in another direction.

"Who were you talking to, Savta Eve?" Enoch sat beside her and stretched to dip his shorter legs into the water.

"Enoch. How did you know where to find me so early?" She put an arm about his shoulders and squeezed, pulling him close to her heart. She kissed the top of his head and released him.

"I've seen you come here sometimes. You always talk to someone, but I have looked and can never find who it is. Do you see something invisible?" His upturned face was round, and his dark hair hung down to his shoulders. Innocent curiosity mingled with seriousness in his expression.

She smiled and took his hand in her older, more veined one. When had her skin begun to wrinkle and the veins grown more pronounced? She still felt young. Not as young as the day of her creation but strong and able to keep up with most in her clan. But looking now at Enoch's smooth skin, she suddenly felt old.

She masked the feeling and met his earnest gaze. "I talk to the Creator like Saba Adam and I used to do when we lived in Eden. The only difference is that He does not respond to me like He did back then. But when I pray to Him, I feel as though He takes my burdens and carries them for me."

Enoch tilted his head as though he were trying to process her comment. "I would like to meet the Creator," he said after a lengthy pause. "I would like to talk with Him too."

"That is a worthy desire, my child. If I have learned anything in my years upon the earth, I would say that the Creator would like to know you too." She released his hand, and he faced the river, kicking his legs in the water and gently splashing her.

He looked up at her again. "Will you tell me what it was like when you lived in the garden? Abba and Saba Seth have told me about the garden, but they didn't live there. I'd like to hear it from you and Saba Adam." He pulled his feet from the water and sat cross-legged, facing her.

She turned toward him and stood, taking his hand and pulling him up. "Why don't I tell you about the Creator as we walk to the place where the cherubim guard the garden to this day? We won't see much, but you will get a glimpse of the world He created and the angels that were meant to help us before we disobeyed the Creator."

Enoch's eyes lit up. "Could I really see the cherubim?" he asked, clearly ready to run ahead of her if he had known the way.

She laughed, delighted with his exuberance. "I imagine you can. I don't think the Creator would have sent them away from guarding the path to the Tree of Life."

"Let's go then!" He tugged her hand, and she stepped ahead of him.

In all her years of bearing children and from all their offspring, she had seen such a desire only in Abel and Seth. Why hadn't Seth brought Enoch here? But perhaps this was God's gift to her, to be able to pass on to one more generation some of what she once knew so intimately. Perhaps Enoch would be the one from Seth's line to bring about the salvation and redemption she so desperately longed for.

She held tight to his hand. "Come," she said, and together they picked their way along a path she remembered well. If only she didn't have to live outside of it now. She longed to see it once again from inside the garden walls.

⁓

Adam stood with Seth as his son examined the work being done on an extension of a wall to make their city larger. Over the years, they had learned to fell trees and quarry stone and make tools of iron and knives of flint. The twins had made musical instruments from the ones they had seen in Cain's city, which had been made by Jubal, one of Cain's many descendants. There were so many grandchildren Adam would never know. But the music that came with the twins had enriched the lives of all, and as the years passed, Seth had found reasons to build a better life than what they began with in their small compound.

"You want to keep the stones varied so they don't slide when they are on top of each other," Seth said to one of his younger descendants. "Make sure the clay, water, and straw are mixed well with the sand and limestone so the mortar holds."

Adam listened as Seth spoke and walked the length of the building site with him. How time had changed the world God had made.

He watched one of the young men laying the mortar into place while another placed a heavy stone on top. Would he himself still be able to lift such a boulder? The last time he'd done so was when he'd finally replaced the altar of earth and made an altar of stone as Adonai had instructed him. But now he sensed the slightest weakening in his bones, and he knew he would not be able to keep up with these younger ones as he had in the past.

The thought saddened him, but with it came the memory of his neglect. When had he stopped going to his favorite area among the trees to pray? When had his worship become too familiar, too routine, and often forgotten?

Did Eve struggle with the same thoughts? They were the only ones who remembered the day they were made and had seen the beauty of the Holy One every day as He came and walked with them.

"Does something trouble you, Father?" Seth asked as he placed a hand on Adam's back.

Adam turned to face him, remembering the day God had shown him that Seth's line would one day bring the Redeemer. Adam was glad of it. If only He would come soon.

"I am just thinking that I must be more faithful." Adam cupped Seth's shoulder. "Perhaps it is time for you to call another meeting, to remind your clan and siblings to call on God's name while there is still time."

What would happen when God sent the Redeemer? Would He save them all or destroy those who did not seek Him? How would they ever be allowed back into God's presence in their current state? Something drastic would have to happen, Adam sensed, though God had never revealed to him what that might be.

He looked heavenward, longing to hear His voice again. *How long, Adonai? How long until we finally meet the Redeemer? Will we know Him when He comes? How will His coming change anything?*

Though Adam waited a moment in silence, there was no answer.

"I think you are right, Abba," Seth said, interrupting his thoughts. "We should also offer another sacrifice and confess our sins to God. It is time."

"Yes," Adam said. "It is."

Eve slowed her step, and Enoch did the same as they neared the area where the garden of Eden stood. Light from the cherubim could not yet be seen. Would she find them gone this time? Might the Creator have opened the way again to the Tree of Life?

The thought gave her both a heady and a disturbed feeling. To eat from the Tree of Life now—what would that do to her? To the whole race of her children? She glanced at Enoch, so young and yet so wise for his age. No, the Creator would not have changed His mind. How could He? Still, a part of her always hoped He would. Perhaps the tree would undo all the wrong they had done.

She continued walking, clinging to Enoch's hand and bracing herself for the vision of the flaming cherubim. "If they are still there," she said, "they will be around that next bend."

Enoch nodded, his dark eyes growing wide. "Are they scary, Savta Eve?"

Eve stopped and knelt at his side, taking his face in her hands. How innocent he was. Should she have reconsidered and not brought him here? "Yes, Enoch, they are frightening to behold, and they wield flaming swords. They have to be stronger than we are or they couldn't keep us from returning to the garden. But God made them greater and mightier than humans. They are guards to keep us out."

"I wish God had not sent you away from Him." Enoch put his arms around her neck and hugged her, bringing tears to her eyes.

She swallowed hard, waiting for the emotion to pass. "I wish that too, Enoch." She kissed his forehead. "But He had to send us out for our own protection. If we had eaten of the Tree of Life, we could never have been truly and forever redeemed." She had always known that.

She shook herself from her wayward thoughts and glanced beyond Enoch for a moment. His upturned face held kindness rarely seen in a child, and she saw only innocence in his eyes.

"Sometimes I think He talks to me," he said. "I think I felt Him touch me once."

Eve stared at the child, searching his face. How could she know whether he had heard from God or from one of the unseen workers of the evil one? He was so young. Could he possibly discern such a thing?

"What does He say to you?" she said at last.

Enoch scrunched his face as though trying to recall. "He said His Spirit would not always strive with men. He said I must be careful to obey His call." He smiled. "I do not understand the first part, but I want to obey Him if He calls me."

Eve felt her strength drain from her, and she sat on the grass, pulling him down with her. "God is speaking to you, my child. I do not understand the first part either, but I sense that He said it because He is angry with the watchers, the demons who bore children with the daughters of men. He is angry with the corruption of the human race."

Enoch pulled up a blade of grass and studied it, and Eve could almost see his mind turning. "When I grow up, I will preach like Saba Seth does against the watchers and the demons. I will speak for the Creator."

How sure he sounded! For a moment, Eve's hopes rose, but he was still a child. So much could change him as he grew to adulthood. "I hope you will always remember this promise," she said, patting his hand. "Now come. Let me show you the cherubim."

Enoch jumped up and followed as she slowly led him around the bend. Had God made Enoch different at heart than the rest of them? To care about the Creator the way he did at such a young age was unusual.

They walked the short distance to the entrance of the garden. As they turned the corner, flaming light blazed from the unearthly being whose sword flashed back and forth and whose eyes seemed to see everywhere at once.

Eve strained to see past the blinding light of the sword toward the garden she once knew, but she could not see more than the dense foliage that had grown up to hide the entrance. Would the cherubim one day no longer be needed because the bushes and trees and climbing weeds, the nettles and thornbushes, would grow over whatever remained of the opening? Or would God one day destroy this garden He had made just for them?

The thought saddened her all over again. A moment later, Enoch released his grip on her hand and walked closer to the cherubim. He stopped just out of reach of the flashing sword and stood staring at the angel.

Silence fell between them, and not even the sound of the sword disturbed it. Enoch's gaze did not waver until at last he knelt and bowed before the angel.

Eve watched, her breath catching in her throat.

The cherubim offered Enoch his free hand. "Do not bow to me. Worship God, child. Not me."

Enoch stood and the angel released his hand. "I will worship the Lord our God," Enoch said.

The angel nodded once, and Eve sensed they had best leave. She touched Enoch's shoulder. "Come, my son," she said as he turned to face her.

They walked toward the city without speaking until they reached the outskirts. Enoch turned to face her. "Thank you, Savta Eve. I understand better now. I'm glad we went."

She smiled. "I'm glad we did too."

28

Eve walked to Tehila's home near the western wall, below the hills that housed the caves where she and Adam once lived. Tehila and Ruel had stayed in what was now Seth's city, for which Eve was grateful. She smiled as her daughter opened the door.

"I see you are ready, Ima," Tehila said, beckoning Eve to enter. "Adva and Devora want to join us. You don't mind, do you?"

"Of course not. We should have a pleasant visit with your sisters. I do hope they are not off somewhere."

Tehila laughed softly. "Where would they go, Ima? I'm sure we will find them somewhere in Jabril's city."

"I'm sure you are right."

A knock at the door brought Adva and Devora, Tehila's daughter and granddaughter, into the house, and soon the laughter and chatter between the young women carried them out of the house to the city gate.

Adam and Seth sat near the gate's entrance but stood at their approach. "So you are off to Jabril's city?" Seth asked. He had not been overly happy with their desire to travel without a male escort but had agreed that the women knew how to wield the weapons they had crafted in past years. "You will be back before nightfall?"

"Yes, my son." Eve patted his arm. "You need not worry."

They slipped through the gate, the women laughing as they left. The distance to Jabril's city was only a few hours' walk, and the sun had been up a short while. Plenty of time if they didn't stop to pick flowers or rushes or to watch the animals they sometimes encountered along the paths outside the city.

Tehila fell behind and joined Eve while Adva and her daughter walked ahead. "It will be nice to be together again," she said, taking Eve's hand. "How different things must seem to you, Ima. So many generations of us living in so many places. It's hard for me to imagine my girls and their children leaving me someday."

"Maybe they won't," Eve said, squeezing Tehila's hand. "Seth and Salema have stayed with us. So you never know."

"Yes, but I never thought Achima and Chania would leave. They were so close to you." Tehila's tone caused Eve to face her daughter.

"You miss them more than I realized." She put her arm around Tehila's shoulders. "You are a good daughter."

"Thank you, Ima." She rested her head against Eve's shoulder for a moment, then together they caught up to Adva and Devora.

The trees grew thick on either side of the path, and Eve's senses heightened to the whisper of the wind above them in the branches. She darted glances in several directions, concerned that the unseen ones could be watching. But they wouldn't travel here, would they? They went to Cain's city because he refused to honor the Creator. God would protect those who were faithful to Him, wouldn't He?

"Keep watch," Eve said as she lengthened her strides. "And let's not linger among the trees."

"Did you see something, Ima?" Tehila asked, worry lines appearing along her brow.

The women easily kept Eve's hurried pace, and when they passed the tree line, she finally spoke. "I did not see anything, but I sensed something. You must remember that the evil one has many fallen angels who were also banned from Adonai's presence and who freely roam the earth. I did not think they would come near our homes because God protects us, but God came to the garden every day and the evil one still seduced us to sin. We can never be too careful." She felt the blade inside the pocket of her robe and kept her hand on the hilt.

"We would never be able to counter the unseen ones, Ima. They are too strong for us. And you said yourself the giants are frightening." Tehila's voice fell to a whisper, and Eve heard the waver of fear in it.

"If we see one, we must call on Adonai to help us. You are right, even our men are not strong enough to fight them." She drew in a breath and quickened her pace yet again until they were half running toward Jabril's city. They shouldn't have come without the men for protection. And yet, what good would the men have done? They could have been killed and the women still taken. Devora was a virgin who stood at risk, and Eve felt the burden to protect her at all costs.

When at last the gate of Jabril's city came into view, Eve breathed a relieved sigh. They were allowed entrance, and all four women stopped to catch their breath the moment the gate closed.

Jabril came from a room near the gate and embraced Eve. "Ima! How good of you to come." He hugged Tehila, Adva, and Devora. "But did you come all this way alone? It is not safe."

Eve accepted the skin of water Jabril carried at his side. "How do you know it is not safe, my son?" she asked, reading the concern in his gaze.

"Nothing has happened yet. Not like what has happened in Cain's city, but there are rumors that the watchers roam these hills. We do not allow our women to leave the city to gather water, which is why we dug a well in the center of town. Each man carries water with him when he goes about to work the fields and keeps a weapon strapped to his side."

Jabril's words caused the younger women to cling to one another.

"How will we get safely home then?" Tehila asked.

"I will take men with me, and we will accompany you on your return. But for now, you are safe here. Go and see Achima and Chania. They will be most glad that you came." He pulled Eve aside as the others moved in the direction he pointed. "Ima, tell Abba and Seth to be watchful. I know God is with them and that they worship the Creator, but so do we, and that does not keep the evil from crouching at the doors of our cities. I've even heard that the giants from Nod have multiplied and are moving about the land in search of other women so they can continue their mixed race." His words were urgent, and his face, no longer young, showed the burden he carried for his entire clan.

"The evil one wants to hurt the Creator by destroying us," Eve said. "He wants to keep the Redeemer from coming and crushing his head."

"He would destroy us all!" Jabril sounded like the little boy she remembered.

"God will not allow that to happen, my son," Eve said quietly. "God is greater than the evil around us or the unseen fallen ones who hate Him. We must call on God's name when we face these enemies and take refuge in Him. He still cares for us, but we need to obey Him and ask for His help."

"I know, Ima. Thank you for the reminder." Jabril kissed her cheek. "We will offer a sacrifice to Him soon. But go and enjoy your girls while there is yet enough light in the day. Then we will take you home."

Eve hurried off to join the others and soon found herself held tight in Achima's and Chania's embrace. Despite the risks, she was glad she had come to see these beloved daughters.

Jabril and his sons, all armed with daggers and swords they had made, spoke quietly with Adam and Seth after seeing Eve and the girls safely home. Eve stood nearby, listening to Jabril's warning again, and saw the men's set jaws and brows drawn in concern.

"We will check the area when it is light and pray that God will give us eyes to see the unseen ones if they are near," Seth said, thanking Jabril for the warning.

Jabril and his sons left and hurried home while it was still light, and Seth and Adam turned to Eve.

"Did you see them?" Adam asked, stepping closer and placing his arm about her.

She met his gaze. They both knew how beguiling the serpent and his followers could be. "I did not see them, but I sensed something foul as we passed through the trees. I did not linger because I was not sure I could keep the girls safe if we encountered them. So we hurried until we reached the gate of Jabril's city."

"You would have been safer if you had turned around and come home," Adam said. "But I'm glad that you talked with Jabril and that he brought you back and told us these things."

"We must offer a sacrifice and confess our sins before we attempt to engage or look for the enemy," Seth said.

"We can announce that tonight. Have each one purify themselves and on the third day offer a sacrifice. Then you and I can walk about the perimeter of the city and see what we can find. With God's help." Adam kissed Eve's cheek and released her. "You are tired. Perhaps you can rest before we eat."

Eve scoffed at the idea. "I have grain to grind and food to prepare. I will rest tonight." Though she wondered if there would be any rest for her thoughts after today.

* * *

Four days later, Adam met Seth at the city gate, weapons strapped to their belts and water skins hanging from their necks.

"Are you sure you want to do this, Abba?" Seth's dark hair was still damp from his morning washing, and his eyes sparked with determination and a hint of concern.

Adam placed his hand on Seth's shoulder. "If I am honest, no. I do not want to go looking for the angels who once worshiped the Creator, whose sole purpose now is to turn my family away from Him. I don't want to be deceived by them or taken captive, if that is possible, or have anything to do with them. Make no mistake, my son. These creatures are a danger to us. These weapons"—he lifted the dagger at his side—"are nothing to them."

The fire in Seth's gaze dimmed a little. "Then why would we go? What purpose is it to find them if the risk is so great?"

"There is power in God's name," Adam said. "And for the sake of the others, we need to know if they are near. We might feel their evil presence, and if they are bold enough, we might see their form."

He wondered at his own common sense in pursuing something that was beyond this world. The unseen ones could be either frightening or alluring and beautiful when it suited them. As the serpent had been to both him and Eve those long years ago.

"May the Creator open our eyes to see them if they are anywhere close to our city." Seth walked ahead through the gate and turned toward the path that led to the river.

Adam turned his keen gaze to the trees, darting glances right and left as they slowly walked, every sense heightened. How much evil would he see before his life's end?

They walked along in silence, stones and twigs crunching beneath their feet. The scents of pine and oak and maple greeted them, but the missing birdsong made Adam pause. He stopped, turned in a full circle.

"What is it, Abba?" Seth whispered. He too looked all about.

"I'm not certain. Let's follow the river and come back near the opposite side of the city."

They walked on toward the river. "Nothing so far," Seth said as they stood on the bank, looking from one end to the other. "But you sensed something in the trees." He faced Adam.

"I thought so. But I may have been mistaken."

They walked among the grasses on the rise above the bank,

looking from one side of the river to the other. They came to another stand of trees and a lesser-used path leading back toward home. Adam took the path, Seth close behind.

In the distance, something moved in the shadows.

They stopped, and the silence grew between them. The shadow had form and a hint of light to it, but Adam could not be sure if it was an animal or one of the unseen ones giving them a glimpse of its presence. They stood still, gazes fixed.

Moments passed until at last the being no longer remained hidden. A fallen angel walked toward them. He was several heads taller than Adam and Seth, his form larger, his bearing intimidating. Seth stood as if stuck to the earth. They should run. But Adam waited.

"What have you to do with me, Adam, son of the Creator? Go home to your city and hide behind its walls. The earth belongs to the serpent, not to you." The angel snarled, revealing a grotesque face.

"You do not speak the truth, watcher of men," Adam said. "The Creator is the only one who owns this earth, and He gave it to humanity to care for, not to you or your master. You will not destroy the race of humans or the creation God has made. Stay away from my sons and daughters or you will regret it."

Adam could not believe those words had come from his mouth. Who was he to tell a powerful fallen angel what to do? Angels, good or evil, were much stronger than men and women. But the words had come as though he could not stop them. Had God given them to him?

"Listen to my father, watcher of men," Seth nearly shouted. "You may think you have power now, but one day the Redeemer will destroy you—all of you. You are not more powerful than our God."

The angel took a weighty step toward them, his look menacing. Adam had a brief desire to stand and fight the enemy but knew even he and Seth together would be no match for him.

"May the Ancient of Days defeat you!" Adam yelled.

He turned as one with Seth, and they ran toward the city gate. They did not stop or look back until they had closed the gate behind them.

Seth called the family together to meet in the center of town, where they had built a gathering place to talk or settle disputes among them. Eve sat on a wooden bench Adam had carved for her near the front of the group. A sigh escaped her as Seth ascended a raised area where he could look over the crowd of his children. The men and women quieted, and she heard her granddaughters hushing their children as well. Silence at last descended.

"I have called you here tonight," Seth began, "to tell you what my father and I have heard and seen. And to issue a warning to all."

He glanced at Adam, who simply nodded.

"Father and I walked today beyond the borders of the town. Our reason for leaving the safety of these walls was to go in search of the watchers of men. My brother Jabril warned us that they no longer remain only in Nod but have begun to walk the earth near other cities. They prowl about, seeking young virgins to snatch when the girls are alone or vulnerable, and force them to mate with them. The girls are powerless against these giant beings, and the children they bear grow into giants themselves, powerful and ruthless."

He paused, and little gasps moved among the men and women gathered behind Eve. Her own heart beat faster as fear attempted to take hold of her. *Please, Adonai, no. Don't let these enemies of Yours have any of these generations of my children.*

"My father and I walked to the river and among the trees not far from the city gate when we happened upon one of these watchers, and he approached us," Seth said. "Make no mistake, these beings are treacherous and evil, and he threatened us when we confronted him. We outran him to the city because our God protected us from him. But we cannot risk anyone leaving the city alone, especially the women and virgin girls. You must always travel in groups or

222

at least pairs. And if you see a watcher, call on the name of the Lord to protect you. You cannot fight them on your own. They are much stronger than any human."

Seth glanced at Eve, then at the rest of his descendants. "Take care to follow the ways of Adonai our God and do not listen to what these creatures say. They will tell you things that will tempt you, but always remember that they can do nothing but lie. You must not allow them to speak to you if you happen upon one of them. I would say it is best for you to run as you call on our God. Escape them if you see them."

He looked from one to another, his gaze seeming to stay longer on Enoch, whose wide eyes held horror and disgust. This child was so young, but Eve knew he would not bear with the evil of the enemy of humankind.

"That is all," Seth said. "If you have questions, ask me or Father anytime. Or Ima, who, like Abba, has seen the evil one, the ruler of the watchers of men. We can give you any help you need." He turned and climbed down from the raised platform.

Eve watched him approach Salema and take her into his arms. He carried a heavy burden to stay true to Adonai. Which one of his descendants would take up the mantle of leading the people when Seth passed on or grew too weary to bear it?

Would she live to see each succeeding generation and know what happened to each of them? She glanced heavenward, but the canopied sky held only varying shades of blues and greens and intermittent white. She could not see to the heavens where God lived, and she could not know the future. Knowing good and evil had not made her wiser. It had brought only suffering and pain.

One day perhaps she would again know only God and all that was simply good. For now, she looked at her family and grasped Adam's hand as he stood and pulled her to her feet. She prayed for each one she could remember. Too many family members filled her mind, and she could not recall every name. It was as though some of them had faded from view and from thought.

Was this how God had intended it to be? Would they have known each child better if Eden had remained their home? Cain would not have killed Abel and the earth might not have filled so quickly.

It did no good to keep going back there, despite her recent visit with Enoch to the garden's edge. Why she could not keep from longing for life to be different, she did not understand. She could only attribute her feelings to the fact that she knew what used to be. And what used to be was so much better.

29

The clamor of voices rose in the center of the town square, where Seth and his many sons dug deep into the earth. Eve watched the group from a distance, her arm around Narit, Enoch's younger sister. Years had passed since Adam and Seth had seen the watcher of men in the trees, but despite their fear, the women with one or two men at their sides still brought water from the river each dawn.

"Do you think they will truly be able to find water in the earth, Savta Eve?" Narit stood nearly as tall as Eve now and had recently reached an age where her father, Jared, would need to choose a cousin to marry her. But the men were concerned with too many other things.

"I hope so, Narit," Eve said, drawing the girl away from the activity of the men. "In the meantime, why don't we use the water we gathered from the river and begin the next meal? The men will be hungry when they are done with this work."

Narit pushed her long, dark hair away from her face and smiled. "I will get the water jars."

"And I will gather your cousins."

Some of them would need to grind the grain while others could accompany Eve to the plots of ground inside the city where they grew seed-bearing plants for food. Still others could pick from the fruit trees that were inside the city.

The olive groves and grapevines were beyond the walls, and the men would have to harvest those soon. Seth's careful planning to include land inside the walls for food had been a wise choice. But what of the future as their population increased? Or would the Redeemer come before then?

Eve shook herself, focusing on the moment as she walked toward Tehila's house.

"Savta Eve," Enoch said, coming alongside and embracing her. "You are just the person I wanted to see."

"Enoch, my son. I am about to call your cousins to help. You can talk with me as we choose the food for the evening meal."

"Of course," he said. They went to each house and called the younger children to help with the weeding.

When they reached the plots of plants, Eve pulled Enoch aside. The boy was no longer a child and was set to marry his cousin Shira at the rising of the next new moon. How quickly time passed. "What is it you want to tell me?" she asked, pulling herself back to the moment.

Enoch brushed the hair so like his sister's, only shorter, out of his eyes. His smile broadened, and the light in his eyes held joy she had not seen in anyone since . . . since the garden.

"What is it, Enoch?"

"I've met with Adonai Elohim!" He lifted his eyes to the heavens, then held her gaze. "He met me as I walked outside the city. I know it was Him and not one of the watchers—it is obvious there is a difference in the good and evil ones. He told me things I dared not imagine."

Eve swallowed the sudden emotion that rose within her. "How blessed you are, my son. God has not spoken to us in many years. What did He say to you?" How she longed to hear His voice again!

Enoch rubbed the back of his neck. "He called me to prophesy and speak out against ungodliness. I think He meant it for now and for a future time that we can't see."

"So you are to tell everyone, not only me." She searched his face, attempting to read his thoughts. What had Adonai entrusted to this descendant so far removed from her first child?

"Yes." Enoch looked beyond her, his shoulders sagging. "It is frightening to think on, Savta Eve. God will judge everyone one day, and we won't be able to stand against His scrutiny."

She touched his arm, and he met her gaze again. "God is also merciful, Enoch. The Redeemer will forgive those who trust in Him."

Enoch nodded, the lines smoothing out along his brow. "You are right, of course. It is a blessing beyond compare to walk with God but a burden to think that He has entrusted me to preach to my family across this city and perhaps to those in other cities. I do not want to disappoint Him."

"If God has given you the words to say, He will not allow you to fail, my son." She took his hand and walked away from the others toward the city wall. "You have grown in grace and the knowledge of God over these many years. You will wed Shira soon, and God is preparing you to do something no one else has done since He created the world."

"I think Shira will understand. She knows of my relationship with Adonai Elohim and, like you, she longs to join me. Perhaps one day everyone will be able to walk and talk with God." He paused. "As you and Saba Adam did in the garden."

Eve smiled, though the memory always brought a hint of pain. Perhaps God was giving her a chance to teach another generation in Enoch and his future children. "There was nothing better there than our walks with God in the cool of the day," she said. "Does He show Himself to you every time or only speak to you? Do you see Him in visions or in dreams as Saba Adam does from time to time?"

"Most of the time, He lets me see Him in some form. He looks like one of us, though His glory shines so brightly He often hides me in the shadows so I am not blinded by Him." Enoch's gaze shifted as though he was picturing his last conversation even now.

"And you have never seen the watchers of men when you go to walk with Him?" How was it possible for Enoch to wander off alone and never be in danger? And yet, hadn't she felt safest when she was at peace with God?

"I have seen them lurking after He leaves as I walk home. But they do not come near. They cannot stand the glory that surrounds Him, and for a short time, while I journey to the gate, the glory stays with me. Once I am inside the gate, it leaves." Enoch looked up at the sound of voices.

"There you are," Shira said to him, coming up behind Eve. "My mother wants you to come. She has questions about the food for the wedding and wants you to taste something new she's created."

He laughed. "I'm sure I will like anything she makes. But I will come because you asked." He embraced Eve once more, then took Shira's hand. "Thank you for listening, Savta Eve."

"I am always here for you both," Eve said, watching them walk off as she had seen so many of her descendants do over the years. But Enoch was different from the rest. Would Shira come to resent his time alone with God?

If Adam had walked with God in the garden without her, she would have missed so much and would have felt abandoned by the Creator. But that would never have happened.

Sin had changed everything. Yet Enoch sinned, so how was it that God had chosen to reveal Himself to him?

Eve returned to the patches of produce where the children had finished weeding, sent Narit for a basket, and picked the cucumbers, onions, leeks, parsley, garlic, and greens she would need for the meal.

"Tomorrow can we go to the river with Saba Adam to get water, Savta Eve?" Narit asked as they finished their work.

Eve nodded without thinking, still trying to process all Enoch had said. "Yes, of course. We will go with the others too." She would not take the girl alone with just Adam. They might feel strong, but they were not as quick or strong as they once were. "Perhaps Enoch will join us." If the watchers did not bother Enoch when he walked with God, perhaps they would stay away from all of them while they were with him.

Eve rose with the dawn and took her water jar to head to the center of the city. The women along with Enoch and Adam had agreed to meet there before heading off to the river. She greeted each one and followed the men through the city gate.

"Savta Eve?" Narit skipped beside her, and her laugh held a musical tone.

"Yes, my daughter? You sound like you are glad to be among the trees again."

"It is nice to be out of the city. I don't like being inside all the time. Why can't we go out like Enoch does?" Narit stopped, waiting for Eve to catch up to her.

"You know why, Narit. It is not safe." Eve searched the girl's expressive eyes, unsettled by the determination visible there.

"I'm not afraid of the watchers of men. I can run fast and could easily get away from them." Narit lifted her chin, and Eve felt a chill run down her spine.

"You speak of things you do not understand, my daughter. You have not seen one of these beings, have you?" Eve continued walking. The rest of the women were already some distance ahead, and Enoch was drawing close.

"No." Narit kicked a stone as though to admit such a thing frustrated her.

"Promise me you will never attempt to leave the city without a guardian. The watchers are not good—not in any sense—and they will hurt you in ways you cannot imagine." Eve silently prayed that her words were getting through to the stubbornness that seemed to hover beneath the surface of this conversation.

Narit turned to Eve with a smile. "I promise, Savta Eve. I just wish I could go about as Enoch does and not have to be protected all the time."

Eve nodded and was about to say more, but the girl ran ahead to catch up to her cousins, leaving Eve more than a little concerned.

Enoch joined her and touched her arm. "Can I carry that for you, Savta?" He pointed to the jar, which she still held on her shoulder.

She smiled at him. "Thank you, my son, but no. I am still able to carry the jug."

"Of course you are," he said, looking to the group up ahead. "What had my sister so intent in her conversation with you?"

Eve released a sigh. She didn't want to tell tales, but if Enoch knew, perhaps he could watch Narit more closely. "She wants freedom to walk about the land without a guardian. She wants what you have."

"She wants to walk with God?" He lifted a brow. "She has never shown much interest in Adonai Elohim."

"She wants to leave the city by herself as you do."

"Ah." He rubbed his chin, then looked ahead again. "She is curious to the point of her detriment, I fear. She is not at all like me."

"No, she is not," Eve said. "She is young and somewhat foolish. She has no idea the danger she courts when she should be listening to her elders and learning wisdom."

Enoch's mouth dipped in a frown, and lines appeared across his brow. "I will speak with her. Thank you for telling me." He quickened his pace, and Eve matched his strides.

The others had reached the river, and Eve realized all of her talking had kept them trailing behind. She glanced about, wary. No sign of the evil one or his followers. If they were near, they were not showing themselves. But that did not mean they were not watching or listening.

30

The day of Enoch's wedding came, and Eve was among the women who helped Shira dress and adorn herself. In the generations since God had given her to Adam, her daughters had added to these festivities with flowers, jewels, special treats to eat, and dancing and singing. The celebrations often lasted for several days.

"You are the most beautiful of women," the younger women sang to Shira. "May you be a fruitful vine in the house of your husband."

Eve listened, emotion filling her throat and tears pricking her eyes. The virgins wore flowers in their hair and encircled Shira, each one coming to her in turn and placing a palm frond in her hands.

A knock at the door brought giddy laughter from the virgins, Narit among them, and Shira's father opened the door to Enoch and his brothers and cousins. Together the whole procession walked through the city streets to the center square where the new well stood. Seth and Adam rose to greet them, and Jared and Shira's father gave Enoch and Shira to one another. Enoch took his robe and covered Shira with it, then led the procession to the house he had built for the two of them on the outskirts of the city.

Adam came alongside Eve and took her hand. "Did you ever think we would live to see so many generations of children fill the earth or attend so many festive occasions?" His smile warmed her heart, and she squeezed his fingers.

"I keep remembering how it was when God gave me to you, and in truth, I think ours was the best wedding possible because God was the one who brought us together. He could not have made a bad choice, as our children have or we have through the years." She couldn't help but think of some of the marriages that had not been good. One of Cain's descendants had married two women, something unheard of since creation.

"Ours was the best wedding," Adam agreed, bending to kiss her cheek. "And our marriage is still the best."

"Let us hope that Enoch and Shira have a long and happy life together," Eve said as they neared the house. Torches lit the night sky, and music played as the young couple entertained their family.

"Enoch is one of the few who understands what we knew in the garden," Adam said as he led Eve to a seat off to the side, where they could watch the others dance. "I've had long talks with him, and I am amazed that Adonai is willing to come to earth again and walk with him. I didn't think another human would ever experience what we did."

"I have heard him speak about Adonai Elohim meeting him as well, and I have to remind myself that this is Enoch's time. Perhaps God is close to us for a time if we have a willing heart. I only wish He saw me as willing, as He does Enoch. I try not to feel jealous, but I miss those moments with God more than I ever thought I would."

"I think we will have them again one day," he said.

She searched Adam's gaze. "How? In this life?"

He shook his head. "I don't know if we will have the privilege of His company in this life, but I believe we will see Him again when this life ends."

Eve felt her heart lift at the thought. "Has He told you this?"

Adam shrugged. "It's more an impression I've received over the years. We have the promise of a Redeemer who will make us right with God again. Since we are made in God's image, I don't think even death means our souls will die. The bodies that were meant to live forever will not go on as they should have, but our souls are connected to Him in a way we can't understand. I think He loves us too much to let us go—unless we no longer want Him."

A sigh lifted her chest. "Like Cain."

He nodded. "Like Cain. And the others who have followed him or come from him and chosen to follow his way."

They sat in silence a moment, the sorrow over their firstborn fresh again in her thoughts.

"Enoch and Seth and Seth's descendants help with that loss," Eve said.

"Yes. I'm grateful for that."

The sun had set fully now, and the laughter and music followed Enoch and Shira as they slipped into the house alone.

"Perhaps it is time for us to go home." Adam stood. "These ancient bodies need their rest."

She laughed. "Yes, I suppose they do."

Eve picked up the baked-clay water jar and walked to the central meeting area to draw from the well. She missed the days when she could travel to the river alone, but since the men had finally struck water, there was no need to take the risk. When they wanted to bathe, they went to the river in groups to lessen the risk, and children were washed in tubs made of cut stone and kept in their homes.

Dawn lit the sky in an array of pink and yellow. As she pulled the jar from the well and lifted it to her shoulder, Seth greeted her. Gray hairs had slipped in among the black hair along his temples, a testament to his age.

"Good day, Ima," he said, leaning forward to kiss her cheek.

"Good day to you as well, my son. How are you this fine morning?"

"I was sent away to find you. Shira is in the middle of giving birth. Enoch is creating a groove in the dirt pacing in front of their house, and the women are crowded in thick around her. They want you to hold the child on your knees when he or she arrives."

"Why did they not call for me earlier? I have delivered more babies than anyone in this camp!" She hurried toward Enoch's home, Seth at her heels.

"They didn't want to burden you, Ima. The younger women need to learn the skills you know so well."

She ignored his comment. "We need water for the day and for the babe. Send someone for more. I will take what I have."

They reached the house, and she set the jar on the ground.

"I will find Narit and the younger girls to draw more water for you, Ima." Seth chuckled as he walked away.

Eve frowned, feeling the need to take charge. She walked into the house to the sound of the baby's first cries. She hurried to the room where Shira and the babe were in the last stages of cleaning and birth.

"It's a boy, Ima," Tehila said, looking up from washing the child.

Tehila had become a good midwife over the years, often taking over when Eve was not available. She quickly wrapped the babe in warm cloths and made sure every part of him except his face was covered, then offered Eve the child.

Eve took the boy and looked into his small face. "What a thick head of hair he has. Much like his father." Enoch had looked similar to the boy at birth, though the babe had Shira's wide eyes and small nose.

"I heard a baby cry," Enoch called from the front of the house. "Is he born?"

The women laughed as they helped Shira to a clean mat and pulled a warm blanket about her shoulders.

"You have a son," Eve said as she turned and walked with the child to meet his father.

Enoch's expression softened to one of awe and love as he looked into the child's liquid, dark eyes. Eve extended her arms, and Enoch took the child from her.

"You are Methuselah," Enoch said, smiling.

"Methuselah. Such a long name for a small boy." Eve laughed. "But what does it mean, my son?"

Enoch lifted his gaze to Eve, but he seemed to see beyond her in his mind's eye. "It means 'when he is dead, it shall be sent.'"

Eve gave him a curious look. "So ominous."

Enoch nodded. "It is the name I was given. God is going to judge the earth, Savta Eve. Not in your lifetime or mine, but after this child has lived all of his days, then it will come."

"Judgment will come?"

"Yes. I do not know how, but I do know that God must judge the earth because of the Nephilim who have corrupted our race." He looked again into the face of his son, who seemed content to be held, though he would soon need his mother.

"I hope he lives a long life then," she said. "And that the judgment waits. God will not simply judge the giants, will He? It will come upon all who do not believe." She searched his face, trying to understand.

"He will judge everyone and convict them of all the ungodly acts they have committed and all the defiant words they've spoken against Him." Enoch cupped the child's cheek. "But you, my son, will not live to see it, for which I am grateful."

"So the world might have hundreds or a thousand years left before God acts." Eve tried to imagine how God would judge the earth. Her children were scattered now, but not so far apart that they couldn't hear the preaching of Enoch or Seth when they visited their relatives. How long would God put up with them all?

Methuselah fussed, and Enoch handed him to Eve. "He needs his mother," she said.

Enoch nodded, seemingly overcome with seeing the child who marked the beginning of the end of all they knew and loved.

Eve turned and took the child to Shira. "He is Methuselah," she said. "Enoch has named him."

"Methuselah?" Shira asked. "He hinted as much if it was a boy." She held the baby to her breast to nurse and closed her eyes.

Eve slipped from the room, her mind whirling. How long would this child live? Would judgment come soon?

There was no way to tell. She left the house, ignoring the young girls who carried more water to Shira's home. Let the others handle things. With this new revelation, she needed time alone to think and pray.

✺

Later that day, the rest of the family gathered around Enoch, congratulating him. Tehila brought the baby to Enoch once more, and in Adam's and Seth's presence, Enoch blessed the child.

"May your days be long upon the earth, my son, Methuselah, and may your name remind us all to turn to God so we may be saved. We have your lifetime and ours to repent and return. May God bless you and keep you and help you to walk with Him always." Enoch kissed Methuselah's cheek and handed the babe to Adam, who also blessed him and then passed him to Seth for the final blessing.

The boy began to cry as Seth finished his final words, and Eve stepped forward and took him in her arms. She carried him into the house to his mother to nurse, kissing his forehead before handing him over. "You are truly blessed, Shira. This child carries a huge responsibility already on his shoulders. You must be the one to teach him until Enoch can take him to the fields." She stepped back, watching as the new life grasped for nourishment.

Contentment settled over Shira's face. "I will, Savta Eve," she said as she brushed the soft hair on Methuselah's head. "Our God will guide us."

Eve nodded, satisfied. She could trust Enoch and Shira to raise their son as God intended. How glad she was again that God had given them Seth to replace Abel. What a godly son he had proven to be.

And how unlike Cain, whom she still missed as the days and years passed. Nothing good came from his city. Only rebellion and sorrow.

No. She could not dwell on the one who had walked away. She would always love him, but she must pour what energy she had left into the children who still obeyed. Preserving Adam's line and keeping them from the unseen evil had to be her singular focus. She must pray for this child and his parents. Perhaps the Creator would honor her fervent prayers.

31

E ve watched Methuselah playing in the dirt with the wooden toys her children had once held, while Shira helped the other women in the central courtyard grind grain. Enoch often left the camp to preach the words God had given him in other cities. In Jabril's growing town a few had welcomed him, but many were indifferent to his message.

"They seem to have lost touch with the Creator, Savta," Enoch had told her one day when they walked outside the camp. He often walked with her after his visits, and sometimes Adam and Seth joined them.

"I am sad to hear it," she said, her heart aching with the knowledge that Jabril and Achima's descendants were not following the beliefs they held dear.

"Though they have worked to keep the watchers from entering their city, I believe some of the young virgins were still taken. I am not sure how." He ran a hand through his unruly dark hair, his penetrating gaze sharp with frustration.

Eve glanced about them. The unseen ones could be near, but if they were, she could not tell.

"I'm glad they have not been able to take any of our family," he said.

What would happen if one of the watchers infiltrated Seth's

lineage? Would that destroy the chance for the Redeemer to come? Could one person ruin God's promise?

"I'm going to visit Cain's city," Enoch said.

She stopped walking, her heart pounding with his declaration. "It's not safe there, my son. And they likely won't listen to your words."

"I have to try, Savta. If I don't give them the chance to repent, I will bear the guilt of not having spoken when I know I should have." He lifted his chin, and she saw the determination in his firm jaw. Then his gaze softened. "Besides, wouldn't you like to know that Cain's descendants heard the word of the Lord and had the chance to escape God's coming judgment?"

She'd nodded and hugged him.

She looked at Methuselah now, so innocent and unaware of what the end of his life would mean for the rest of those living on the earth.

Enoch's sister Narit walked toward Eve from her father's house and knelt beside Methuselah. "How is my new nephew today?" She smiled in that carefree way she had and cupped the baby's head with her hand.

"He is already growing too fast," Eve said, taking a closer look at the young woman who was usually off with her cousins and rarely took time with her nephew or older grandmothers. "As have you." How tall she had grown. She was younger than Enoch by several years but seemed to have matured into a beautiful young woman without Eve's notice.

Narit laughed, the sound light and musical. "I suppose that happens to all of us." She sat on the rock beside Eve and bounced as if she could not keep still.

"Do you have a cousin in mind that you prefer to wed?" Eve asked. Narit's wedding day would soon be upon them.

Narit laughed again even as a blush colored her cheeks. "There is one. My mother is trying to convince Abba to work something out with his father."

Eve wondered which one of her many descendants would marry this girl. If Jared wanted someone different for her, it would only cause a problem if Eve sided with the girl's choice.

"Have you been to the river yet this week, Savta?" Narit asked, lifting her long hair in both hands and placing it behind her. "I want to go, but Abba says that we can wait a few more days. Will the watchers ever go away so we can live freely again?"

"Not until the judgment comes," Enoch said, coming up behind Eve and snatching Methuselah into his arms. The boy giggled, and Enoch tickled him until they were both laughing. When he set the boy down again, he knelt at Narit's side. "You know better than to expect these evil beings to leave, my sister. The Almighty One has warned us of them, and until God Himself destroys them, we will always face them as enemies. God has warned us to stay away from them, and we dare not take His word lightly."

Narit's expression sobered. "I know. And I do. I've just never seen these watchers you talk about all the time. Perhaps if I saw one, I would fear. But it is hard to fear what you cannot see."

Eve touched Narit's knee. "My child, the unseen ones are not always frightening to look upon. They make themselves beautiful and charming, and they woo you with words that are hard to resist. Once you are caught in their lies, they would snatch your soul if they could. You would never be able to marry this man you desire if one of them got hold of you."

Narit looked at her feet. "I know, Savta. I was simply curious. Have you seen them since the first time?"

"I saw the giants when we visited Cain's city years ago. Adam and Seth and Enoch have seen them more recently." Eve glanced up at Enoch, who now sat beside his sister.

"When I walk with God near the garden or in the forests, I see them in the shadows," he said. "They won't come near the cherubim or the presence of God, but they do make themselves known when I walk toward home. They stick to the shadows because God is with me, but they flicker their limited light in the darkness."

"If God is with you and you are safe, why wouldn't He also be with me and my cousins?" Narit frowned as though she still thought the whole situation unfair. "Sometimes living in the city stifles me, and I want what you have."

Enoch placed his arm about her shoulders. "Do you desire to walk with God and know Him as Savta Eve once did in the garden?"

Narit did not immediately answer. At last she looked at her brother. "If we lived in the garden, I would. But if I have to stay inside these walls, there isn't much point, is there?" Her eyes held a hint of defiance.

Eve's heart sank. *Oh, child. If you only knew what you would lose if you left here.*

"If you want to truly know our God," Enoch said slowly, "I will take you with me when I meet with Him one day. But I have to know that you want Him, not just freedom to do what you desire."

Narit smiled, suddenly her happy self again. "Of course I want to know Him. Would you really take me to meet the Creator? How do you walk with Him? Do you actually see Him?"

Enoch studied her. Did he believe her? "I will talk with Him about bringing you to meet Him. Then I will answer your questions. Now go and do the work Ima wants you to do." He shooed her away, and she skipped off, laughing.

Enoch moved closer to Eve, and Methuselah climbed onto his lap. "I do not know if I can trust her, Savta. She is too eager."

"If I recall, you were young and eager to visit the garden with me not so long ago." She smiled. "Perhaps she truly wants to know Him."

Enoch nodded, looking unconvinced. "Perhaps."

He set Methuselah beside Eve after kissing his forehead, then stood and walked off, leaving Eve to wonder whether Narit was sincere in her desire to know God or simply wanted what she shouldn't have.

Enoch kissed Shira, then bent to cup Methuselah's soft cheek. "I am taking Narit and her cousins to the river for a short time," he said. "My turn has come up, and of course they cannot go alone."

"No, they cannot," Shira said. "I would like to go as well, but today is not a good day. Besides, I want you to take us. Just us." She gave him a coy smile, and he returned it.

"You tempt me, dear wife." He kissed her again, then walked away to meet his sister and cousins at his father's house.

He expected to see Narit and the girls impatiently waiting for him, but there was no sign of them in the courtyard. He opened the door and entered his father's home, turning this way and that looking for the girls. He stepped farther into the room. "Narit? Ima? Where is everyone?"

Silence met his ear. Strange. But perhaps his mother was working with the other women at the grinding stones. Narit must have gone with her.

He tamped his frustration as he left the house. His father would be with the other men in the fields, caring for the animals. Even they did not go out alone. Everyone knew the watchers were stronger than a single man. One or two were lookouts while the others worked.

Enoch walked briskly toward the central courtyard where the fire pit was the largest to feed the most people. He saw his mother working alongside Savta Eve and some of his other aunts and cousins.

"Ima," he called above the noise of the grinding stones. He stepped closer and touched her shoulder.

She stopped turning the stone and glanced behind her. "Enoch. I thought you were taking Narit and her cousins to the river today. Why are you still here?"

Confusion filled him, followed by a heightened sense of fear. "I just came from your house looking for her. I cannot find her.

242

Did she tell you she would wait somewhere else? Near the gate, perhaps?" He knew how impulsive she could be. But the girls wouldn't leave the city without him, would they?

Savta Eve stood, her expression matching the tightening in his gut. "I will help you look for her."

He walked off with her close behind. Adam and Seth met them near the gate.

"Have you seen Narit?" Enoch asked, his panic rising. His sister could not possibly be so foolish! But she did carry a bit of rebellion in her attitude.

Adam shook his head and Seth did the same. "We just returned from inspecting the wall where they are adding another portion. We have not seen her," Seth said.

"Or Hana and Devora? I am supposed to take them to the river. But they were not waiting for me at the house as we planned." Enoch looked from one to the other and then glanced heavenward. He closed his eyes for a moment, praying for wisdom.

Help me find her, Adonai. Please.

"I am going to the river to search for her," he said. "Perhaps, Savta Eve, you can gather some women to search the city?" He glanced at Adam and Seth. "Do you want to join me?"

"Of course," Seth said, following beside him.

The three of them walked through the small door beside the gate. Eve hurried off, her voice rising in the distance as she called Narit's name.

"They could not have left the city without someone seeing them," Seth said as they moved quickly downhill, through the trees, past skittish animals that fled at their approach.

"Hopefully not," Enoch responded, his eyes darting here and there, looking for the unseen ones who could be lurking nearby.

"Hana and Devora were with her?" Adam asked.

"They were supposed to be." Enoch ran a hand through his hair as the sound of the rushing waters met his ears. He stopped, listening.

A cry like that of a wounded animal pierced the air. Enoch looked from Adam to Seth, then ran in the direction of the sound. What if it was a wounded animal? He could be hurt if he interrupted a cat or bear killing its prey. But he had to take the chance.

The cry came again. Footsteps sounded behind him, and he knew Adam and Seth were at his heels. They came to the bank of the river, where the water fell over the rocks and wound through the land to meet the other rivers that bordered Eden.

Enoch stopped, straining to see into the foliage near the river. Trees grew tall here, and the underbrush hid beavers and waterfowl.

"I see a flash of light," Seth said, pointing toward several large oaks with roots going deep beneath the waters.

Enoch ran in that direction, praying for eyes to see what was so often hidden from their view.

"Let me go!" Narit's voice was unmistakable.

Enoch ran faster as her cries grew in intensity. She was a fighter, which might work in her favor. But the watchers were strong. One young virgin could not resist them on her own. Was she alone? Or were her cousins fighting with her?

He came closer. The watcher was visible now, his large hands clutching Narit about the waist while Hana and Devora each tugged on one of his arms. They kicked and fought and pulled and intermittently screamed. But the watcher's grip on Narit held.

Any moment now, this one would be joined by others who would each take one of the girls. Then Enoch would not be able to save any of them. He crept closer, breathed a prayer for strength and the power of God, and shouted, "In the name of the Almighty One, release them at once!"

He ran forward, repeating the words again and again. He grabbed Narit and pulled, giving a loud shout. Hana and Devora released their hold on the watcher and ran back the way Enoch had come. He pulled on Narit one more time while calling on God's name, and the watcher released his hold on her.

Enoch turned and ran with her in his arms, then set her down and urged her to run ahead of him. They reached Adam and Seth, and the men surrounded the girls and ran with them toward the city. Once they were inside, the gate shut behind them.

Seth turned to Adam. "It is time we diverted the river to come to us rather than us going to it. We need more than a well, and it appears no one is safe anymore."

Enoch's heartbeat slowed as the girls hurried to their mothers. No one had ever saved a virgin from the watchers. Against the name of his God, the beings were not so invincible. He would not fear to step outside these walls to walk with God. But Seth was right. They couldn't let the virgin girls travel even in a group with men as their guards. Why had his sister been so foolish?

He shook his head. He preached consistently against these creatures. If the men and women of this city began to think of them as less than powerful—or worse, something to be worshiped in place of the Almighty—they would lose Seth's city just as surely as Adam had lost Cain's.

Enoch could not let that happen.

32

Adam worked alongside as many men as could be spared from keeping the flocks and herds to divert a portion of the Euphrates River. Eventually the waterway would run under the city wall and turn back toward the main river. Sweat poured down Adam's back as he dug into the soil with the iron tools he had fashioned, and he rubbed his brow with the back of his hand. He sank onto the dirt and drew in a breath to rest for a moment.

"We are not going to finish this soon," Seth said, frowning as he sat beside Adam. "We will still need to go to the river to bathe until we do." He drank from a skin of water at his side.

Adam did the same and tied the skin shut when he finished. "We will simply have to be diligent to watch those who watch us." He glanced about him, suddenly wistful. How much had changed in his years on the earth. "After we complete this task," he said as Jared and Enoch joined them, "we should take a group of men and travel to each of the cities. Not to preach this time but to see if there are giants in the land. We need to see how great the enemy's reach has become."

"What can we possibly do about it if we find they have spread their evil influence?" Jared asked, glancing at Enoch, who had far greater knowledge of this threat than any of them did.

"I know we can defeat them in the name of the Lord," Enoch answered, "but I don't know if they can be killed. We cannot kill the demon watchers, but we might be able to kill their offspring."

Adam listened, his heart thudding harder with the thought of bloodshed. There had been more of it since Cain murdered Abel, at least among Cain's descendants, but to go out and hunt down the giants . . . who was strong enough to do such a thing?

"I'm not sure God would send us into battle against them." Seth's words broke through Adam's thoughts. "You're talking about killing our kinsmen."

"Not our kinsmen but the offspring of these unholy alliances." Enoch lifted his hands in supplication. "I do not favor war or battle either, Saba Seth, but if the giants are allowed to live, they will continue to bear children until there are few purely human people left in their cities."

"But what if our brothers and sisters rise up to defend these giants or stand in the way of such a battle?" Jared asked. "We could end up annihilating the good along with the bad."

"No one is good in God's eyes, Abba," Enoch said, tenting his hands beneath his chin. "But you all do have a point. I have no direction from God to wipe out the giants. There are too many of them. If Cain had destroyed them from the beginning . . . but I suspect the devil and his followers would have just kept coming and perhaps still do. They will continue until they corrupt us all."

"Our sin has already corrupted us," Adam said, rubbing the back of his neck.

"But God promised us a Redeemer to take away our sin, did He not?" Enoch held Adam's gaze, zeal in his expression.

"Yes, He did." Adam's heart again yearned for better days, and he wondered why his mind drifted to the past, to days that held less evil and more kindness. He was becoming too much like Eve. Or perhaps it was a sign of his growing old.

"The Redeemer will come one day, Saba Adam. But He won't be able to redeem the giants who are not fully human. I am repeating what we already know though. I agree that we should see how far this corruption and poison have grown. We can't fight against or defeat an enemy that we cannot see. We can only see the effects of his work." Enoch stood and brushed the dirt from his tunic. "I'm rested enough. I will dig more. You can join me when you are ready." He walked back to the area where the men were still digging alongside the river.

"Enoch is right about one thing," Adam said as Jared and Seth also stood. "We must fight this evil among our kinsmen whatever way we can."

"Yes," Seth said, offering Adam a hand.

Adam stood, though he wasn't sure he was quite ready to help with the work again. Yet a part of him did not want to admit that he was aging, despite his many years.

Several months passed, and the project to bring the river to the city was finally completed. The younger men carried heavy rocks to create a narrowing of the flow so no one could swim under the wall, and in the end, the city had a pool where the men and women could bathe. Structures to keep privacy intact were built around the pool, and days were set when the women and children could come separately from the men.

Eve looked on the project with awe, amazed at how much they had learned to do since the early days when they didn't even have fire or a house or soft beds to rest on. God had given them great wisdom.

"There you are, Ima," Tehila said, coming up behind her. "I was hoping to find you."

Eve turned and embraced her. "What do you need?" she asked, releasing her.

"The younger women have asked me to ask you to teach us.

Not how to do things, though that is always good, but to help us to be better wives and mothers and to tell us of Eden. I know you miss the garden, and none of us have seen it." She took Eve's hand. "Ima, Enoch has taught his wife and sons and daughters and sisters and brothers to make pictures in clay to record things of the past so future generations do not forget. Narit enjoys working with the clay and carving the symbols. And since her experience with the watcher, she is anxious to help Enoch record what used to be so her children and ours will remember our God. So, will you?"

Eve laughed heartily, and when she caught her breath she smiled into Tehila's eyes. "You spoke so fast, my head is spinning, my daughter. But yes, I would love to tell each of you of the beginning. You say Enoch has found a way to write things in clay so that others will know what he means?"

Tehila nodded and gently pulled Eve along with her. "I will show you. He has made a cone of clay with symbols on it. Each symbol stands for a word or phrase or person or animal. Once you see it, you will understand."

Eve left the pool and allowed Tehila to lead her. Record their words and thoughts? What more would they think of, the longer they lived? Nothing would be impossible for them!

A sudden check in her spirit made her pause. No, that was not true. Only Adonai could do the impossible. If her descendants began to think they could do what only He could do, would His judgment come more swiftly? Would Methuselah's life end sooner if they began to think that way? *When he is dead, it shall be sent.*

She couldn't bear to see him die soon because of their sin.

"It's right here," Tehila said as they approached Enoch's home. "He keeps it here in this stone trough." She lifted the lid and pulled the cylinder from it.

Eve took the cylinder and turned it this way and that. "This is wonderful," she said. Writing the past for future generations would keep them from thinking they could do anything. She and Adam, Seth and Enoch, and whoever else remembered the good of the past and had seen the works of God would remind them that the Creator was the only one to be worshiped. Not the evil one or his followers. "I want to learn to read what these things mean."

"And Narit will teach us as you tell us the stories of long ago." Tehila smiled, took the cylinder, and replaced it in its case for safekeeping. "Enoch allows any of us to have access to it so we can all learn," she said as they walked toward Eve's house. "But the women are already waiting for you."

"You were that certain you could convince me then?" Eve chuckled. How good it felt to have something to look forward to, something wonderful to share with her children and all those who followed after them. To be needed. Wanted.

"I was fairly certain, and Enoch told me you would teach us. He said you have never forgotten Eden."

"He is right. I never have."

"And you would go back if you could."

"I have tried to go back, but I cannot. So now and then I visit the gate where the cherubim guard the entrance. I think they know I would not attempt to slip past them, which of course I couldn't. But I enjoy seeing a glimpse, at least in my memory, of what used to be." Eve placed an arm around Tehila's shoulders. "I should have taken all of you, but until Enoch asked, I never thought of it."

"Perhaps you still can," Tehila said, her voice low and tempered with awe. "I think it would be a frightening thing to see though, and all of us fear leaving the city now. This is why your memories matter to us. Tell us what we cannot see."

There was so much to tell.

As they entered Eve's house, where many of her descendants had gathered, she settled onto a wooden seat and looked at their eager faces. *This is good. Thank You, Adonai.*

"I guess the best place to start is in the beginning," she said. "I was formed from a rib that God took out of Adam, and He fashioned me to be Adam's helper, his mate to populate the earth. He made us to complete each other. But the real origin of all things was before I was made. God told us that in the very begin-ning He made the heavens and the earth out of a formless void. So everything you see here had its birth as God spoke each thing into existence."

She watched each upturned face and smiled at their rapt at-tention. Perhaps these women would help keep the evil one from destroying Seth's clan, and as the words spread, maybe God would convince her other children to return to the truth. To the God who had made them too.

33

Adam filled the goatskin pouch at the well in the city center and lifted it over his head. Two heavy pouches were strapped to his belt, one filled with nuts and dried grapes, the other with stones for his sling. His short dagger was tucked in with the sling.

Seth and Enoch emerged in the early dawn and met him at the well. "You are up early, Abba," Seth said. He and Enoch filled their skins, and they all walked toward the gate.

"It is a long walk to Jabril's town and the ones beyond. If Enoch is going to prophesy to his relatives, we need to give him plenty of time." Adam offered Enoch an approving smile.

They followed the path through the trees, ever mindful of the dangers from the wild animals as well as the evil spirit world. Gooseflesh prickled Adam's arms as they made their way down the long path. This place used to be one of his safe havens where he talked with God in prayer, but for years now, it had no longer given him that sense of security. Had God abandoned this forest?

"What do you plan to say to the people?" Seth asked once they emerged from the trees to wide-open fields where wildflowers waved in the breeze.

"Repent, for the judgment of God is coming," Enoch said.

"That's all?" Somehow Adam had expected more. "Will you explain the judgment? Has God told you more?" A hint of longing filled him, and he wished he had been called by God to know such things.

"He told me to tell them, 'Listen! The Lord is coming with countless thousands of His holy ones to execute judgment on the people of the world. He will convict every person of all the ungodly things they have done and for all the insults that ungodly sinners have spoken against Him.'" Enoch glanced at Adam. "I have to make sure every city hears the words while there is still time."

"Of course," Adam said. "I remember the holy ones in the assembly of the Creator's council. There were far less than thousands upon thousands there, but many more angels filled God's holy city."

Enoch stopped walking and faced Adam. "You were privileged to see such things, Saba." He gripped Adam's arms and kissed his cheeks. "I hope one day to see them myself, if God will allow it."

They walked on in silence until they reached Jabril's city. Jabril met them at the gate, where he often sat to judge the people in his clan and settle disputes among them.

"Abba!" He held Adam close. "How good it is to see you." He looked to Seth and Enoch, greeting each one. "But why have you come? Is something wrong?"

Enoch stepped closer. "I have something to say to the people here. Shall I call out the message as I walk through the city, or do you prefer to gather the people to meet? It cannot wait for nightfall, as we have more cities to visit today."

Jabril's brow furrowed. "What sort of message do you have?"

Enoch studied Jabril as if weighing his expression. "It is a message from the Creator. He has sent me to speak to those who will listen."

Jabril glanced from Adam to Seth, who both nodded their agreement. He released a sigh, looking uneasy. "It might be easier for you to walk the streets and proclaim your message than for me to gather everyone so early in the day. The men will be leaving for the fields and will not like the interruption. You may find some of the women willing to listen."

Enoch's piercing gaze held Jabril's, and Adam saw Jabril squirm under the scrutiny. "The men need to hear this too," Enoch said. "They need to hear it before they go to the fields, and if they are already with the flocks, call them home."

Jabril bristled at Enoch's forceful tone. "What gives you the right to speak to us this way?"

Enoch straightened, his eyes like fire. "Thus says the Lord, 'Listen! The Lord is coming with countless thousands of His holy ones to execute judgment on the people of the world. He will convict every person of all the ungodly things they have done and for all the insults that ungodly sinners have spoken against Him.'"

Jabril did not respond for a weighty moment, and Adam remembered the years when this son's faith was strong. Ever since Abel died, Achima and Jabril had been true to the Creator. Had that changed?

"I will call them together," Jabril said at last, his shoulders sagging a bit. "I do not know if they will listen or accept your words, as the more recent generations have not cared to keep the sacrifices as we did in the early years. There is much more concern about the pleasures and trials of life." His cheeks colored as though he were ashamed to admit such a thing.

He turned, reached for a ram's horn, and blew into it three times. The call carried long and far, and as they watched from the steps at the gate, men and women came from all directions to the center of the city.

Jabril stepped down, and Adam, Seth, and Enoch followed as he led them toward the central meeting place. Adam glanced at Enoch, but his gaze was fixed on the gathering crowd.

I hope he has truly heard from You, Adonai. Be with him. Adam sensed peace as he prayed, surprised to feel God's comfort so quickly.

Jabril climbed onto a low rise, and the crowd quieted at his lifted hands. "My people, we are privileged to have my father, Adam, here today, along with my younger brother, Seth." He pointed to both men, and the crowd lifted their voices in a hearty cheer. He lifted his hands again for quiet. "And with them is our relative, Seth's descendant Enoch. He is a prophet of the Lord and has come with a message from Him for us and for all the cities of the earth. Please listen to him."

Murmurs swept through the crowd, but the people slowly quieted.

Enoch took Jabril's place on the rise and lifted his hands toward the heavens. "Thus says the Lord," he began, repeating the words he had said to Jabril moments before.

Adam stood to Enoch's right and Seth to his left. When Enoch finished with a call to repent and walk with God, some of the people wept while others walked off, scowling.

"We have sinned," one man said, and those surrounding him nodded in agreement. "What should we do to walk with God?"

"Keep the sacrifices," Enoch said. "Pray. Tell God you are sorry for the things you have said and done against Him. Surely His mercies are great." He walked among those who remained, giving them advice and comfort. "Jabril can give you instructions on how to keep the sacrifices," he said as the sun climbed higher in the sky. "I must hurry and tell the others lest judgment come sooner than we anticipated."

The group of those whose hearts had softened surrounded Jabril while Adam and Seth told him a quick farewell. Enoch was already two steps ahead of them, walking toward the city gate. Once outside it, he turned west, where another of Adam's sons had gone to build a city for himself.

"I think they reacted well," Seth said as he and Adam caught up to Enoch. "Many seemed to want to walk with God."

Enoch nodded. "So it would seem. Let us hope they did not simply have a quick attack of conscience but not a heart change toward the Lord. There is a profound difference."

Enoch was right. Jabril's city was the one Adam had thought would all turn to God in repentance and faith. But only some came, and how long would their faith last? When the others continued in their revelry and sin, would those convicted of their sin remain true to the Creator?

If Jabril's city was already so caught up in the ways of the world and not of God, what would they find in the next one? Or in Cain's, where they already wondered if even one relative still believed? Suddenly, coming judgment did not seem as urgent as it did frightening. Adam could not bear to think that his descendants would suffer God's wrath rather than His redemption.

"Why do you come to visit us, oh persecutor of men?"

The voice came from a man who stood half again as tall as Adam. The sun had reached its midpoint, and Enoch stood in front of them at the gate, gazing up at the giant.

Adam's stomach dipped. So the Nephilim had also infiltrated the city of Nachom, descendant of Jabril. Was this why Jabril had been so hesitant to have Enoch preach in his own town?

"You are no man," Enoch declared loud enough to be heard beyond the city gate. "I call on Nachom, descendant of Jabril, to open the gate and let us enter!"

The giant laughed. "You will not enter here. Nachom does what we tell him to do, and he will not listen to you."

"Let me speak to him," Enoch insisted.

The giant scowled. "You cannot tell me what to do."

"I can in the name of the Lord Almighty, who is coming to judge the world. I will speak to this city now."

Enoch did not flinch or move even though the giant shouted curses on him and paced the area behind the gate, which he towered above.

"Listen! The Lord is coming with countless thousands of His holy ones to execute judgment on the people of the world. He will convict every person of all the ungodly things they have done and for all the insults that ungodly sinners have spoken against Him," Enoch shouted over and over again.

His voice carried louder than the curses of the giant, which could only be an act of God. Only Adonai could give a man the ability to preach from beyond the walls and actually be heard.

Adam listened in silence to Enoch's repeated warnings and the giant's vile curses. The men of the city appeared above the wall and seemed to be straining to hear over the giant's noise.

Enoch turned away from the giant and walked the length of the wall, his voice clear as he shouted, "Get rid of the giants among you and any offspring of demons and women. God will judge the earth for this vileness. Repent of your acceptance of these creatures of hell and return to the Lord who made you. Sacrifice right sacrifices to God, and do what pleases Him." He turned and walked the other direction. "He has shown you, oh mortal, what is good. And what does the Lord require of you? To act justly and to love mercy and to walk humbly with your God."

Enoch paused, looking into the many faces gazing down at him. "But you do not do what pleases God. You have spoken defiant words against Him and done all manner of evil things He did not create you to do." He drew a deep breath and gave one last shout. "Repent! Judgment is coming if you don't."

With that, he turned and walked away. Adam and Seth hurried to catch up with him. The sun had begun its slow descent, and they would barely make it home before it set.

"They will not listen," Enoch said once they had walked some distance in silence.

"Perhaps some of them will," Seth said, touching his shoulder. "Only God knows those who will listen and believe and those who won't."

Enoch nodded. "Of course, you are right. But I know in my heart, from those whose eyes bored into mine as I spoke, that they are a hardened city that has embraced the ways of Cain. They have invited the watchers into their town and actually celebrate the giants that have been born to the virgins there. They are proud of their sin."

Adam pondered Enoch's words. How could he know so much from simple glances? Had God given him such discernment that he could read men's thoughts or intentions?

They were proud of their sin? Adam supposed pride was at the forefront of every sin. Pride led every man and woman to think they knew better than God. That they didn't need God. That they were strong enough to handle anything they faced in life. Hadn't that also been the underlying reason he and Eve had tasted the fruit? Had disobeyed God? They'd thought they could disobey and still live the life they had always known. They'd thought any change that might come would be good and make them wise— something they desired more than they desired God.

The memory settled like a heavy weight in his gut. How foolish he had been. He would change the past in a heartbeat if he could. Why had they eaten the fruit?

Now his descendants were parading the giants in their cities and inviting demons to mate with them, dine with them, and live with them. And they were proud of what they had done, if Enoch was right.

How far his race had fallen.

34

Adam took Eve's hand, and they walked through the city gate toward the river. Enoch had visited Cain's city last but had found no welcome there either. And though Seth's remained alert to the watchers and they had diverted the river, Eve still longed for times outside of the city, in a place more like the garden.

"Do you think we are safe here, my husband?" she asked as they walked through the underbrush and listened to the birds twittering and singing and calling high above them in the trees. Their music, all in different tones, soothed her. "I've missed this," she said, gazing up at him.

He stopped, and they looked above them at the spreading oak and then toward the heavens. "None of these are the original birds from the garden." Adam rubbed the back of his neck and leaned closer to the trees as if seeking a better glimpse among the leaves. "I wonder how long a lifespan God has given the animals and the birds and fish of the sea in comparison to us." He looked at her. "And yes, we are safe here."

Eve smiled and squeezed his hand, enjoying the beauty despite the differences from what they once knew. "We have seen many changes in the animals over the years. Many of those that once ate only grasses became predators of other animals after we disobeyed the Creator. But even if they live without becoming another's prey, I doubt they live as long as we do. Perhaps a few hundred years instead of many hundreds as you and I have."

"They seem bigger than they were in the garden." Adam led them toward the river that beckoned. "Have you been back to visit the cherubim again?"

Eve shook her head. "Not since I took Enoch as a boy. I guess I finally decided that I can't bear to look upon them anymore. It's not like I will one day find them gone. God isn't going to change His mind and allow us to eat of the Tree of Life. Not until the Redeemer comes."

Adam nodded, and silence filled the space between them. They reached the water's edge and sat, dangling their feet in the cool water. "I miss so much about that place," he said, admitting to her something she had rarely heard him say. Perhaps they were both growing too inward and reminiscent in their advancing age. "Do you ever wonder what it will be like when we see God again?"

Eve faced him. "All the time. When I'm not worrying about one of our children or their children, of course." She laughed lightly, but she could not hide the distress she felt. "I wish we had taught them better of Adonai right from birth. I regret so many things— our disagreements and arguments with them as they matured. Even now we all seem to find reason to be at odds."

"Enoch's preaching has brought division between the cities, more than there was before, and even here where most of Seth's descendants get along, they can't seem to agree with Enoch's strict devotion to Adonai." Adam intertwined their fingers. "I fear even his wife and children do not understand him. He's been spending more and more time alone in his walks with God."

"He told you this?" She hadn't spoken to Enoch in some time, but she spent more time with his wife and children than she did with him. "I miss our talks."

"I do as well. Since we came back from our visits to the cities, he seems to leave early and return late to his home." Adam ran a hand over his beard. "I wonder . . ."

"I miss God too," Eve said, reading his thoughts. "He seems to spend more time with Enoch than He did with us in the garden. Do you think Enoch will do any more preaching against the watchers, or did he complete his work?" She glanced around, always wondering if the unseen ones were listening to their conversation. But there was no sign of them, and she could not see or sense them.

"I think the unseen ones have left us for now to focus on the other cities, or perhaps to find a new way to break through our defenses. That does not mean we should stop being vigilant, but I do not feel the fear I once did."

"Perhaps the prayers of the elders are keeping them away," she said, wiggling her toes in the water, breathing deeply of the clean air.

Footsteps in the distance caught their attention, and they pulled their feet from the water and stood.

"Abba." Seth hurried to them, out of breath. "You must come. Ima, you as well."

"What's wrong, my son?" Adam pulled on his sandals and Eve did the same.

"Methuselah is very sick. Shira does not know how to help him, and no one has seen Enoch. If Methuselah dies, judgment will come much sooner than we expected. Hurry!"

Eve had rarely seen Seth so rattled. "Tell me what symptoms he has. A cough? Trouble breathing? What?"

"His breathing is labored, he's in pain, and he appears to have been bitten by something."

Eve's heart nearly stopped. Bitten by a snake? A bat? Something that crawled along the ground?

"We should look for the leaves of the velvet bean if it is a bite. The extract can work against the venom." She slowed her steps and searched for leaves of the vine that she'd used among other herbs in healing for years. "There are some herbs drying in our

261

house. Go and gather those as well and have Shira crush them so we can use them in a poultice."

Seth nodded and ran on ahead.

Adam helped her look for a moment until she spotted the leaves. She snatched them from the plant until she had a handful. "Hopefully, this will be enough. I can only hope this works. I don't know what type of bite he's had. We must pray, Adam. This child cannot die yet." They needed more time. More of God's patience toward those who did not believe so they might not perish in His judgment, whatever it might be.

"We will pray," Adam assured her. "Right now, we must meet Seth and Shira. I'm sure God will help you choose the right remedy."

She ran ahead, fear carrying her faster than she'd gone in years. *Please, Adonai, do as Adam said, have mercy, and help us. Don't let Methuselah's time be yet.*

Adam searched outside of Enoch's home and the surrounding area, Seth going in the opposite direction. Eve and Shira were in the house with the sick boy, who had grown far too fast and was nearly the height of a man. One look at the wound had shown the marks of a snakebite, something Eve had learned over the years to treat, depending on the type of snake. The more poisonous ones could kill quickly.

Adam's heart raced as he searched for the scaly reptile, pushing away the foliage surrounding Enoch's home. The beast could be far away by now and have even slithered beneath the city wall.

Seth met him after both of them had covered a large portion of the area. "Do you think we should search the entire city, especially near the trees and foliage?"

Adam looked into an overhanging tree, reminded of the serpent of old, the dragon of the garden who had become a large snake once God cursed him. Yet the devil didn't remain a snake all the time. They weren't looking for a beast as large as he, were they? Would one of the watchers have coerced a snake to bite Methuselah? Was that even possible?

"I think it would be wise to search every part of the city, and let's also call a meeting tonight to have everyone be on the lookout for this creature. There may be more like it. If they've buried eggs in the earth, we could have a problem." Adam tapped the dirt with his walking stick. "But they typically live under rocks and in hidden areas."

"They could live under one of the houses, then, if they burrow below the rock walls." Seth fisted his hands, a sign of his anxiety. "Please, Adonai, show us where they are hiding," he prayed.

Adam prayed the same, only silently.

They walked on, this time searching each house along the outside where a crevice might have formed, allowing a snake to burrow beneath. It was late afternoon when they returned to Enoch's house, defeated.

"How is he?" Adam asked Eve as she met them in the main room.

"Better." She released a long-held breath. "His breathing is normal and the swelling in his leg seems less. Did you find the snake?"

Seth shook his head, and Adam said, "No. We searched the entire town under every rock, even along the outskirts of every house. It probably slipped beneath the wall and has left by now."

"Or we scared it away by all of the noise we were making," Seth said.

"Methuselah was going to gather fruit from one of the trees near the wall. It's possible he climbed the tree." Eve glanced at the room where Shira remained with her son. "Is Enoch back yet?"

Adam looked toward the door. "I have not seen him. I wouldn't know where to look if we tried."

"He'll come home soon." Seth sank onto one of the cushions, and Adam did the same. Eve joined them.

"It's been an exhausting day. If the snake was in the tree, it's likely Methuselah didn't see it," Adam said.

"Unlike the one who made himself very visible in the garden," Eve said, her brow creasing. "I wish Methuselah would have been the one to crush the serpent's head."

"Or Enoch," Seth said, tenting his hands beneath his chin. "I think we are going to have to call that meeting before Enoch returns. People need to be aware. Strange that we haven't seen poisonous snakes enter the city until now."

"Do you think the unseen ones had something to do with this?" Eve asked, looking into Adam's eyes. "Could they have power over the animals and creatures? Would God have given them that ability?"

Adam shrugged. Hadn't he thought the same as they searched? "I suppose it is possible. Or it was simply a snake that found easy prey when Methuselah disturbed him in the tree."

"More likely that's what it was, Ima." Seth stood despite the obvious weariness in his expression. "I'm going to call the people together."

"And I will gather the women to feed us." Eve stood as well.

"I will go to the gate to watch for Enoch. Surely he will return soon," Adam said.

"Send him home as soon as you see him." Eve slipped into the back room while Adam and Seth headed to the door. It was going to be a long night.

Enoch walked along the path between the trees some distance from Seth's city, following Adonai Elohim's light. They came to an opening where the ground was smooth and a log lay on it. Enoch sat, enveloped by the light, and listened as Adonai spoke to him.

Your son Methuselah is sick in bed. He has been bitten by a poisonous snake, but I have given Eve wisdom on how to help him. He will not die yet.

Enoch's heart pounded at the news, but peace quickly followed at Adonai's pronouncement. He would not be forced to bury his son. "Thank You."

When you return home, I want you to make plans to go again and preach to the people in every city and village you find along the way. Some of the people have left the cities since you visited, and they need to hear the message. Do not take anyone with you, as I will be with you each step of the way.

"Will they accept the message?"

Most of them will not. Some of them will follow Me for a time, but their faith will not last. Only Seth's line will remain true to Me. But you must give the others the opportunity to hear the truth before the end comes.

"Will the end come in my lifetime?" Why he wanted to know such a thing, he could not say. But something in him said he did not want to be around when God exacted such judgment.

You will not be here to see My judgment. You will be with Me.

So he would die before it happened. Relief filled him, though another part of him mourned, knowing that few of Saba Adam and Savta Eve's descendants would stay true to Adonai.

The light swirled about him in multifaceted colors, some he had never seen before, shimmering and radiant. How could anyone not love the Creator? It was a question that troubled him often.

I know that you love Me.

"With all of my heart, Lord. You alone are God. You alone are good."

You will be with me where I am.

"When I die, I know I will see You as I cannot see You now."

You will not die.

Enoch stilled, unable to respond. He would not die? Everyone died. It was part of the curse.

Because you have been most faithful to Me, you will escape death. I reserve this gift for a select few. You are the first.

His heart filled with awe and wonder, and he fell to his knees, his face touching the earth. "I am not worthy."

I know. But you are forgiven.

Forgiven. During the sacrifices, sins were forgiven, but he had to repeat the sacrifices over and over. This was a different kind of forgiven. He could sense it.

It is time to return. Your family is seeking you.

He stood, sensing Adonai Elohim's touch on his shoulder. And then He was gone, leaving Enoch alone in the forest without the comfort of the colorful light.

He turned and headed home, led by the light of the fading sun, a light far dimmer than the one he had just enjoyed. How he missed God's presence already! Oh, to be with Him always!

You will not die.

He had actually said that. Enoch had not imagined it. But he could only imagine what God meant. How did one not die?

35

A mixture of conversation filled the central area of the city as Eve took her seat near the front of the crowd. Seth stood in his usual spot a step above them in order to be heard. Enoch had just returned, and Methuselah had greatly improved, almost as if God Himself had healed him. A poultice normally took longer, but Eve sensed that God's hand was on the boy. Perhaps he would have recovered without their help.

Seth raised his hands for quiet as Enoch came and sat beside her. "Greetings, Savta," he whispered in her ear. He patted her hand. "It is good to be home."

She smiled at him. "I'm glad you are back."

"I've called you here for several reasons," Seth said, his voice carrying, silencing all who still talked among themselves. "First, for those who have not heard, Methuselah was bitten by a snake earlier today. Thank the Creator he has greatly improved. But be on the lookout for snakes in trees or under rocks. Now that one has gotten inside the city, we don't want more causing harm."

Murmurs passed through the crowd.

"Has there been a search for their dens?" one man asked.

"Abba and I searched the entire city but found nothing. You are welcome to search as well. In fact, we would ask that you do. It is very possible that we missed something." Seth took a few more questions, then quieted the crowd once more. "Enoch is going to speak to us for a moment," he said, stepping down and motioning Enoch to take his place.

Eve glanced behind her. To her relief, expressions seemed open and the people eager to hear his words.

"Good evening," Enoch said, lifting his arms to the men and women. "I come to you with a message from the Creator." He waited a moment. "He is sending me to speak again to every city and village where men and women reside. I wanted to begin here at home where you know me. I know that most of you accept and follow the ways of Adonai. The sacrifices are kept, and none of the watchers have infiltrated our people. This pleases the Almighty One. But He would warn you to remain diligent. Stay true to Him. Repent of any sins as you commit them. Do not wait for the day of sacrifice to humble yourselves before Him. He is near to those who call on His name, and He will bless you for your obedience."

He took a breath as though waiting to see if there were questions, then continued. "Teach your children the ways of the Lord, and do not give in to the desires of this earth, the things that are passing away. Keep your eyes fixed on the coming Redeemer and hope in Him. Our God will not forsake us if we obey Him."

Silence followed his remark, and a moment later, he stepped down from the raised stone.

Eve stood as Seth dismissed the group and the people returned to their homes. "When will you leave for the other cities?" she asked as Enoch fell into step with her. Shira had remained at home with Methuselah, so Eve walked with Enoch to his house.

"As soon as I can. I will wait until Methuselah is up and working with the others again. But God's message is urgent, so I dare not wait long." He stopped and took her hands. "Savta, you have my deepest thanks for teaching me of Adonai when I was but a child. For taking me to the garden's entrance. I owe my faith to your teaching."

Warmth spread through her. So few of her children had said such things to her. She squeezed Enoch's hands. "It does my heart good to hear you say that, Enoch. You and your family will surely be blessed for your devotion to Adonai. I must admit, I wish I could walk with Him again as you do now. I miss the time we had with Him in the cool of the day in the garden. But I am glad He comes to speak with you. You have a tender heart and a love for Him I don't think I've seen in anyone before or since you came into our family."

Enoch bowed his head, and she kissed his forehead.

"I know God will go with you when you travel," she said, "but do be careful. Evil is not to be trifled with. The devil and his angels are very real, and they know God has His hand on you. For that reason alone, they will want to harm you. Be watchful, my son."

Enoch released her hands, and together they walked on toward his house. "I will be watchful, Savta. I know God is with me. He told me to go alone for that reason. My life is in His hands."

A prick of fear touched Eve's heart when she thought of him going off to these places without Seth and Adam. But if God had told him to go alone, who was she to stop him? Who was she to argue?

"I will pray that you return safely," she said as they reached the house.

"Thank you, Savta Eve. I treasure your prayers."

Enoch came and went to the neighboring and distant cities, and as the years passed, God continued to send him, as though the message could not be spoken often enough.

One morning, Eve met Enoch at the gate as he carried a pack over his back. She had water and food tied to her sash as well. "I want to go with you to Jabril's city," she said at his approach. "I haven't seen Achima or Chania in far too long. Will you take me?"

Enoch rubbed a hand over his beard, searching her face. He

closed his eyes as if praying, then opened them and nodded. "You can stay with them until I return for you," he said. "You are ready?"

"I'm ready." Her heart lightened at the thought of seeing her oldest daughters again. Word had come some time ago that Hasia had gone the way of all the earth, but Achima and Chania still lived, as did Kaelee, Lasaro, Kalix, and Naava. She longed to hold each one close again.

"Saba Adam did not want to come with you?" Enoch asked once they passed through the tree line where the unseen ones sometimes hid.

"Not this time," she said. "He was working on some new project with Seth. He said as long as you were with me, he did not mind me coming."

Enoch's brow furrowed, but he said nothing. Eve did not understand how a project could matter more to Adam than seeing his family, but they were surrounded by family at every turn, so she supposed he did not long for the others the way she did. But he had not given birth to them.

"I have a question for you, Savta," Enoch said, giving her a sidelong glance.

"You always have questions, my son." She laughed softly and touched his arm. "Ask me."

Enoch glanced behind them. "I've noticed that Saba Adam rarely speaks of Cain. If someone happens to mention him, Saba grows silent and his expression is grim."

"Cain killed his brother, Enoch. Saba Adam found Abel's body. You have to know how hard it has been for him. To lose a son so young, and to have him die at the hand of his brother . . ." She swallowed hard. She had forgiven Cain, but she had never stopped missing Abel. Time did not heal a wound such as losing a son whose life had barely begun.

"I know, Savta. I fear only for Saba's spirit. He harbors bitterness, and such feelings do not please Adonai." He stopped to face her. "You know this."

270

Eve took his hand and squeezed. "You have a tender heart, my son, and that is good. Saba Adam loves his children. All of them, including Cain. But he struggles to forgive Cain when he is reminded of Abel or hears of the way Cain's descendants have turned from the Creator. He grows silent because he does not know a better way to handle his anger."

"Forgiveness is not something that happens only one time, Savta. Sometimes one act needs continual forgiveness because the pain still causes us to grow bitter." Enoch turned, her hand still in his, and continued walking. "I hope Saba Adam forgives even if he can never forget."

Eve stared straight ahead, slowly releasing her grip on Enoch. Was Adam causing Adonai grief by bearing his hurt for so long? "Are you suggesting, my son, that God wants us to forgive what He Himself does not forgive? God sent Cain away. He has not forgiven him."

"God would forgive Cain if he repented. Even he is not beyond God's aid. But Saba would do well to forgive Cain even if he is not repentant because God does not want us to harbor hatred in our hearts. It hinders our walk with God, and Cain is not bothered in the least by Saba's unforgiveness. So Saba hurts himself, not Cain." Enoch pushed his walking stick into the earth as Eve pondered his words.

"Have you spoken to Saba about this?" she asked, recalling her conversations with Adam. Would he listen to Enoch over her?

"Once or twice. He does not like to talk about it." The gate to Jabril's city approached, and Enoch touched Eve's shoulder. "I will pray for him. I hope he can release his anger toward Cain. God will deal with Cain one day, but Saba would not want God troubled by his attitude. It is wrong to hate another made in God's image, no matter what they've done."

"You have learned much in your walks with God," Eve said as they stopped at the gate and knocked.

"There is much I have yet to understand," he said.

The gate opened to them, and they entered.

Jabril met them. "Ima! How did you know we needed you?" He glanced at Enoch.

"Needed me?" Eve searched Jabril's face. "What's wrong?"

"I was about to send word for you, but things have happened so fast. Achima is not well. You must hurry to Chania and see if you can help her." He faced Enoch. "You are here to speak to the people?"

"Yes," Enoch said as Eve left them.

The sound of the horn startled her as it called the people to gather and hear Enoch's words. But she rushed through the unfamiliar streets toward Chania's house, her heart pounding. *Oh, Adonai, not Achima.* She couldn't bear to lose another.

36

I ma," Chania said, holding Eve tight the moment she'd found the right house and knocked on the door. "How did you know to come?"

Eve took a step back and searched Chania's face. "I didn't *know* to come. I just missed all of you. But Jabril told me that Achima is not well."

"Achima is failing, Ima. I am so glad you are here."

"Failing? It's that bad then?" She looked into Chania's stricken face and saw her nod. "Take me to her."

Chania led the way to a house nearby, where several younger women had congregated. She pushed past the daughters and granddaughters of Achima and Jabril until she found Achima on a pallet in an inner room.

Eve knelt at her daughter's side and took her limp hand. She did not stir. "How long has she been like this?" Eve asked, meeting Chania's worried gaze.

"Several days. We thought she would improve, but then Jabril was ready to send for you because she did not. She cannot eat and does not wake." Tears filled Chania's eyes. This daughter had always been so giving and so close to Achima.

"How did it happen?" Eve had seen a few people besides Abel pass into the next life, but not like this. Usually an accident—a fall or an altercation with a wild beast—caused their death, despite the care they took to avoid such things.

"She just didn't awaken one morning. Jabril found her still abed when he awoke, which was not normal, and tried to wake her but couldn't. She still breathes, for you can see her chest rise and fall, but she does not open her eyes or eat or speak. Is there anything we can do for her, Ima?" Chania's voice wavered.

Eve studied Achima's prone form, lifted the covering, and looked her over for any signs of a bite or infection, but found nothing. "I don't know," she said at last. "Something struck her in the night. Something internal that we cannot see."

"So there is nothing we can do?"

A sob rose in Eve's chest, and Chania wept. Eve looked at her firstborn daughter, remembering the little girl who had cared for her younger siblings. Who had married Abel and was so distraught at his death. Who had married Jabril and followed the instructions of the Creator even when they moved away.

"We can pray," Eve said softly. "But I do not know what we can possibly do other than that."

"I've been praying since it happened, Ima. Jabril has too, but nothing has changed. Why does God not answer our prayers?"

It was a question Eve asked herself often. Yet why *should* God answer their prayers? They had no reason to hope they deserved anything from Him after all the sin that roamed freely on the earth. His judgment was coming. Why should He care about the life of one creature whose time might have come?

And yet, a child should not die before the one who bore her. Hadn't she felt the same way with Abel? To lose a distant descendant was hard, but to lose one she had carried in her womb was far different.

"God doesn't answer yes to all of our prayers, Chania. Certainly He has never given in to my requests to undo the past and return to the garden. But then, what we did was irreparable until the Redeemer comes."

"But she can't leave us yet. She's still young!" Chania dipped a cloth in a bowl, then placed it on Achima's forehead. "I need to do something, Ima. Can't we make God see that we still need her?"

Eve released a deep sigh. "We cannot *make* the Creator do anything we might want Him to do, my daughter. You know that. He is the Almighty, and we cannot control Him. We can humbly ask things of Him, but He has the right to deny our requests."

Chania's tears fell again, and she knelt at Achima's side and laid her head on her sister's chest. "Please don't leave us," she whispered.

Eve's own tears came then, and her heart cried out the same words. But she knew that if Achima was to wake, God would have to awaken her. There was nothing they could do to help her.

Eve stayed an extra week. Enoch took word to Adam, who quickly joined her, keeping vigil at their daughter's bedside. Jabril seemed too stricken to rise and constantly sat with his head in his hands. On the seventh day, Achima stopped breathing, and the entire city fell into mourning.

A cave not far from the city had already been secured, and for the second time in her life, Eve walked with her family to bury one of her children. She hadn't even gotten the chance to say goodbye, for Achima had not responded to anything said to her. Had she heard the many words Jabril and their children had spoken to her? Had she heard Eve and Adam when they told her of their love?

There was no way of knowing. The smallest hint of gratitude filled Eve that she had been here, for over the years she had seen so little of Hasia. To be here for Achima and to know she had been spared the coming judgment brought Eve the slightest bit of comfort.

They came to the cave, and Jabril's sons rolled a large stone from the entrance. Some of the young men, grandsons of Jabril and Achima, carried Achima's body into the cave, and Jabril wept as the stone closed her in.

Eve swayed, the grief too strong to hold in. She wept as they walked back to the city. Adam held her tightly against him, as though he feared he might lose her as well. Each family group supported another, and soon the town gathered to weep and eat and finally celebrate Achima's life.

Adam rose to speak, telling everyone what a wonderful daughter she had been, but emotion was too close to Eve's heart to allow her to say a word without tears.

They slept in Jabril's home that night before the trek home the next day and tried to comfort their grieving son. But Jabril would not be comforted.

"Why did God let her die before me, Abba?" he asked. "Why were our prayers in vain?"

His plaintive cry pierced Eve's heart every time she thought on it on the way home, and throughout the days to come.

Why hadn't God heard their desperate cries to spare Achima? Eve knew she would never be able to answer that question.

Adam walked with Seth outside of the city, inspecting the wall and checking on the men tending to the flocks and fields. "The wall remains sturdy," Adam said as he placed one hand against the stones. "Despite the years, I see no obvious crumbling."

Seth bent to look at the base of this last section of wall. He straightened. "You are right. So far, God has kept our city safe and our wall intact." He turned and pointed toward the pastureland. "Shall we?"

Adam nodded and fell into step with him.

"Ruel is with his great-grandsons in the fields with the sheep and goats today," Seth said. "It would be good to see if they are left at peace or if the animals notice the unseen ones. They can be more attentive than we are." He glanced at Adam. "Even the donkeys grow fearful when the unseen ones are near."

"I have not seen one in years," Adam admitted, not sure whether to be grateful or to wonder why his ability to see the unseen realm had dimmed. God had not spoken to him in visions or dreams in some time either. Eve would say the problem was with him, not with God, but he tended to resist her suggestions or advice. Was she right?

"I think they are staying away because of Enoch," Seth said, interrupting his thoughts. "God walks with Enoch, and I doubt they would come near when God is present."

Adam rubbed his tense shoulder and continued walking. "You are probably right." He sensed that his own heart was not where it should be. Was a sacrifice needed to restore his lost relationship with Adonai?

But was it lost? Or had he simply outgrown the visions and dreams of long ago when he'd needed them more?

They come less often when you think of Cain.

He tried to ignore the thought, pushing it down as he always did when thoughts of Cain surfaced. He could not dwell on what had happened generations ago. Cain had suffered for his choices and his unwillingness to repent. It was no business of Adam's any longer.

But the twinge of anger still surfaced.

"What has you so quiet, Abba? Something surely troubles you." Seth glanced at him as the flocks came into view.

"I was thinking of things I should be able to forget by now. Things I think I have forgiven but that rise up again when I least expect them." He lifted his hands. "The thoughts come and haunt me, but then they disappear. I just had a memory that I didn't want."

Seth stopped walking to face him. "I've never known you to remain unforgiving with any of us."

"With you and your family, I am not angry," Adam said. "It is something that happened before you were born that rises up to haunt my memories."

Seth tilted his head and searched Adam's face. "This has to do with Cain, doesn't it?"

Adam glanced beyond Seth. "Did your mother tell you this?" Could he not trust his wife to keep his admissions to herself?

"No, Abba. Enoch sensed it and mentioned it to me. He worries about you." Seth placed a hand on Adam's shoulder. "Cain has not sought forgiveness, so you have felt no need to release him of his guilt."

"God Himself does not forgive us if we are unrepentant, my son. I have repented of my anger toward Cain, but sometimes the memories take me back to that day when I found Abel in the woods." He searched Seth's face, reading understanding in his son's expression. "Your mother feels compassion for Cain, but even on our visits to him, I simply cannot."

Seth's hand fell to his side, and he shifted his weight to the other foot. "I must say, I am grateful that Ima loves us no matter what we do or say, even when we hurt her. But I understand why you do not see things the same way. Enoch sensed that you struggle, so he mentioned it to me."

"I appreciate your concern, my son. But I do not hate Cain. He is my son. I simply cannot understand how he could have done such a thing and how he could choose to walk away and stay away from the Creator all these years. It is as though we gave life to an evil man. What could have possibly led him to such jealousy against his brother? Perhaps it was something we did . . ."

Seth's brow lifted. "Neither of you are to blame for our foolish actions or choices, Abba. God gave each one of us the ability to choose to obey Him or to disobey. Cain chose to disobey."

Adam rubbed the back of his neck. "You are right. But if we had not introduced you to sin, life would have been very different. I fear your father is flawed and foolish and has many regrets."

Seth's expression softened, and he slowly smiled. "My father

278

is an honest man who is like every one of us. I am glad you told me. I will not repeat your words. But I do hope you can let God deal with Cain. I think He already has."

Adam patted Seth's back as they continued walking toward the sheep. "Thank you, my son. I will talk with Adonai again and confess my inability to let this go. Perhaps He will help me to do what I cannot seem to do on my own."

37

E
ve awakened at dawn after a restless night of sleep. The cushions that she had remade only a few years ago did not seem to keep her body from aching, something she could not get used to. All her long life she had felt youthful and vigorous and rarely felt pain unless she cut herself while cooking or crafting something new or was delivering a child. So this waking in pain where every bone and joint ached troubled her. Was her body finally coming to that point where she would return to dust as God had said?

She discarded the thought as she stiffly rose. She moved from her mat to the pegs where her day clothes hung, slowly pulled off one tunic, and exchanged it for another. Relief filled her as the aches lessened. Perhaps she just needed to make a thicker cushion.

She walked to the door of the house, not surprised that Adam had already left, grabbed the jar that sat by the door, and lifted it to her shoulder. The walk to the well at the center of town invigorated her as she breathed in the morning air. Other women soon began to make the walk from their homes, and Eve smiled. It was good to have her daughters and descendants gather each morn, to talk and plan the work for the day.

Shira greeted her as she reached the well and waited her turn with the rope to lower her jar.

"Savta Eve, did you happen to see Enoch this morning?" Shira's face was pale and her wide eyes held worry. "He did not come home last night."

Eve studied Shira, thinking to reassure her. Hadn't Enoch often been late in returning? But something in her spirit and in Shira's eyes made her stomach dip with an unusual sense of fear. "When did you last see him? Didn't he say he was going to visit the cities again to preach to them?"

Shira nodded. "Yes, but that was weeks ago. He returned and then went out again to walk with God. I thought he would return last evening, but he was not in our bed this morning, and I never heard him come home."

"But he could have come home and left again without telling you, couldn't he?"

"He's never left without telling me. I don't know if he ever came home." She glanced about, and Eve noticed the women had gathered around and were listening.

"Should we send someone to look for him?" Tehila asked, coming up beside Shira. "Ruel would go, and I'm sure Seth and Abba and our sons would search if you are worried."

Shira looked at Eve, uncertainty in her eyes. "I don't know. Perhaps he will return today."

"You don't think the unseen ones could have captured him, do you?" Devora asked.

Eve turned to look at her. "Let's not try to guess what happened and cause more fear than we already feel." She set her jar on the ground. "I will find Adam and Seth and ask them if they have heard from Enoch. They talk to him often enough. They might know."

"I want to go with you," Shira said, leaving her jar behind as well.

"We will wait here, Ima. Please return and let us know," Tehila said.

Eve and Shira hurried toward the gate where the men usually

281

sat to discuss the business of the city before they were called to the morning meal.

"Ima, is something wrong?" Seth stood and walked toward her, Adam at his side.

"What is it, Eve?" Adam held her gaze, and she knew he could read her fear.

"When was the last time you spoke to Enoch?" Eve asked. Shira stood beside her, and Eve placed an arm around her. "He did not return home last night, and we are concerned."

Adam's thick brows drew down, and he glanced at Seth.

"He returned from his preaching a week ago, but the other day he left to walk with God," Seth said. "It was near evening when he told me he was going out to meet with God, but I went home before he returned."

"I did not see him go or come," Adam said. "When did you say he left?" He faced Seth.

Seth stroked his beard. "It wasn't yesterday, so it had to be the day before."

Shira clutched her arms, visibly shaken. "That is when he told me he was going to be late, but when he didn't return that day, I assumed he got delayed longer than he expected. But when he didn't arrive by this morning, I began to worry. It's not like him to stay away without telling me. You don't think he ran into one of the watchers or a wild beast, do you? He could be hurt!"

Eve searched Adam's face, and though he hid his fear well, he could not keep it from her. He would be remembering Abel all over again. But no one would have hurt Enoch, would they?

"Seth and I and Ruel and some of the others will set out to look for him," Adam said.

They started down the steps, but Eve stopped them. "At least take something to eat with you on the way. You will miss the morning meal."

"There are fruit trees and nuts to be found as we search," Adam said, hurrying after Seth and Ruel.

Eve watched them go. Ten men filed through the gate in search of Enoch. Memories of the search for Abel rose to the surface, and she nearly stumbled as she walked with Shira back to the well where the women waited.

Please, Adonai, don't let them carry Enoch's bloodied body back to us as Adam once carried Abel's. Let them find him in his right mind and in one piece. But let them find him, please!

Adam's heart pounded as the men moved away from the city toward the places where Enoch walked with God. They searched in groups of two, and Seth's presence with him brought a small amount of comfort. But his mind whirled with memories of long before Seth was born.

Would they find Enoch's body as he had found Abel's? Perhaps someone had killed him for his constant preaching against evil and sin. Or one of the unseen ones had captured him and hurt him somehow. Yet wouldn't God have protected His prophet?

Adam's breath came hard as they passed through the trees, searching for signs of blood or the wispy light of the watchers. Was the devil laughing at the pain in his heart? Could the enemy possibly know what this search was doing to him?

Is this because I can't completely forgive Cain?

But he'd tried. Since his talk with Seth, he had asked God to help him, and he had some measure of peace because of it. Why did forgiveness need to be offered over and over, every time the memory brought pain?

"Do you know where else Enoch might have gone? Where God might have led him, Abba?" Seth had stopped walking at the end of the forest and looked at Adam. "I don't want to overlap where the other men are looking, but would the Creator have led him to a cave? Would he have returned to the garden? I know Ima took him there as a child."

Adam lifted his hands in a defeated gesture. "I have no idea.

The garden is possible. But the cherubim would not have allowed him entrance. And I'm not even sure I could find the garden again. Your ima is the one who visited often. I couldn't bear to return to the place where everything changed."

"But surely you could find it if we walked in that direction. Or should we get Ima to help us?" Seth's look held the same fear Adam felt.

"I think I can find it without Ima's help. She would take us, but every step would cause her to fear that we will find Enoch as I once found Abel."

Adam turned and headed west toward Eden. Did the garden still exist? Would Enoch have come here as Eve had? Would God have allowed him in?

The thought troubled him in a way he didn't expect. Of course God would not have allowed Enoch entrance. By now He could have destroyed any evidence of the garden without them even knowing it. If the Creator could speak the world into existence, nothing was too hard for Him. He could remove the garden and carry it to the heavens, or simply remove the Tree of Life and make the garden like any other place on earth.

"You are quiet, Abba," Seth said as they looked under bushes and in the shadows for some sign of Enoch.

"The garden is farther away than I remembered." Adam stopped after they had walked long past the place where he thought it stood. "It's not here," he said, facing Seth. "If it is here, the cherubim are not."

"Are you sure this is the place?" Seth glanced about them.

They had traveled so long, nothing seemed familiar. "Maybe we should get your ima," Adam said. The thought sent a feeling of defeat through him, but he had to be sure. Perhaps her memory about this was better than his.

Eve and Shira met the men as they returned in groups of two. "Anything?" Shira asked each one.

"He wasn't in any of the caves above the city," Ruel's group told her.

"We went halfway to Jabril's city but found nothing," said another.

"He wasn't headed toward Cain's city either. If he was, there is no sign of him," the third group said.

"We searched all the way to the river and followed it for a distance. Unless he fell in and got caught under a fallen tree or some rocks, he wasn't there," the fourth group said.

"Abba and I tried to find the garden, Ima," Seth said, coming at the last. "Abba couldn't find it in the place where it should have been. We thought perhaps you might recall where it is better than any of us do since you have returned to it most often."

Eve stepped forward. "I will take you there." Her pace quickened with the beat of her heart.

Shira followed. "I want to come."

Eve looked at her, then at Adam and Seth. At their shrugs, Eve nodded. They walked through the gate with her leading the way. How long it had been since she had held Enoch's hand and led him to see the cherubim with the flaming sword. Would she find things as they had been then? She hadn't returned in years. But her heart was certain it knew the way.

Shira came alongside her and slipped her arm through Eve's.

"You're trembling." Eve stroked Shira's hand. "Perhaps you would feel better if you waited in the city?"

Shira shook her head. "I want to know. I want to see the place Enoch talked about, and if he is there . . . even if it is just his broken body, I want to find him."

Eve tilted her head to better read Shira's expression. "You are braver than I expected."

"Not brave, Savta. Afraid."

Shira tightened her grip on Eve's arm as they searched for the unseen ones or evidence of Enoch's body. A garment or a piece of his belt or sandal. Something. *Not blood. Please not blood.*

They walked the distance Eve knew so well and came to the place where the cherubim had always stopped her. But no flaming sword guarded the entrance, no holy one of God. It was overgrown with briars and brambles. Had God abandoned this place? What was it like beyond the entrance?

"This is it," she said, looking at Adam. "Did you bring something to cut away these thorny bushes?"

"The cherubim are gone," he said, looking as surprised as she was. "No wonder I walked past it. It's not the same at all."

"Perhaps it is on the other side of these thorns." She looked to Seth, who pulled a blade from his belt to cut away the bushes. Adam and Ruel helped him, and soon there was a path that led into Eden. Or what used to be Eden.

Eve stepped carefully through the opening they had created, Shira following, and joined the men inside. Nothing looked as it had those long ago years. The grass had grown tall, still watered by the mist. Seth and Ruel swung their blades to make a walkable path farther toward the center of the garden.

"This is where we used to walk with Adonai," Eve said, looking up at one of the fig trees where she had taken leaves to first cover herself.

Memories flooded her. She pushed beyond the many fruit trees they had been given for food, looking for the two trees that had occupied her thinking for years after their banishment from this place. She stopped when she reached the Tree of the Knowledge of Good and Evil. It still stood, and when she glanced to the side of it, she could almost see the shining, scaly serpent angel beckoning her forward.

"It's gone." Adam's words behind her startled her. She glanced behind her, and he pointed to where the Tree of Life once stood. "God took it away." He placed a hand over his forehead and squinted as though his eyes deceived him.

"No wonder the cherubim are gone. Once the tree was removed, there was no need to keep us out." Eve walked slowly to the place where the tree had brimmed with different luscious fruit each month, its leaves green and its scent strong and clean and full of life. "I wonder where it went."

"Perhaps God took it to His home in the heavens," Adam said, joining her. Shira had remained behind with Seth and Ruel, all staring at the tree that had caused their parents' downfall. The tree they should have run from rather than walked to.

"Perhaps. I wonder if God would tell us if we asked. Should we also ask Him where Enoch has gone? It seems as though you have looked everywhere. If he is in the garden, wouldn't he have made a path before we got here? This place looks undisturbed."

Adam's hand rested on her shoulder. "Unless God brought him here without need of making a path." He rubbed the back of his neck.

"Yes, but wouldn't we see footprints at least? I see nothing out of place, just overgrown." Eve brushed a strand of hair from his eyes. "This brings back so many memories."

He nodded.

Adonai, where is Enoch? And where did You put the Tree of Life?

If she and Adam wouldn't pray together, she could at least pray on her own. She looked far and wide from where they stood.

Seth approached them. "I think we should look throughout the entire garden. Abba, will you lead us?"

Adam nodded again. "Yes." He took Eve's hand, pulling her along with him. If he forgot something, she might remember it.

They spent the next few hours searching the tall grasses, the rivers that met and meandered through the garden, the places where they used to find privacy though none was needed, and at last the place where they had hidden from God.

"He must not have come in here," Seth said when they ended up back at the entrance. "I don't know where else to look, Abba."

Eve glanced from her husband to her sons. "I have asked God to show us where he is. I think we should return to the city and call the men and women to pray. Perhaps God will speak to one of us in a vision or dream as we sleep. But if we don't ask Him, we won't know."

Ruel agreed. "I think Ima has a good point. Unless Enoch left to stay in another city or was captured and taken somewhere by the unseen ones, we will never know. God knows. We should ask Him."

Adam led the way back through the entrance they had carved, and the group walked in silence toward the city.

38

Enoch followed Adonai Elohim to the entrance of the garden, where Savta Eve had taken him as a young boy. The cherubim greeted him and bowed to Adonai Elohim, then disappeared. Adonai Elohim moved into the garden and spoke to the briars and brambles to cover the entrance behind them.

Their feet glided between the tall grasses, leaving no trace of footprints, and Enoch watched in awe as the Creator transformed the overgrown garden into exactly how Savta Eve had described it to him. Animals scampered along the ground and came to Adonai Elohim, seeking His touch. He pulled a piece of fruit from an apricot tree and offered it to Enoch.

Enoch tasted the fruit and smiled. Nothing outside of this garden tasted as good.

He moved with Adonai Elohim throughout Eden until he'd been shown every part of what used to be. At last they came to the center of the garden where the two infamous trees stood. The Tree of Life glimmered in Adonai Elohim's glow.

Adonai Elohim took hold of the tree with one hand and Enoch's hand with the other, and in an instant Enoch was transported above the earth and ushered into the presence of the Almighty Ancient of Days. From the throne, light flashed and thunder rumbled.

Seven lamps of fire burned before the throne, and a crystal sea spread out from the throne and beyond where Enoch stood. As he gazed about, he saw that Adonai Elohim had placed the Tree of Life on either side of the river. Had the one tree become two?

He turned around to gaze on the glittering, glorious throne again and saw four living creatures floating about with eyes covering them in front and behind. One was like a lion, another like a calf, the third like a man, and the fourth like a flying eagle. Each one had six wings full of eyes.

"Holy, holy, holy is the Lord God, the Almighty, who was and who is and who is to come," they cried continuously.

Enoch watched them, mesmerized, unable to take it all in. He looked down at his own body, exploring his arms and legs with both hands. Did he look the same? He could tell this body was purer, healthier. When he took a step, he hovered, as if there was nothing to hold him to the surface beneath him. His body had changed, but he was still Enoch.

He looked into Adonai Elohim's fiery gaze. "I am not the same. What has happened?"

"Did I not tell you that you would not die?"

Enoch nodded. But he had not known what Adonai Elohim had meant. "I will not be returning to earth, will I?"

"No." Adonai Elohim offered his hand, and Enoch took it. He led Enoch throughout the golden city, showing him jeweled buildings and lush gardens rich with flowering plants and bulging fruit.

Angels floated rather than walked along the golden streets, and Adonai Elohim introduced him to the archangels Michael and Gabriel. Enoch sensed that in time he would come to know the names of each one of the millions of angels who moved in and around the city.

The throne room of the Ancient of Days, where the council of God met, grew quiet at his approach. He bowed low before the great King, the Creator. Adonai Elohim touched his shoulder, and he stood again, facing the Ancient of Days, Lord God Almighty.

The Spirit floated about the room in ribbons of color and yet held a form Enoch could not quite describe. The Three in One spoke among themselves and gazed upon Enoch as they spoke words he could not comprehend. But the intensity of the love directed at him made his knees weak, and he felt a deep longing to weep. No love on earth compared to this. No human relationship came close to this.

Thank You. He knew they understood his thoughts, and he could not bring himself to speak aloud. To be transported to this place without first passing through the shadow of death—he knew no other human had done so. Why had he been given such a privilege?

And what of Shira and his family? Would they know what had happened to him? He could imagine Shira frantic with worry. *Please assure her I am with You.*

Adonai Elohim stood before him and cupped his face. "She will know. There are no fears or reason for tears here."

Enoch nodded, overcome. A moment later, he was embraced by the Creator. Tears did come then, for his family, who would surely miss him. But each one was wiped away by Adonai Elohim's celestial hands.

"Come. I have a few humans I want you to meet." Adonai Elohim led Enoch to another part of the city, where he saw three people, two of whom he had met.

"Achima, Hasia," he said. He glided toward them and embraced each one. He looked at the third person, and though he'd never seen him before, he knew him. "You are Abel, whom Cain killed."

"Yes." Abel beamed, his smile lighting his entire countenance. "While I would not have wanted Achima to lose me so soon," he said, looking at the woman who had once been his wife, "there is no place like this in the universe God has created. I have been here a long time, and yet it feels as though I just arrived."

Enoch glanced behind him at Adonai Elohim, who smiled His approval.

"Death is just the doorway to be with God," Abel said, drawing his attention again. "If we believe in Him and worship Him on earth, then when death comes, He takes us to be with Himself. I've been waiting a long time for others to join me here."

"That's right. You were the first," Enoch said, wondering what that must have been like for him.

"I actually felt quite privileged to have all of this and be the only human among all of God's mighty ones. And better yet, the only human in perfect fellowship with God Himself." Abel stepped forward to embrace Enoch. "There is so much to show you."

Enoch did not want to leave the Creator's side, but Adonai Elohim assured him that he would never be without immediate access to Him again.

Reassured and still feeling the change in his body and mind, he went with Abel, Achima, and Hasia to explore the vast city. They had so much to talk about! He supposed as more people joined them, all the years of eternity would never grow tiresome or boring.

His step lightened as he learned that he could walk or glide or even lift up off the streets and hover in the pure air. He would never stop being grateful for this amazing transformation.

Adam awoke with a start, heart pounding, sweat beading his brow. He sat up and took a deep breath. The dream came again into his mind's eye, and he blinked twice, trying to be sure that God had given it to him.

Eve stirred at his side and opened her eyes. "Is it morning already?" She sounded groggy, but she sat up and faced him. "You've had a dream."

He nodded. "Yes."

"Just like you did when you knew where to look for Abel."

"Yes . . . and no."

"No?" She reached for the lamp and held it between them.

"What do you mean, no? It's either yes, you know where he is, or no, you don't. How can it be both?"

"I know where he is, but we cannot go to him. We will not find his body as we did Abel's." Adam ran his hands down his face, still trying to reenact the vision of the heavens. "Enoch did not die, Eve." He took her hand. "God took him straight to His kingdom in heaven. I saw him there with Abel and Achima and Hasia."

"Hasia was there?" The joy in Eve's voice matched his own feelings. "I was certain she would be condemned along with Cain."

"I have a feeling each person is responsible for their own sin. A wife is not condemned for the choices of her husband or her children." He smiled, still seeing the joy emanating from their faces and the brilliant light he'd long forgotten. "They are with God in a place like we used to see when He allowed us into the council chamber with the angels, before the unseen ones fell and evil entered the world. Even now my heart pounds with longing to return there. How blessed Enoch was to be taken and miss death." He released a long-held breath and briefly closed his eyes. But the memory of that place had already faded.

"Taken without death. I would not have thought God would ever do such a thing. Not after the curse." Eve yawned, though Adam wondered if either one of them would sleep again that night. "I wish we could all escape death and had never brought it upon our children. I have always felt unworthy of God's love, like I continually fail Him."

Adam studied her. "I would not have guessed you thought this way. You have always spoken of how you miss Him and our time with Him in the garden."

"I knew He loved me then. I could sense it every time He looked at me. He knew me. He wanted me. And then I pushed Him away because I didn't want to do what He said." She cupped the lamp in both hands, looking at the flame.

"I don't think He ever stopped loving us, Eve. We disappointed Him and hurt Him by our actions, but I don't think He can stop loving us. It is a part of His nature." Adam wasn't sure how he knew that, but he'd seen it in the Creator's actions from the day he was made.

"It's one thing to know something in your head and another to believe it in your heart." She met his gaze. "I don't deserve His love, whether He offers it or not."

"None of us do, beloved."

Her eyes widened. "You've never called me that."

"And I don't tell you I love you often enough either." He took the lamp from her hands and set it aside, then pulled her close. "One day you will believe that God still loves you. For now, be happy for Enoch and in the knowledge that death is not the end. Those who trust God will be with Him again."

"It is a comforting thought," she said, resting her head against his shoulder. "Shira will miss him though."

"Yes, as will his children. Perhaps she will marry again, as Achima did."

"She will enjoy her grandchildren and helping her daughters in the meantime." Eve yawned again, and Adam chuckled.

"Perhaps we should try to get a little more sleep. It is too early to wake the others and tell them the news." He pulled her down beside him and listened as her breathing grew even. But all he could think about was the beauty of Adonai's city and the day when he would be with the Creator again.

Morning came too soon. Eve woke with a start, but her heart felt light. Adam rose with her, and despite the aches that apparently came with aging, she fairly jumped as she stood.

"I don't know if it is simply because you told me your dream, but in the night, God also showed me where Enoch is." She took his hands and did a little dance. "Oh, Adam, it is such a beautiful place! Better than Eden."

He laughed. "Yes, it is. I'm glad you saw it too."

"We must hurry and tell the others before Shira sends her sons to search for their father. She won't rest until she knows." Eve donned her sandals and pulled a robe about her.

Adam did the same, and together they half ran to Shira's house, stopping to get Seth along the way.

"We have both been given a dream from Adonai," Adam said to him. "We will tell Shira first, but then the entire city must know."

Shira ushered them inside the moment they knocked. "What is it? Did someone find him?" she asked.

"The Lord spoke to us in our dreams last night," Adam said, looking from one to another. "He showed us His heavenly home, and we saw Enoch and Abel and Achima and Hasia there. Enoch did not die, so we will not find his body. God took him straight to heaven without death."

"How can this be?" Seth rubbed his chin. "Such a thing has never happened. Are you sure the dream came from the Lord?"

Adam nodded. "God has spoken to me many times over the years in visions and dreams. This was like that and yet completely different. I knew in my heart that Enoch had been taken the moment I saw him there with the Lord."

Shira sank to her knees, one hand covering her heart. "Enoch is gone?" She wept and then laughed, as if she couldn't decide how to feel. "I will never see him again, and yet I cannot say goodbye because his body was taken by God?"

"Yes," Eve said, kneeling beside her. "He walked with God, and God took him. He will never have to suffer again in this life, and he fulfilled what God called him to do. We will miss him, but we know that if we trust our Creator, we will see him again one day."

Shira clung to Eve and wept again, and Eve felt her own tears rise to the surface. She would miss Enoch's greetings and their long talks about Adonai, but she couldn't wish him back to this earth. She didn't want him to put up with preaching against evil to people who did not listen or to be in danger of the watchers any longer. He obviously was not the Redeemer God had promised, but perhaps his transport to heaven was a taste of good to come. Perhaps others would please Adonai so much that they, too, would escape death. She could only hope.

More than that, she hoped one day she felt worthy in His presence. Not because of anything she had done but because He truly loved her. Like He obviously did Enoch.

Was Adam right? Did God love every one of them? Even Cain? Was it possible that God would never stop loving them, despite what they did to hurt Him?

39

Eve rose from her bed, gripped the stick Adam had made for her, and slowly stood, grateful that the pain eased and the muscles loosened with each step. How old was she now? She could not remember how long it had been since her creation.

In the years since Enoch had gone to the heavens, Eve's heart no longer cared for the things of earth. She pined for God.

She left the house and moved to the central courtyard, where the women ground the grain and cooked the flatbread. Large clay bowls of date honey and fruit lay on a large rock, and she sat down nearby and set her walking stick on the ground beside her.

After dipping the flatbread into the honey, Eve chose a pear to eat with her food. She sat opposite the women, who no longer expected her to help them. She was not sure she could rise from the ground if she sat over a grinding stone so long.

"Ima," Tehila said, bringing her own fruit and flatbread to sit beside Eve. "I was hoping you would be here."

Eve chuckled. "Where else would I go, my daughter? There is so little I can do to help anymore, but at least I can eat."

Tehila smiled, her own eyes showing the lines of age. "They won't let me help either. I never thought my life would come to this. I thought Devora would remain with us until I pass from this life. But now she has married and moved to begin their own city. How many cities do we need, Ima? Was it hard for you to have so many children so far away?"

Eve looked into Tehila's earnest gaze. "The hardest was Cain, for he was sent away by God, and he was young. Hasia carried our first grandchild, and we didn't get to meet him until many years later." She took a bite of the flatbread. After sipping from a cup of water, she smiled at Tehila. "I've been very grateful that you have remained with us. You and Seth and Ruel and Salema and so many more. But yes, it has been hard to raise children and have them move away and never return. I didn't know what to expect away from the garden, but it wasn't a life like this."

Tehila looked at her food but didn't eat. "You mean more than just the children, don't you?"

Eve nodded. "I didn't expect that the enemies of the Creator would work so hard to destroy the human race. I did not realize what we would face in dealing with the watchers and their offspring."

"I'm glad we have no Nephilim walking about here." She shivered. "Do you fear them as I do?"

Eve looked into the distance, remembering when the unseen ones were good, standing or sitting in God's presence. Why did the devil and those who followed him ever think that God was someone who could be defeated?

"I fear the Creator, Tehila. He has the power to cast us out or welcome us home, as He did Enoch and the others who died believing. I don't fear the watchers for myself." She had never actually said the words aloud before, but they were true. She no longer feared the enemy of their souls. God alone was to be feared. "I am not past disobeying God, but I know that He will protect me from the evil one. It's my children the enemy wants. He can hurt me more by going after them."

"I fear for my descendants," Tehila said. "I can't know what they are facing now that they are no longer near. I hope they remember what we have all taught them."

Eve nodded. "I hope so too. And I pray."

Tehila took her hand and squeezed. "I'm glad you are still among the living, Ima."

Eve laughed as she looked beyond Tehila toward the heavens. "I am glad as well. But if God calls me to join those above, I am ready to be with Him again."

"You have always missed Him, Ima." Tehila took a bite of her flatbread while Eve pondered her daughter's comment.

"His was the first face I saw when I opened my eyes to the world. I hurt Him terribly when I took the fruit from the tree and ate of it. I could see the anguish in His eyes. And though He has promised another chance for the humans when the Redeemer comes, I always felt as though I needed to do something to take away that pain."

She took a sip of water as others gathered around to listen. "Your father tells me that God loves every one of us, no matter what we've done. We can be forgiven, which the sacrifices show us. But I have always felt I had to earn that love. I thought I'd lost everything when we left the garden." She straightened and clasped her hands in her lap.

"You have told us this for years, yet even now you question His love for you?" Tehila asked.

Her words pricked Eve's conscience. *Do You love me?* She glanced heavenward, then looked at her daughter and the small gathering of women sitting at her feet. "Since I seem to be interesting to so many of you, old as I am, I suppose you want me to answer the question?"

A chorus of yeses followed.

"Even now I question God's love for us. For me in particular. Obviously He loved Enoch, but I lost what Enoch gained. And I've never quite found it again. Not as he did."

"If Abba says that God loves us all, then He loves you, Ima. Otherwise I must conclude that He doesn't love me or any one of us sitting here. Perhaps you are too hard on yourself." Tehila patted Eve's knee.

Eve smiled. "I'm sure you are right. Don't doubt His love because of me. I have the disadvantage of knowing that life could have been so much better for all of us if not for me."

"No one blames you, Ima." Tehila took her hand again. "If we had been born in the garden, what would have stopped us from eating of that tree? If it hadn't been you, it might have been one of us."

Eve pulled Tehila into an embrace. "Thank you, my daughter."

Eve found Adam at the city gate. The sun was barely halfway to the sky, and birdsong floated on the air. "Come with me to the river?" she called up to him.

Adam descended the short stairs and met her. How was it that he had no trouble walking or even running, yet she felt as though her body was falling apart?

"Why the sudden desire for the river?" Adam asked. He took her hand as they walked through the gate onto the well-worn dirt path.

"You know it reminds me of what Eden used to be. I want that feeling of closeness to God once more." She offered him a wistful smile.

Adam nodded and led her closer to the river, the rushing sound soothing to her ears.

"Do you think the Creator ever forgets any of His creatures? There are so many. Sometimes I forget the names of my great-grandchildren."

"I have a feeling the Creator remembers every single one of His creations, down to the smallest insect. Even the stars are called by the names He's given them," Adam said.

"How do you know so much? Though you were created first." She laughed, for they had been "born" on the same day.

"These are just things God has shown me over the years. When Enoch learned to imprint our stories into clay, I had him write some of this down for future generations. Many of his writings will be added to mine and Seth's, and we will have much to pass down to Methuselah's children."

They sank down along the bank, and she tucked her feet beneath her. She looked into Adam's handsome, rugged face. His muscles were still visible in his strong arms, as though he had hardly aged.

"I can't say for sure," Eve said, "but God may call me to Him soon. I think my time on the earth is nearing an end." The thought should have brought sadness, for she didn't want to leave Adam alone, but all she could feel was joy.

He grasped her hands and turned her to face him. "You are young yet. Well, we are older, but you have many good years ahead of you, beloved. I think you need to let go of the memory of Eden and heaven and find something worth doing here and now." His brow furrowed, and he did not look happy with her comment.

He feared losing her.

"You love me," she said, smiling at his discomfort. "I did not say I would pass from this earth today. But don't you long to return to what we had with God? I've missed it most of my life."

"I've missed Him too, when I'm not so distracted with the things of this life. I think you have thought about Him more than I have."

She took his hand and felt the strength of each finger against hers. "I could be wrong," she said, wanting to cheer him despite the continual pain in her body and occasional throbbing in her chest. "I don't want you to worry. We will be together again one day."

"I know." He pulled her close.

She could feel the beat of his heart, strong and steady, but she felt as though her heart could not keep the same pace. Each beat carried a hint of pain. Was this how death came to some? Apparently there were many ways to die, though how many humans had passed, she could not know. Too many distant descendants roamed the earth now, and though she was sure it could hold many more, she would never know where they wandered to.

The river lapped against the bank and raced over nearby rocks.

Birds sang in a symphony in the trees above them. Some of the smaller animals crept closer, and one of the bunnies allowed her to touch it. She closed her eyes and leaned against Adam's strong frame.

This was a taste of Eden. But why were the animals coming to her all of a sudden?

The birdsong grew louder, and light shone down on her as though the sun had broken through the surrounding trees. Only this light shimmered and splayed into more colors than she had ever seen on earth.

And then she saw Him. Adonai Elohim held His hand out to her, and in that moment, love poured over her until she could feel nothing else.

You do love me!

She felt His approval and saw Him smile.

I have loved you with an everlasting love. You are Mine.

"I understand at last how much God loves me," she said, tilting her head toward Adam. He was looking at her with alarm. "What's wrong?" She tried to touch his face, but she was no longer able to lift her arm.

Adonai Elohim took her hand, and she turned toward Him.

"Come," He said, drawing her closer.

"Adam will miss me." She wanted to tell him she was fine, and he would be happy for her if he could see what she did. God had her now.

As Eve flew upward with Him, she knew she was not only loved by her Creator, but she was finally forever home.

Note to the Reader

The story of Adam and Eve has drawn much debate over the years as to whether they were real people or not. I believe that if God included people in Scripture, then they were historically real. We may not be able to prove that, just as we will never find the Garden of Eden, but that doesn't mean that the garden didn't exist or that those people didn't live.

That said, please remember that this book is fiction. As an author, I will sometimes make minor historical timeline tweaks to create my stories. Call it creative license. This is why I ask my readers to go back to their Bibles and read the account there for themselves because ultimately God's Word is the only truth.

This truth in Scripture shows us more than the creation story in Genesis. It also teaches us that there is an unseen realm, which God created before He made humanity—the angels and demons (angels who had their own kind of fall), principalities and powers that inhabit the spiritual world. And they hate the humans God has made.

In this book, I have attempted to show the beginning of creation and the beginning of time in a way that incorporates that unseen realm and how it played a very real part in the fall of humanity. The rebellion that began in the heavens came to earth when the first humans became the target of the evil one and brought death upon us all. Eden was not lost simply because of Adam and Eve's sinful choice. It began with a diabolical plan to convince them to make that choice.

I hope as you read this book that you were able to glimpse what might have been, both in and out of the garden, and better understand the hidden enemy of our souls. Where my fallible, human imagining of how things might have been doesn't agree with your understanding or view of things, I pray that you would always hold my ideas lightly and keep the truth of Scripture above any biblical novel you might read. Only God is true.

May you also realize that nothing we can do will ever stop God from loving us. As Paris Reidhead once said, "It is possible to die unsaved, and many do, but it is impossible to die unloved."[1]

Adam and Eve's story is about God's plan to redeem them—a plan set in place even before they ever sinned. God was not taken by surprise by anything that happened, and in His great wisdom, He already knew how He would make things right again. He's already made a way in Jesus Messiah. One day He will make Eden come to earth again and all will be made new.

In His Grace,
Jill Eileen Smith

1. Paris Reidhead, "Not to Be Wasted" (sermon, 1967), https://www.sermon index.net/modules/articles/index.php?view=article&aid=45959.

Acknowledgments

In early February 2022, I had a Zoom call with my agent, Wendy Lawton. We talked about the possibility of upcoming projects, and I admitted to her that I wasn't yet satisfied with Eve's story. She said, "This is about that time in every book that I hear you say this." Anyone who knows me well would say the same thing. The perfectionist in me is always certain that the book I'm writing is the hardest yet.

Eve's story, however, really did hold greater challenges for me than anything else I've written to date. Why? Because I was tackling an era before time existed, along with the beginning of time and what followed. There is no archaeological evidence to prove anything I wrote. We have Scripture, but even Scripture suffers much debate about the story of beginnings.

There were moments I truly wasn't sure about this. But Eve's character reflects how I see someone who has met the God of the universe, known His love, and walked with Him face-to-face—and then lost all she had with Him. I think at some level we can all relate to how she might have felt.

This book would not have been written, however, without the support and faith of the team at Revell, who allowed me the chance to tell a difficult story. Thank you to each one of you, especially Rachel McRae, Jessica English, Michele Misiak, and Karen Steele.

A special thanks also goes to my fellow authors and dear friends Hannah Alexander and Jill Stengl, who both gave me feedback on the earlier drafts. I'm not sure I will ever have confidence in what I do, but good friends make me believe the work is possible.

During the writing of this book, my personal life went through a lot of stress and upheaval. This was the year of a breast cancer diagnosis and the loss of my brother. And at this writing of the final draft, I am preparing to travel to attend my mom's funeral.

My husband and I also took two trips to Oregon to help our kids and bought and sold a house. We are settling in our new home, and I am happy to say that though I still have boxes to unpack, we are no longer tripping over them. We are very happy with God's gift of this move.

As always, I thank God for my family and friends, especially Randy, the best friend a girl could have. Soon after I turn this book in, we will celebrate forty-five years of marriage. God is most gracious.

And like Eve, who longed to be with Adonai Elohim her Creator once again, I could not end a book without thanking God for His grace, mercy, and amazing love that is greater and higher and deeper and wider than we will ever imagine. One day, if we trust in Him, we will behold Him face-to-face. And meet Adam and Eve and all who walked with Him before us. What a day that will be!

TWO BROTHERS.
ONE BETRAYAL.

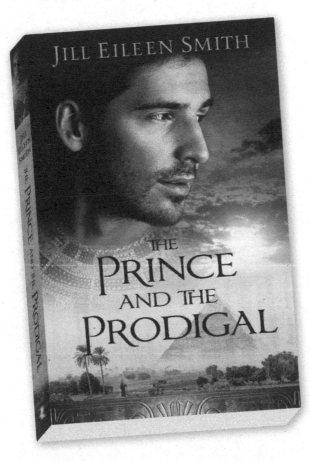

Jill Eileen Smith delves into another piece of Scripture with *The Prince and the Prodigal*—the story of Joseph and Judah and the history between them.

Turn the page for a sneak peek at their story . . .

Prologue

Mamre, 1842 BC

Jacob paused at the outskirts of Mamre near Hebron, taking in the familiar hills and fields where he had spent the early years of his life. Memories filled him, along with an ache in his heart over the news that his mother had long ago passed into Sheol. Why had he been forced to stay away nearly thirty years? He closed his eyes against the glare of the setting sun, remembering his mother's tenderness, her way of speaking, her smile. If only things had been different. He should never have allowed his uncle Laban to keep him away so long. He should have been here for her.

His heart skipped its normal rhythm as anxiety flared with the memories. Would his father welcome him now? Isaac had spent years alone without wife or sons, with none but his servants to care for his flocks, his fields, his needs. Jacob should have been here for both of them. The moment he had wed Rachel, he should have made plans to return. But Laban had tricked him again and again, and the regret he felt gave way first to anger, then to acceptance. He had done what he had to do. There was no use in trying to change the past.

He slowly pushed his staff into the dirt and limped closer to the encampment, which spread far and wide before him, a testament to his father's wealth.

"Are you all right, Abba?"

The voice of Rachel's firstborn, seventeen-year-old Joseph, caused Jacob to turn and smile. How often had he thanked God for Rachel's oldest son? Every day was not often enough, but every day the thought of Rachel surfaced, and Joseph was his memory of her. He was so like her in looks and in spirit. So unlike his brothers. A better, wiser son.

Jacob patted Joseph's hand where he had placed it in the crook of Jacob's arm. "I am fine, my son. It has been a long time since I have laid eyes on my father. He will not see us coming, but he will hear us. And he will know my voice." He hoped. "My father will be pleased to meet you. Come. Let us not delay lest the sun sets before we arrive and the servants think we are strangers come to harm them."

Joseph glanced behind them, and Jacob turned his gaze as well. Their caravan of sons, wives, children, and animals would need more room than Isaac now possessed. Jacob would do his best to include Isaac in their home—to give him a family again.

He picked up his pace despite his apprehension and moved toward the black goat-hair tents, spotting the largest one in the center, right where his father's tent had been when he left it for Paddan-Aram. God had promised to be with him when he left, and now He had brought him home again. How fitting.

The thought pleased him more than he expected. And to know that he had finally set things right between himself and his brother still filled him with awe. God really could do the impossible.

He looked at Joseph once more, marveling again that Rachel had borne him after so many years of longing. Yet why did God take her upon Benjamin's birth? And why did Joseph's brothers so often look on his favorite son with disfavor?

Jacob shook the thoughts aside. "Come," he said again. "There is my father's tent. It is time for you to meet your grandfather."

Joseph followed obediently, and Jacob said no more as they reached the tent, where the flaps were lifted. Isaac sat in the doorway upon cushions with a young servant girl close by.

"Father." Jacob could barely choke out the word, and emotion suddenly overtook him. He knelt with difficulty due to his bad leg, drew up beside Isaac, and carefully touched his knee. "It is I, Jacob."

Isaac turned his head toward Jacob, his eyes unseeing. He cleared his throat. "Is that really you, Jacob, my son?"

"Yes, Father. It is really I. I have come with the wives and children and flocks that the Lord your God has given to me. I have come so that they can know you, Father." He paused, swallowed hard, and felt the strong grip of his father's hand in his. "I have come home," he said, this time letting his tears flow.

He leaned closer, and he and his father embraced as though they never wanted to part again. Isaac's tears wet Jacob's robe, and they wept together for all that had come between them. For all of the loss they had both suffered. And for the joy of coming home again.

1

1841 BC

Joseph walked the ancient path from the fields near Hebron to his father's tent beneath the oaks of Mamre. The shepherd's staff rested in his right hand, but his gait felt weighted, despite the brilliant colors of the setting sun and the cool whisper of the breeze in the trees above him. He wasn't sure he wanted the role his father had placed upon him. His brothers certainly would not approve.

The scent of roasting lamb wafted to him, and a moment later the cry of a child met his ears. He hurried closer as Dinah emerged from his father's tent, carrying his brother Benjamin.

"You are back," Dinah said, smiling above his brother's wiggling body. The boy was nearing his first birthday and did not often like to be held except by Joseph, though he seemed to tolerate Dinah above the other women in the family.

"Yes," he said, dropping the staff and reaching for Benjamin, who now tried to fling himself into Joseph's arms. "There you are, baby brother!" Joseph held him high above his head until Benjamin squealed with delight. They played their little game until Joseph finally set Benjamin in the dirt and held his hand to help him walk toward their father's tent.

"How did it go?" Dinah asked before he could walk away. "I know it has not been easy for you of late. Our half brothers—and my own brothers, for that matter—seem to consider you a pest more than the grown man you are."

Joseph gave her an appreciative look. He lowered his voice and leaned closer while trying to keep Benjamin from tugging him away. "It's nice to know that someone understands. I fear our father does not stop to consider that having me report to him on their behavior will not help their feelings toward me. He already favors me overmuch because I'm Rachel's son."

"Abba loves you, Joseph. He does not see clearly where you are concerned—or that he puts you in difficult situations." She touched his arm. "Perhaps I can speak to him about this sometime."

Joseph shook his head. "No. Don't worry yourself over it. If I have too much trouble, I will talk to Father."

Dinah lifted a brow, her expression dubious. "Sometimes he listens to me better than to any of you. Keep that in mind if you need me." She turned, then tossed him a smile and walked off to her mother's tent.

Joseph chuckled as he led Benjamin to greet their father. Jacob was sitting among his cushions just inside his large goat-hair tent. The sides were up to let in the breeze, and Jacob smiled as he saw them coming.

"Greetings, Abba. Did you rest well?" At over one hundred years, Jacob often rested in the heat of the day. He no longer had the strength to shepherd the flocks as he once did. Rachel's death seemed to have aged him, despite the joy Benjamin brought to both of them.

"I did, my son." He motioned with a veined hand for Joseph to come closer and sit beside him. Joseph did as he was asked. "Tell me, how did it go in the fields today? Have the sons of my concubines returned with you?"

Joseph glanced at Benjamin, who had picked up a wooden stick and was attempting to put it in his mouth. Joseph took the stick

314

from him and offered him a small wooden toy he used to play with. He looked once more at his father. "They are taking the flock to greener pastures and staying in one of the caves tonight. They did not wish to return to camp just yet."

Jacob straightened, and his brows knit in a frown. "Was there good reason to travel away from the camp? Why not set out for greener pastures tomorrow? Did the sheep not find enough to eat throughout the day?"

"The sheep found plenty of green pasture to eat and rest in today. I told them we should bring the sheep to the pens tonight and set out elsewhere tomorrow, but they did not listen." Joseph did not enjoy bringing such a report to his father, but he withheld the things he suspected his half brothers were really intending to do this night.

"If they will not listen to you, send them to me. I will see to it they listen to you, my son." Anger filled his voice but quickly abated as Joseph held his gaze. "My son." He reached for Joseph's hand. "You always do what I ask. I never have to wonder or worry about you. What a gift from God you have been to me in my old age."

Joseph patted his father's hand and nodded. "Thank you, Father. I desire to please you, as I know this also pleases our God." Hadn't he known at his mother's knee that God watched over them, that it was God who had given Joseph to her after years of barrenness? That it was God whom they were to serve and obey, for He had created all things?

"You are a good son," Jacob said, attempting to stand. Joseph jumped up and helped his father, offering him his staff to steady him. "I smell something good—roasting lamb? Let us go now and meet your grandfather and let the women serve us."

They walked toward the tent door, Benjamin toddling unsteadily ahead of them.

"Do you know if Leah's sons will be joining us?" his father asked.

"I have not seen them. Perhaps they will send a servant to tell us."

Leah's sons rarely joined the family at mealtimes, even though it was one of the few times they had to spend with Isaac. They often took the flocks too far to return to camp in one day. He supposed Zilpah's and Bilhah's sons just did as they saw Joseph's other brothers doing. Though they often argued, they seemed to get along better with each other than they ever had with him.

Jacob led Joseph and Benjamin to the center of the camp, where stones were placed about a fire. "They always came home when we lived in Shechem. They should not stray so far here. How do we know the Canaanites will always be friendly toward us?"

Joseph sat beside his father and pulled Benjamin onto his lap. "I don't think you need to fear for Leah's sons, Abba. They are grown men, and so far the men of Canaan have never troubled us."

"They are young and foolish," Jacob spat, scowling as if remembering things Joseph wished they could all forget.

Moments later, Isaac's servants helped him walk to the central fire and settled him on a wide rock. A servant sat beside him to help with his food.

"Greetings, Saba," Joseph said. He rose with Benjamin and walked over to kiss Isaac's cheek.

"Ah, my son Joseph. I know your voice. You smell of the sheepfolds."

Joseph chuckled softly. "That I do. I spent the day with the flocks, but now I am here."

"And you are well?" Isaac's voice sounded thin and reedy as though passing through little air.

"I am well, Saba. And hungry!"

Isaac laughed. "Then I will not keep you from eating."

Joseph moved back to the rock beside his father and allowed Dinah to take Benjamin again. He listened to his grandfather and father speak for a few moments, until Leah stepped from her tent and brought food to Isaac. Bilhah and Zilpah also emerged from the tent and served Jacob, Joseph, and Dinah, who fed Benjamin from her plate.

Joseph smiled at his father, then wrapped a piece of lamb in flatbread and took a bite, grateful for the silence. He did not miss his brothers. The only one he longed to see daily was Benjamin. Though they had left his grandfather Laban and endured the death of his mother, coming back to Mamre had not brought the peace his father expected. Or Joseph had hoped for. The only thing he had found here that brought him joy was the chance to learn more about the God of his father from Jacob and Isaac. Both men had told him the tales of their encounters with the God of Abraham and repeated the history of their people. Even the deceit of his father and God's overwhelming grace afterward were not withheld from Joseph.

Joseph found great comfort in the stories. And in times when he lay awake upon his mat and stared at the tent above him, the comfort of knowing that God cared for him too kept him believing that one day things between himself and his brothers would improve.

⁓

The bleating of sheep met Joseph's ears as he climbed the low rise to the vast pens where his father's sheep were kept. Reuben and Judah called the sheep to follow from two of the pens, while the other four sons of Leah came behind, making sure none strayed as the men led the ewes with their young to the lush green pastures just over the rise.

Dan, Gad, Naphtali, and Asher took the goats and headed in the opposite direction without a single look at Joseph. Joseph tapped his staff into the dirt as he followed behind, wishing again that his father had not asked him to report on the actions of these sons of the concubines. Did they suspect his change in roles?

He glanced at the cloudless heavens, the place where God lived, grateful for the gentle breeze that offset the heat of the rising sun.

His turban protected him from the glare as he searched ahead of him, where his half brothers seemed in a hurry to put distance between them. They were going to ruin the goats at that pace. The young could not travel quickly. As he watched, Asher struck one of the goats for lagging behind.

Anger flared, and Joseph picked up his pace. He hurried to Asher's side. "Why did you strike him?"

Asher waved Joseph away as though his words meant nothing. "You worry too much and have obviously not spent enough time with these ornery animals to know they need a firm hand. Forget about it."

"Our father would not appreciate you mistreating the goats." Joseph straightened, but Asher still towered over him and laughed at his concerns as if Joseph were a child to be coddled.

"It was merely a tap. The animal needed to keep up." Asher walked away, still laughing, as though their exchange was nothing more than a humorous spat.

Joseph stood still a moment, assessing the situation. His father had put him in charge of these sons because he did not fully trust their work. But they didn't know his position, and he didn't like telling tales on them. If only they acted as they should so that there would be nothing to tell!

He followed his half brothers again, determined to watch them and the goats, whether he spoke to them again or not. He felt the sacks at his side and the sling tied to his wrist.

When they came to a large field, Dan and Naphtali went in one direction while Gad and Asher went in another. Joseph knew neither group welcomed his presence, so he spent the day moving from one to the other.

He finally stopped where Dan's herd had settled and leaned against a large oak tree. He pulled a handful of almonds from one of his sacks and slowly chewed as he looked from one end of the field to the other. Dan and Naphtali were not together now—only Dan was visible against the rising sun's glare.

Joseph moved about, trying to locate Naphtali, but he had disappeared from view. Puzzled, he strode the length of the area where the goats had spread out. He walked toward where Asher and Gad had gone, but there was no sign of Asher either.

He glanced from Dan to Gad, debating whether to stay with them or continue his search for Asher and Naphtali. They couldn't have gone far. Or had they planned to go to the city or some other place all along?

He looked at Gad still sitting beneath a tree and occasionally looking at the animals. Frustrated, he looked back toward Dan, but he was no longer there. When Joseph came to the low rise in the field, he found no sign of Dan, and the goats were moving away from him. Where were they going?

Irritation spiked at the thought that they were purposely trying to avoid him or play some spiteful trick on him. To what end? What could they possibly be doing that they must keep secret?

He dug the staff into the dirt and hurried down the slight hill, shading his eyes to look in all directions. Had Dan known where Asher was and joined him there? They would weaken the herd and kill the young if they did not take care to go at the animals' pace. They knew this. Every shepherd knew this.

After a lengthy jog, Joseph found the goats near a row of caves. Naphtali was there as well, but this time Dan was missing. Joseph closed his eyes, telling himself to remain calm. They were toying with him, trying to upset him. Obviously they did not want to include him as they once did. But why? Did they not care what their father would say to them when he heard of this?

Suddenly Joseph wished he were anywhere but here. He did not want to care for the flocks with these brothers, with any of his brothers. They refused to treat him as their equal, and while they might have tolerated him in his youth, they had grown more frustrating with each passing year.

He walked toward the caves in search of a place to escape when he heard laughter coming from within. Female laughter. He stood still, listening. The distinct voice of each brother interrupted what could only be a liaison with women.

Disgusted, Joseph returned to the goats and approached Naphtali. "Is this how you care for Father's flocks and herds? By meeting with women and ignoring the animals?"

Naphtali shrugged. "What are you going to do about it? Run to Father and tell tales? We will deny what you say, so don't trouble yourself."

Naphtali waved him away as Asher had done, as though he were a troublesome gnat. Joseph looked him in the eye and then turned and walked off. He hated to disappoint his father, but watching his brothers was a waste of time. Surely there was something else he could do to help. Obviously he was not wanted here.

Of course, there was no way he could keep his brothers' actions from his father. They would soon like him even less than they did now. But what else could he do?

Jill Eileen Smith is the bestselling and award-winning author of the biblical fiction series The Wives of King David, Wives of the Patriarchs, and Daughters of the Promised Land, as well as *The Heart of a King, Star of Persia: Esther's Story, Miriam's Song,* and *The Prince and the Prodigal.* She is also the author of the nonfiction books *When Life Doesn't Match Your Dreams* and *She Walked Before Us.* Her research into the lives of biblical women has taken her from the Bible to Israel, and she particularly enjoys learning how women lived in Old Testament times. Jill lives with her family in southeast Michigan. Learn more at www.jilleileensmith.com.

Meet

JILL EILEEN SMITH

at **www.JillEileenSmith.com** to learn
interesting facts and read her blog!

Connect with her on

f Jill Eileen Smith

🐦 JillEileenSmith

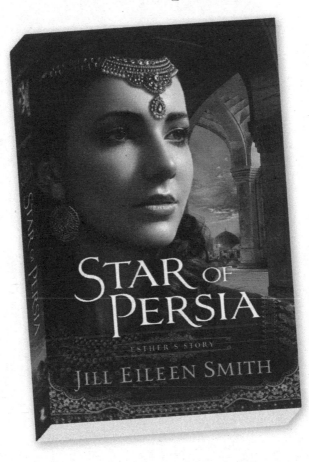

"Smith does an excellent job of bringing her characters to life. . . . A memorable and noteworthy rendering of the atmosphere and figures of the Scriptures."

—*Booklist*, starred review ★

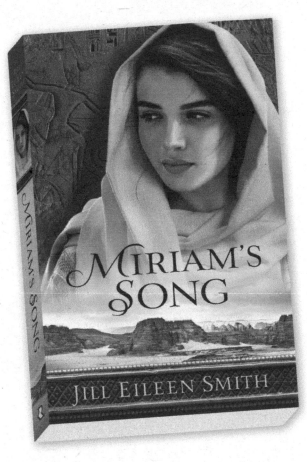

Miriam and her people have prayed for deliverance from the cruel tyranny of Egypt for generations. She believes her brother Moses is the long-awaited answer to their pleas. But how can the exiled prince-turned-shepherd stand against the most powerful man in the world?

Revell
a division of Baker Publishing Group
www.RevellBooks.com

Available wherever books and ebooks are sold.

Against the Backdrop of
OPULENT PALACE LIFE, RAGING WAR, AND DARING DESERT ESCAPES
Lived Three Women . . .

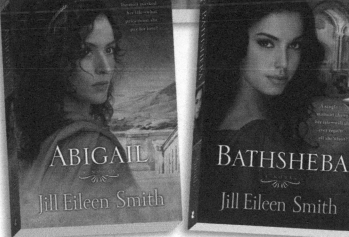